WIN ☐

LOSE ☐

KILL ☐

DIE ✗

Delacorte Press

Text copyright © 2022 by Cynthia Murphy
Cover art copyright © Getty Images

All rights reserved. Published in the United States by Delacorte Press, an imprint of Random House Children's Books, a division of Penguin Random House LLC, New York. Originally published in paperback by Scholastic UK, London, in 2022.

Delacorte Press is a registered trademark and the colophon is a trademark of Penguin Random House LLC.

GetUnderlined.com

Educators and librarians, for a variety of teaching tools, visit us at RHTeachersLibrarians.com

Library of Congress Cataloging-in-Publication Data is available upon request.
ISBN 978-0-593-70547-6 (pbk.) — ISBN 978-0-593-70549-0 (ebook)

The text of this book is set in 11-point Adobe Garamond Pro.
Interior design by Cathy Bobak

Printed in the United States of America
1st Printing
First Edition

WIN

LOSE

KILL

DIE

This one is for the godkids . . .
Kyla Somerville,
Grayson Coffey,
Dominic Kelly . . .
always remember to follow your dreams.

1

I DIDN'T MEAN TO KILL THE FIRST ONE.

Honest.

It was just . . . too *easy, I suppose. She was already in the water, and when I plunged my hands in to help her out, I kind of . . . changed my mind.*

Something inside me snapped.

I held Little Miss Perfect's head down and waited for her to stop thrashing around.

It took longer than I thought, and then she just . . . floated there. Limp. Pathetic, really.

"Accidental death," according to the experts. That's nearly right. Like I said, it's not like I set out to do it.

It felt good, though.

2

I CAN'T BELIEVE WE'RE BACK HERE ALREADY.

Summer had passed by in a daze thanks to the bang to the head I took at the end of last year. Instead of going to beach parties with my friends and staying up to watch the sunrise like I'd planned, my days were full of police interviews and PTSD. That last day of school had started so perfectly, and then . . .

"Liz." A sharp hiss and an elbow in my ribs bring me back to the present. Taylor is standing up straight, her gorgeous hazel eyes focused on the stage, for all the world playing the perfect mourner. I mimic her, my gaze following hers to a large easel draped in black cloth. It's displaying a blown-up photograph of Morgan.

The girl who drowned on the last day of school.

"Pay attention." Taylor says this out of the corner of her mouth, like she's a bad ventriloquist with one of those creepy puppets. She does it so effortlessly—not one muscle in her face moves. I guess I haven't recovered as well as I thought, even after all those hospital visits over the summer. I try to concentrate, I really do, but my mind wanders as the headmistress's words blur into one long sermon, each pause punctuated by the squeaking sound of rubber heels on the parquet floor. Autumn is seeping into the corners of the building already and the air smells of rain and damp, freshly laundered uniforms.

I study the picture. Morgan was pretty, in a preppy, Reese Witherspoon in *Cruel Intentions* kind of way. She looked so sweet and unassuming, which I know was total bull. Truth is, Morgan had the personality of a venomous snake. You did *not* cross her, if you knew what was good for you; she'd make your life at Morton a living hell if she felt like it. It had been her idea to take the boat out on the lake that night, her big moment after being sworn in as head girl. She'd bullied most of us into it, from what I remember, though admittedly I don't remember much. Not after the boat flipped.

Dr. Patel, the headmistress, ends her monologue with a request for a moment of silence. She's flanked by several members of the faculty—some of them are crying, dabbing handkerchiefs or tissues at their faces. Her sharp black trouser suit is conservative, appropriate for a pupil's memorial, but super stylish and paired with some killer heels. I can't help admiring anyone who can walk in shoes that high, never mind run the country's most elite boarding school in them. The rest of the staff look frumpy in comparison. I watch the clock and sway slightly. I'm not used to standing up for so long after spending the summer in bed watching nineties teen movies.

Taylor ignores me, her head down, eyes closed: the perfect pupil. And mourner. Her long, naturally red hair falls like a curtain, spilling over the gray tweed of her blazer. Morton Academy's very own Cheryl Blossom, standing right next to me.

Dr. Patel calls the memorial to a close and bodies start to shuffle toward the exit in silence.

"So," I whisper as we wait our turn to file out of the hall, "how does it feel?"

Taylor looks at me as we emerge through the tall, wooden doors into the corridor, smiling with her mouth but not her eyes. "How does what feel? Being passed over for head girl? Being so close to that full-ride scholarship I could practically taste it? Great, thanks for asking."

"Oh, come on. You're deputy! That's still pretty sweet. Plus"— I lower my voice, even though everyone else has resumed their own conversations too—"you know what that means for Jewel and Bone. Being deputy in the society means you get your pick of colleges."

Now the smile reaches her eyes.

"Yes, I do. I am very excited for this year. If I can just find the right sponsor, schmooze the right rich person, then I won't have to worry about working through university at all. Just think of all the people we're going to meet, the events we'll get to go to. . . ."

"*You'll* get to go to," I correct her, smiling ruefully. "Some of the perks of the society don't stretch past head and deputy, remember?"

"Yeah, sorry." Taylor chews her lip and avoids my eyes. "I know that if you hadn't helped me and Kat with the scavenger hunt, you would have finished it before us. You'd be the one being sworn in as deputy head tonight, and—"

"Hello, gorgeous!" A deep voice interrupts her as two heavy arms thump down around our shoulders. I'm kind of grateful for the interruption. Marcus's aftershave is so strong I start to cough, but Taylor immediately twinkles up at him. I duck out from under his arm and let them have a moment.

4

"What do you both look so serious about?" He looks good, like maybe he actually slept over the summer. Lucky him.

"Oh, you know—life, death." She waves her polished fingernails in the air. "How I spent half an hour choosing a shade of lipstick that didn't clash with the funeral flowers." Taylor glances around furtively. "Actually, we were just talking about my ceremony at JB tonight." She stands on her tiptoes to kiss him. "You know your girl is moving up in the world."

"I sure do. I still think you should've gotten the top spot instead of Jameela, though. I mean, if there was anything I could do . . ." He walks out of the hall with us, but I stop listening as we start up the corridor to the entrance hall.

God, I missed this place. I breathe in deeply, as though I can inhale the pure essence of Morton into my very soul. I love the feeling of belonging, being one of a handful of kids from all over the country who are invited to attend such an exclusive institution. It doesn't matter who we are or where we're from—we're here because of our brains. Rich, poor, it doesn't matter at Morton. We're all here because we are damn clever—and the truth is that most of us wouldn't have gotten the chance otherwise. It's in the middle of nowhere and boarding is compulsory. There's no internet access without supervision, either—that's one of Morton's unique selling points: good old-fashioned bookwork. You win some, you lose some, I guess.

I take a second to remind myself it's all real. The stone ceiling soars over us, and our shoes tap softly on the ancient stone floor as we weave through bodies clad in gray blazers that are piped with an almost lurid acid green. The mahogany wall panels glow, sunlight streaming through the long windows that allow us glimpses of the vast, manicured gardens beyond them. We pass the headmistress's office and start to climb the large, curving staircase that always makes me feel like I'm in a Disney film. The handrail is gleaming, so polished that it's slick beneath my hand. The whole place smells of wood and citrus and I adore it. It smells like home.

"Hurry up, Liz." Marcus and Taylor are watching me with amusement from the landing above, and I realize I've zoned out a bit. "Stop daydreaming."

"Sorry." I duck my head to hide my flaming cheeks as I take the remaining stairs two at a time until I reach the landing beneath a huge stained-glass window. I walk slowly, following them through the wide double doors into the West Wing. Yes, I said West Wing—that's how big this place is.

This floor is all classrooms and the science labs are right next to classics, so I watch the perfect couple disappear into their room and then enter my own class. Classics is my main subject—all students do three in total, but we have been hand-selected for these classes in particular. It's kind of like a specialty, something we will take on to college, maybe even get fast-tracked. The teaching here is the best in the country—expectations are high. There's hardly anyone here yet; the assembly interfered with the timetable for the first full day back, so I choose a desk in the middle row, by a window that looks out onto a wide expanse of water.

The lake.

Morgan.

I move quickly, my flesh crawling as memories of that night once again try to claw their way to the surface. I take a seat at the opposite side of the room, as far from the window as I can get.

The classroom fills up slowly and I'm pleased we have a small group—not that we ever have large classes, with only fifty chosen to attend Morton in each year group. The teacher arrives last, and I'm happy to see we've got Professor Insoll again. The man's a legend—in the world of ancient religious artifacts, anyway. He used to teach at a university, but I guess Morton pays pretty well—plus it has to be a bonus when you have a bunch of kids who are desperate to learn rather than perpetually hungover undergrads.

We go through all the usual first-day-back motions—new textbooks, a prep schedule that looks ridiculously full, and a winter exam timetable. I'm busy writing my name on everything when a note slides across my desk.

"Pass this to Jameela," a voice hisses.

Jameela? Hmm. I wonder if it's Jewel and Bone business, maybe a note about the first of the donor meetings, where we'll get to meet prospective sponsors who will hopefully pay our way through college, but a quick glance around reveals that hardly anyone else in the class would have that kind of information. I shrug and pass it on to Frank, just in case. I can't go handing out potential secret society information to just anybody. "For Jameela," I mouth, nodding to the girl with long, dark braids sitting in front of him. I go back to signing my name with a flourish and forget all about the note.

Until Jameela shoots out of her seat, screaming, and drops the paper like it's on fire.

3

"THEN WHAT HAPPENED?"

"Nothing." I shrug. Taylor hoots a laugh, though there's not much humor in it.

"Trust Jameela to get away with making such a scene," she grumbles. "How did Insoll not confiscate the note?"

"She hid it pretty quickly, told him there was a spider on her desk."

We fall silent for a moment and I enjoy the sound of the gravel driveway crunching beneath my new shoes as we walk away from the main school building. I glance back, watching it get smaller and smaller, its myriad windows reflecting the late-afternoon sun in a hundred different directions.

I divert my attention back to the path and smile over at Taylor, irresistibly reminded of the first time we walked this way. We're still in our uniforms, a JB requirement, and the stiff wool of my pleated skirt tickles my bare legs with every step as I try to keep up with her.

"She looked pretty shaken up," I say. "I wish I knew what it said. Why didn't I look at it? I mean, I was holding it!"

"Because you're Liz Williams, the nicest girl in all of Morton." The main gates into the grounds, large metal things that hide us away from the real world, have come into our line of sight, so Taylor veers off to the left. We decide against the driveway for the mani-cured lawn and head toward a dense copse of trees. She's right, of course. I am nice.

"Boring, right?" I say. She pauses and turns back to me, linking an arm through my own.

"Never." She grins, bumping my hip. "You're my moral com-pass, Lizzie. What would I do without you? Besides, it was probably just another of her nudes from last year."

She has a point, on both counts.

"Come on," I sigh. "We don't want to be late for this."

"Agreed." Taylor drops my arm as we approach a thickly wooded section of the grounds. She holds open a small wooden gate as I take one last glance around for any stragglers. The long, sweeping driveway is clear, with Morton House tiny in the distance. It's al-most seven, so everyone else will be doing prep after dinner. Per-fect. We both ignore the No Entry sign hammered into the flaking wood—it's not for us, after all—and within seconds the darkness of the trees has enveloped us.

It was last summer when I first realized this part of the grounds even existed, after the riddles appeared on our pillows and we fol-lowed the clues that had been scattered around the building. No one really comes out this way, which is kind of the point, I guess. The rest of the grounds here are so picture-perfect: grass always cut, flowerbeds freshly dug, hedges pruned. This bit is wild, like a fairy-tale forest, full of snapping twigs and tiny, scampering feet. As if on cue, a squirrel appears in front of us, his bushy tail twitching in time with his tiny nose, ears pricked and alert. He eyes us bravely but scampers the second we move.

"Aww, cute!" I whisper.

"Why are you whispering?" Taylor whispers back.

"Why are *you* whispering?" I giggle. She rolls her eyes at me, but the laughter is contagious and a smile starts to tug at the corner of her mouth.

"Stop it," she whispers back, and we both dissolve into silent laughter. It's the nerves, it must be. Last time we were all here was *that* night.

The laughter dies in my throat.

"Hey." Taylor pauses. I'm sure she can read my mind sometimes. "How are you feeling? Are you ready for this?"

"Yes." My voice comes out as intended, firm and unwavering, though I'm not sure I *am* ready. Taylor reaches out a hand and for a second, my vision blurs and it's hers, *Morgan's,* reaching desperately from the black water.

Then it's just Taylor's hand again, nails perfectly manicured, not blue and dripping lake moss. I stare until she drops it and sighs.

"Come on, then. Like you said, we can't be late—you know what she thinks about starting on time. I don't know about you, but I want to be charming all those rich donors once we start meeting them. I heard a rumor that two girls from last year were so late to a meeting that they were stuck serving canapés during their first sponsorship party as punishment. . . ."

We delve deeper into the trees and I keep my head down, away from the low-hanging branches that threaten to tangle their bony fingers in my hair. The path is narrow here, fringed with wild orchids that are taller than both of us. Their dark purple tongues leer as we pass, and they stink of decay, a sweet, sickly odor that burrows into your nostrils and doesn't go away. We should have taken the other path, the one that's maintained, but that would have brought us past the lake, and I don't want to deal with that until I have to. I realize Taylor has brought me this way on purpose—she knows I'm avoiding the lake. I thank her silently.

The area ahead of us begins to widen and I can just make out glimpses of roughly hewn gray stone through the brush. Brambles have been left to grow wild here and my brain dredges up a memory of an old DVD I would watch on repeat, when the witch curses Sleeping Beauty and the thorns surround the princess's castle. These vines are almost welcoming, though, the way they have woven together, arching over us to create an entrance of sorts. We duck and pass through, then follow the short stone path to an ancient wooden doorway where we pause for breath.

"Ready?" I whisper.

Taylor straightens her shoulders and nods once. "Ready."

We push open the door, which, despite its obvious antiquity, is well oiled and guides us into the chapel in silence. It's dark inside and the thick walls immediately muffle any sounds of the outside world. We close the door gently and give our eyes a second to adjust to the flickering candlelight at the opposite end of the aisle. You'd almost think it was a fully working church, not a front for something else. I guess that's kind of the point.

I follow Taylor down the aisle and pause in front of the altar, my good-girl Catholic school upbringing making me drop a knee and bow my head quickly before catching up with her at another wooden door. This one is behind the altar, where the priest goes at the end of mass. We pass through it in silence and it feels wrong, like it usually does, but I remind myself it's not a *real* church and keep my head down as we walk past the others. We stop at the far end of the room, in front of one of the wooden benches that line the walls. My mind flashes back to the last time I was in here, snatches of memory seeping in. Puddles of lake water on the worn stone floor. Morgan, her blank face, lips blue . . .

I shake my head, hard. No. Not now. The doctor warned me this might happen once I came back to Morton, but I didn't expect so many flashbacks so soon.

I shrug off my blazer, hang it carefully on a peg, and run my fingers over the small, gem-encrusted pin that's attached to the inside pocket, the one that sits over my heart. I smile as I remember finding it on my pillow, its sharp spike pushed through the paper that invited me to the hunt. I take a second to smooth down my skirt and make sure my shirt is tucked in neatly—not that anyone will see it. Only then do I pick up the long, folded gown from the bench and slide it over my head. I remove the little skull-shaped pin from my blazer. The sharpness of the gemstones pricks my fingers as I fasten it onto my cloak. The thick velvet flows down over me, swallowing my uniform and pooling around my feet. I brush my hair back and tuck it behind my ears, pulling the hood up and over so it sits low, casting a large, hollow shadow where my face should be. I glance at Taylor, now hidden behind an identical robe, before following her and half a dozen other figures down the staircase that is hidden in a shadowed corner.

To the crypt.

I trail the dark procession to the bottom step, and, as usual, I am the last one. I wait as everyone else takes their positions, and when it's my turn, I step out onto a narrow platform. I am standing on a raised stone pathway that forms a circle, more paths spiking off toward the center, so from above they look like the spokes of a wheel. My robe, always too long, drags in the inches of floodwater below and cold fingers spread up through the velvet as though they are clawing at my ankles. I shake the thought from my head and finally arrive at my platform, taking my place in the circle.

I try my best to ignore the dead body in the center.

4

I KEEP MY HEAD DOWN, SO I'M COCOONED IN MY OWN LITTLE world of velvet and icy cold. Around me the air gradually stills, shuffles of feet and whispers of swishing robes quieting down as the rest of the group settles into their positions. Only when the room is silent do I allow myself to look up and focus my eyes on the stone plinth in the middle.

I won't lie—the first time I saw Old Josef, I was pretty freaked out. I'd just trekked through the woods, following the final clue in the library—the image of a small, jewel-colored chapel wrought into one of the stained-glass windows. When you stand at a certain angle, at the right time, the sun shines through and practically points at this part of the woods. The clues in the hunt had all been so cryptic—kind of the point, I guess, so not everyone could solve them—but I'd worked my way through them, dropping hints for Kat and Taylor, who had both received riddles too. When I found the chapel, they were there as well. I let them go in ahead of me, not quite realizing what it would mean, and we followed the music down into the crypt. We weren't the first ones there. I was handed a robe and led to my place—there were five others ahead of us—while we waited for the rest of the platforms to fill up.

When the room was full and we took off our hoods, it was explained to us that this revealed the hierarchy of the society. Marcus had been the first male to arrive, and out of the girls, Morgan was in the top spot. They were sworn in as head girl and head boy, along with their deputies, and the rest of us became prefects. I would have been slightly higher in the pecking order if I hadn't let Taylor and Kat in before me.

I refocus on the present and narrow my eyes at Old Josef again. The more you look at him, the more fascinating he becomes. He rests in his coffin of glass, like some twisted medieval version of Snow White, and has been there for as long as Morton has been a school. Some people say he came from Poland, others Germany, though all that is left of him now is in this casket, so we'll likely never know either way. He was some kind of saint, apparently, who ended up here when the school's founder needed something new and eccentric for his cabinet of curiosities.

My eyes travel along the skeleton, and I imagine trailing my fingers along the rough golden brocade that wraps around each individual rib, the central panel of fabric encrusted with precious stones that decorate his sternum, and the magnificent collar that envelops his bony neck. His face hangs open in a rictus grin and the top of his skull is encircled by a glorious crown of hand-carved crystals, all wired together with gold. His skeletal hands are beringed and rest gently on his stomach—or where his stomach would be, I guess. His bottom half is out of sight, draped in moth-eaten velvet and shadows.

"Bow to our hallowed companion, in honor of our founder."

I do it automatically, following the instructions of the disembodied voice, as though the words themselves curl around my spine and push me gently forward at the waist. The words echo around the room and I dip my upper body forward in as deep a bow as I can manage without falling into the water below. Once I straighten up, I glance at Old Josef once more and whisper the same words as everyone else in the room, though this time they are directed at the grave that lies below his casket—the final resting place of Patrick Morton, founder and first headmaster of Morton Academy. The man who decided he would help the *really* clever kids succeed by matching them with people who would pay for their educations. He's kind of a Jewel and Bone hero. "Thank you, founder. We honor you with jewels and remember you with bone. May we succeed."

"Acolyte Asanti, step forward," the voice calls, and I pinpoint its location to the plinth that would be at twelve if this were a clock. The figure in Jameela's spot glides forward on the narrow stone ledge that connects the outer circle to the inner sanctum. As soon as she steps onto the island that holds the bones of our founder, another command is given. "Remove your hood."

Jameela is pretty and petite, and the cloak swamps her more than most. Taylor must be gutted. Jameela was the second girl to complete the hunt, so she's been promoted from deputy and now has the pick of any university she wants to go to. Like, *any:* Oxford, Harvard, Stanford. She can walk right in and the whole thing is covered. I allow myself to daydream for a second, imagining attending classes at Yale or Cambridge, all paid for. No student loans, no work-study jobs.

I refocus and watch intently as Jameela removes her hood. To be fair, the girl is clever—she was plucked from a nowhere town as some kind of mathematical genius. I hate math—too many numbers, too much logic. I much prefer the history of people, delving into the reasons behind the beauty they have created and left behind, whether it's in artwork, architecture, or just good old stories. I think it's why I was so smitten at the idea of a secret society—it's like stepping into an as-yet-unwritten part of history.

Jameela's smooth skin gleams golden in the flickering candlelight, but she is biting her lip. She looks nervous, and I just know that Taylor is screaming on the inside. She would never allow herself to show fear. She would appear brimming with poise and confidence even if she didn't feel it.

Especially if she didn't.

"Acolyte Asanti, do you dutifully ascend to the coveted position of head girl? A role that will not only afford you status within Morton Academy and beyond, but also within the Society of Jewel and Bone?"

Jameela clears her throat. "Yes. I do."

"Then may you succeed."

"May you succeed," I repeat with the rest of the group. It feels like a lifetime ago that we stood here doing the same ritual for Morgan, but it has only been weeks. Six to be exact. Maybe that's why Jameela looks so worried—does she think the position is cursed?

"Acolyte Fox, step forward."

Here we go—this is how it should be done. In her gown, Taylor strides down the narrow path like a supermodel and takes the place next to her superior. She drops her hood, and even from here I can see the sparkle in her eyes, the perfect flick of her eyeliner. I stand a little straighter, proud to be watching her. She's a natural.

"Acolyte Fox, do you respectfully ascend to the position of deputy head girl? A role that will not only afford you status within Morton Academy and beyond, but also within the Society of Jewel and Bone?"

"Yes, I do."

"Then may you succeed."

"May you succeed," I say through a smile. I want to applaud, but the most important part is coming.

"Are you both ready to swear your blood oath?"

"We are." The girls clasp hands, and the figure who has been speaking breaks away from their platform and joins them in the center. A shining silver blade slides from an oversized sleeve and is presented to Jameela, who I swear goes a little gray even though she's done this once before, when she was sworn in as deputy last summer.

Taylor keeps her head held high as Jameela takes the knife. It's an old blade, as old as the body they are flanking, I'd guess, and just as encrusted in jewels. The blade is kept sharp, though, something that is evident as Jameela slices into her own palm, and then Taylor's upturned one. They both step toward the skeleton, and, as the glass case is opened for them, they each lightly grasp an arm bone, smearing their blood upon the blood of hundreds of previous pledges. On top of Morgan's.

"Esteemed acolytes, please welcome the new head and deputy head girl of the Society of Jewel and Bone. As you know, this grants you the same esteemed positions within Morton Academy. Many congratulations."

Applause and a loud whoop from someone who can only be Marcus echoes around the cavern, and I join in enthusiastically. That feeling of belonging floods through me again, and I remember how intoxicating it can be. No matter what happens outside these walls, this place right here is mine. I am part of something special. Something important.

Jameela and Taylor embrace and the third figure removes her own hood, a shiny sheet of hair swishing as Dr. Patel, the headmistress of Morton, kisses each girl twice, once on each cheek. She then turns to the crowd and holds up one hand, a signal to silence our applause and remove our hoods. I tear mine off like a doctor pulling off a mask after a seventeen-hour surgery and relish the tickle of the cold air on the sweaty nape of my neck. The space to my left is empty, meaning Kat hasn't returned yet. I hope she doesn't get in trouble for missing the first meeting.

"Welcome back, acolytes." Dr. Patel gestures around the room with the blade she has retrieved from Jameela, before it disappears back into her robes, still bloodstained and dripping. "Our first meeting of the year is usually brief, given that it is the first day back. Tonight, however, we had to undertake the somewhat unusual task of welcoming a new pair into the hierarchy. Thankfully our head boy and deputy are both present and well." Dr. Patel nods toward Marcus and Frank, respectively. They nod back. "Now that is over, I will proceed as normal and ask the traditional question of our new head girl and the head boy." She turns to face Jameela, who holds a thick, bloodied piece of gauze to her left palm. "First, Acolyte Asanti, do you have any business you would like to discuss with the group?"

"Yes." Jameela's answer is a shock, and judging by the whispers around the room, not only to me. What could she have to discuss so soon?

The note?

"I see." Dr. Patel's voice is hard to read, as usual. That woman gives nothing away. "Well, the floor is yours."

"Thank you." Jameela looks less nervous and more terrified as she pulls a piece of paper from within her robes. She clears her throat. "I got this today."

It *is* the note. I lean forward a little.

"I didn't want to believe it, but I don't think we can ignore it." She hands the crumpled paper to Dr. Patel, who reads it with an inscrutable expression.

"It could be a sick joke," she says to Jameela.

"It could," she agrees, "but Morgan was my best friend. I think we should take it seriously."

"Very well." Dr. Patel hands the paper back to her. "You may address the group."

Jameela swallows hard and holds the crumpled paper aloft. The room is swathed in silence. "It's . . . it's a photo. Of Morgan, from her memorial." I strain to hear as her voice drops. "With her eyes scratched out." There's a collective intake of breath as she clears her throat and reads aloud from the page in her hand.

"Morgan's death was not an accident. I killed her. And you're next."

5

THE LOOKS ON THEIR FACES WHEN SHE PULLED OUT THAT *photograph! I could not have planned it any better. I didn't expect her to take it so seriously, though. Let alone make it public. I thought it would just make Miss Look-at-Me-I'm-the-New-Head-Girl squirm.*

In hindsight it was arrogant of me. I just couldn't help it. It's getting hard to suppress the urge to do whatever I want. To tell the whole truth, officer, it's getting hard to suppress the urge to do a lot of things.

So, what now? I suppose there's no way I can let her start investigating, especially not with the whole society behind her. Though that might be fun . . . it was such a bad idea to share it with everyone there tonight. Such a bad idea—I had only intended to scare her. Maybe make her drop out. I wasn't going to do anything . . . bad.

Oh, who am I kidding. Of course I was intending to do something bad.

So, Jameela. Target number two.

6

"WHAT DO YOU THINK?"

I tear my eyes away from my battered copy of *The Secret History* and frown at Taylor. Some people think reading equals doing nothing and love to interrupt right when you get to the juiciest parts.

I cast an only slightly interested eye over Taylor's outfit from my cross-legged position on the bed. The first day of school traditionally ends with a pajama party on the roof for seniors, and our long hallway is full of girls laughing, running in and out of each other's rooms and posing in their best pj's. I should have known my old leggings and oversized hoodie wouldn't cut it. I wasn't able to work over the summer, thanks to my head injury, so I'm stuck with last year's stuff.

Taylor is wearing a silky ivory two-piece: short-shorts trimmed with black piping and lace and a fitted, long-sleeved button-down shirt, the cuffs open and rolled up to her elbows. Her name is embroidered on a pocket over her chest, and the remains of a summer tan on her legs contrasts beautifully with the white fabric.

"Those must have cost a bomb! Don't tell me you waitressed all summer just so you could spend your entire paycheck on new clothes?"

"Of course I did." She sighs. "I saved all my tips for day trips, though—we should be let out of this place every month this year. I just wanted to look good, you know?" Her voice shrinks. "And now it's even more important. I need to look deputy-head-girl-worthy."

"You look amazing," I reassure her as I look down at my own chest, where DO NOT DISTURB—MENTAL-HEALTH DAY IN PROGRESS is emblazoned on my sweatshirt. Taylor flips her immaculately straightened hair over one shoulder and pouts down at me. I missed her over the summer, more than I thought I would. Thank God for FaceTime.

"Thanks. And you look super cute! So cozy—I think I'll freeze up there."

"You'll have Marcus to keep you warm."

"I know." A wicked smile crosses her face as she leans down to look in the mirror on her bedside table. I take the opportunity to carry on reading. "Are we going to get you a little plaything this year?"

"Oh, stop." I close the book, surrendering, and watch as she slicks another layer of gloss across her full lips. "I've got enough to think about without boys getting involved. Anyway, they all kind of suck and I am not searching the juniors for new blood."

"OK, OK." She waves her blusher brush in surrender. "Consider me told. . . . Ouch! What the hell?"

"What is it?"

Taylor puts the brush at arm's length and checks her face in the mirror again. "Something sharp in my brush, it just scratched me."

"Seriously? Let me see." I hold a hand out for the brush and she shoves it at me, patting the skin of her cheekbone gingerly.

"Ugh, that stings. What is it?"

I study the bristles and pull out the offending object. "Here's the culprit." I wince, holding up a small rusty nail. "How did that get in there?"

"Eww, gross! Who knows—it's not exactly designer. One day I will have decent stuff, I swear." She paints on a smile, straightens, and slips her feet into black fluffy slippers. "Can you see the scratch?"

"No," I answer honestly. "Not a thing."

"Good." She wiggles her eyebrows at me. "Ready?"

I unfold myself and swing my legs off the bed, pushing my feet into battered rubber flip-flops.

"Ready," I answer.

The hallway has pretty much emptied out now, the last girls trailing up the spiral staircase in the corner of the corridor, footsteps echoing on the iron structure. We start to follow them up to the lounge, but Taylor stops me.

"Here," she hisses, thrusting a small glass bottle my way. "Keep hold of that, will you? I've got some mixers upstairs."

Vodka. I haven't drank since last summer term. My stomach turns just thinking about it.

"No chance." I thrust it back, but she steps away. "Taylor, you know I'm not supposed to drink on my meds. I could have a seizure."

"I know, you don't have to. I just need you to hide it in your sweatshirt, please? Just till we get on the roof." She gestures at her flimsy pajamas and sticks her bottom lip out in another pout. "I don't have anywhere to hide it."

"Fine," I huff, shoving the cold bottle into the kangaroo pouch on my sweatshirt. "But only because it's for you. I am not getting caught with this and I am not helping you drink it, OK?"

"Of course." She beams at me and catches hold of my hand, giving it a squeeze. "Thank you. Now, let's start this year off right!"

Taylor skips over to the spiral staircase and begins to bound up it as I follow, careful not to drop the glass bottle on the metal steps.

The lounge is packed with girls from our year, most of them wearing some variation of Taylor's outfit matched with pristine hair and makeup. I touch my own sleek bob and slide my fingers into the patch where the staples had been. The hair there is rough and bristly from being shaved and growing back in the weirdest ways. I wish it was long again, but my head injury last summer didn't leave me with much choice but to cut it short.

"Lizzie!" A loud squeal shakes me from my self-pity as strong arms crush my shoulders from behind. "God, you're skin and bone! How the hell are you?"

"Hey, Kat," I squeak. She releases me and I turn around to give my friend a big squeeze. "I was wondering when I'd see you. I didn't see your stuff in the room."

"Literally just got back from Cyprus this morning; we had a family wedding. I've been traveling all day, walked through the door about five minutes ago, so I just dumped it and followed the noise."

"I can tell—you're so tan! You look amazing, as usual."

"I spent the summer at the gym." She flexes one bare arm and I see muscle there that would put most of the boys to shame. "You should come with me now that we're back." She squeezes my arm through the thin hoodie and I wince. "It'd be good for you, like rehab or something."

"Er, yeah, maybe." She grins at me; she knows full well I have no intention of going with her. "Hey, come say hi to Taylor. We have got to fill you in on what you have already missed."

We weave through the room as I regale her with the events of the day: the memorial, Jameela's note in classics class, and, finally, the JB meeting.

"Wait." She stops and stares at me. "Someone is claiming they killed Morgan? Seriously? Who knows about this?"

"Only the other acolytes, I think." I shrug. "Jameela was pretty freaked out, anyway."

"Did Patel take it seriously?"

"Hard to tell," I muse. "She doesn't give much away."

"True. What does Taylor think?" Kat asks.

"Not sure. I bet she thinks Jameela is playing it up, looking for attention. She's still a bit sore on Jameela automatically being sworn in as head girl. She thought there'd be some sort of new challenge or something, so she could prove herself. Don't tell her I said that, though!"

Kat shakes her head. "Of course I won't. I wonder if it's ever happened before. Someone not finishing the year as head girl."

"I dunno. Maybe Taylor's right. I mean, Jameela is a bit of a drama queen."

"This is true. Come on, enough morbid talk for now. I need a drink and to see if Caroline is still wearing that crop top she loved so much last year. . . ."

I giggle. "Perv," I say. We start moving again and I try my best to soak up the atmosphere. Seniors at Morton, finally. God, I dreamed of this last year. There were always whispers of parties and I never thought I'd finally be at one, but here I am, a Jewel and Bone acolyte, no less.

I take in as much of my surroundings as I can. It's not that different from our lounge from last year, but the excitement in the air now is real. There's a whole dark academia vibe to the room: age-worn leather armchairs and wood-paneled walls. One side of the room is decorated with miniature portraits of head girls gone by, Dr. Patel among them. Morgan's picture is up on the wall already—no matter how brief her reign, if it happened at Morton, you could bet it would be documented. The photographs go all the way back to 1906, when the academy was founded, and I suddenly feel queasy with the eyes of a hundred more girls on me.

"Lizzie?" Kat is staring at me, concern in her eyes. "Are you feeling all right?" Her thick Northern accent is soft.

"Yeah, yeah, of course. Just being a space cadet. Sorry—a side effect, you know?" I rub the bristles over my scar.

"OK." She doesn't look convinced. "You'll be fine, I promise. We've got you."

"I know. Thanks, Kat. Now come on, this vodka Taylor made me carry is burning a hole through my conscience. I need to get rid of it."

We approach the back of the room, where two huge balcony doors provide a view of the countryside for miles around. A small kitchen area in the corner comes into view and, sure enough, Taylor's there, rummaging around in the tiny fridge. She stands up, triumphantly brandishing a bottle of Diet Coke, half of which she promptly pours down the sink.

"Vodka?"

"Vodka." I slide the bottle out and hand it to her. We close ranks, Kat on one side, me on the other, as she pours it into the Coke bottle.

"Voilà!" She gives it a swirl and takes a swig. My own mouth waters, my stomach turning just thinking of the sting, but as always, Taylor's face doesn't give anything away. "Right!" she shouts to the room of girls. "Now I'm ready to party!"

"Did someone say party?" A thick Essex accent interrupts and the room falls silent as Jameela emerges from her room. That is a definite perk of being chosen as head girl—your own room on the top floor, your own bathroom, everything. Another reason Taylor's jealous—imagine not having to wait in line for the shower. "Seniors, are we ready to welcome the new school year?"

A chorus of *"Hell, yeah!"* fills the room as Jameela squares her shoulders and glides through the crowd, flanked by her old roommates, Emily and Ayesha. They smile and nod, and as Emily passes me, she pats the place over her heart where her JB pin would be, a gesture from one acolyte to another. I return the gesture.

A shiny black badge decorates the lapel of Jameela's pajamas, which are a deep, dark red that perfectly matches her lipstick. She strolls toward the balcony doors, the one thing our junior lounge did *not* have, and flings them open, allowing a soft, late-summer breeze to filter into the room.

"Seniors"—she smiles—"I declare this year officially open for business."

7

THE ROOF GARDEN IS *GORGEOUS*, EVEN MORE SO IN THE dying light of late evening. Last year, when we were in the junior lounge, we used to stare out the windows and wish we could come out here. I think a couple of the girls tried once, but as far as I know, it did not end well for them.

The walls that enclose the roof garden are magical, castlelike battlements, just high enough to see over. There's fake grass underfoot, so I kick off my flip-flops and let the blades tickle and scratch the soles of my feet as I pad over to peek at the view.

Nothing but acres and acres of fields surround us, a patchwork quilt of lavender, densely knotted pockets of woodland, and a hundred shades of green. I turn back to the terrace. Tiny bistro tables and chairs dot the area, each a different vibrant color, yellows and pinks and peacock shades of teal and violet. Long strings of solar light bulbs arch overhead, anchored on the walls and all sweeping up to a flagpole that juts ceremoniously from the center of the building, giving the illusion of a skeletal circus tent. Small flickering tea lights have been placed into plant pots and these line the long wooden benches that cling to the inner walls. I take a deep breath and turn to smile at Kat and Taylor. They grin back—I think Taylor is even a little teary-eyed. Not that she'd show weakness in front of all these people.

"Come on." She swigs from her bottle again and marches through the roof garden, turning the corner around the junior lounge.

Our side of the terrace is an upside-down L-shape, so once you're around the corner, you can't see our lounge anymore. We *can* see the other side, though: a mirror image of our own.

The boys' side.

Morton is totally old-school when it comes to sleeping arrangements, even though all the lessons and extracurriculars are mixed. The girls' dorms and lounges are in the West Wing and the boys' are in the East Wing. From what little that Taylor tells me, the layout is pretty much the same over there. Out here, though, in front of the flagpole and directly between the wings, there's a wall to separate us.

Well, it tries to.

Marcus, of course, is the first one over. The wall itself is low, but there's a tall, metal fence on top of it, capped with spikes. There's no way to climb it, and even if you did, getting skewered by one of those spikes would definitely mean a trip to the nurse's office—and how would you explain that one? Marcus doesn't even attempt it. Instead, he hoists himself onto the outer wall battlements, swings a leg around the edge and sits there, one leg on either side of the metal pole. His large hands are wrapped around the end fence post, letting it take his weight.

I swear you can hear the collective intake of breath from forty-nine other kids as his body hangs over the four-story drop.

"Yes, Marcus!" someone shouts from the boys' side, and others start to join in, chanting his name. If I didn't know Taylor so well, I'd say she wasn't bothered about the fact her boyfriend was risking his life to climb over the wall, but I'm close enough to see faint tension lines around her mouth. I reach down and squeeze her hand while her eyes stay fixed on him as he swings his other leg over. She doesn't let her breath out until both of his feet are firmly planted on this side of the wall. Then she takes a huge swig from her bottle.

"Easy." Marcus shrugs, turning to look at the crowd of girls before him. His eyes land on Taylor and he points at her. "There she is," he booms, "the only girl I'd risk my life for."

"Oh, please," she says, but her tension has melted away and she laughs as everyone bursts into heckles around us. She saunters over and I feel that familiar tug of longing in my chest as she smiles up at him. Not jealousy, exactly, but a definite ache of . . . something.

The party starts to erupt around us. The rest of the boys follow Marcus's lead, and pretty soon all of the senior class is crammed onto our side of the roof garden and drinks start to appear from ever more innovative places. I look around for Kat and see she's already doing some kind of push-up competition with the guys from the football team, so I take a wide berth around *that* and stop to say hi to Frank and some of the other kids from my history class.

That's when I see him.

Now, I'm not the most dramatic person ever, but for a second I swear that the noise dulls a little, the crowd parts ever so slightly, and everything moves in slow motion. I know every student in our year, and I've never seen this one before. He's tall and slim, taller than me, and his skin is light brown. He cracks a smile and I see the most amazing set of teeth outside Netflix. I'm staring, I know I am, but I can't help it. A small group surrounds him over in the far corner of the garden, right by the corner wall, and it takes me a second to realize that Taylor and Marcus are part of that group. In fact, Tay is waving at me and from the look on her face, it's clear that she hasn't just started. I hustle over.

"Hey," she says, shooting me a meaningful look as I join the group. "We were just talking about you, weren't we, Marcus?"

"What? Oh, yeah. Hey, Liz, meet Cole. He's new here."

"Hey." Cole nods at me and up close I can see that he is, in fact, one of the best-looking people I have *ever* met. He's wearing loose black trousers and a high-necked shirt made from the same type of material. Linen, I think. It has those little buttons on it, at the throat and cuffs, and I wonder if it's some kind of martial-arts uniform.

"Not quite," he says with a laugh, and I realize I've just voiced my thoughts aloud again. Damn it, I really need to watch that particular side effect of my medication; it could get me in a lot of trouble. Especially while he's around.

"Sorry, I didn't mean because you are . . ."

"What, Chinese?" He laughs again. "Don't worry. Nah, they do look like something out of *Cobra Kai,* but they're my honest-to-God pj's." He holds up two fingers in defense of his story, the rest of his fingernails pink from the pressure of his long fingers holding a green glass bottle. "They are from my Cantonese grandma, though. Hong Kong specials. Think they cost her about sixty dollars at Mong Kok market."

"Oh." *Oh?* Is that all I've got? My cheeks heat up. I'm literally feeling myself blush, right in his face.

"Yeah." He takes a swig of his beer and holds it out to me. "Want some?"

"No, thanks, I don't drink."

He grins at me and takes another drink. "Sensible. Interesting."

Seriously, how much blood do my cheeks need right now?

"Hey." Taylor nudges me and nods toward a small group by the central wall. "Look." A couple of the boys have climbed back over and disappeared inside and now they emerge with a small box of cigarettes in tow, which they pass through the metal railings to the group on our side. A red-clad arm reaches out to grab it—Jameela, with her entourage. From the look of her, she's wasted already. I wonder if they started drinking in her new room after the meeting. I check my watch—they must have been. We've only been out here half an hour.

"Smoking." I wrinkle my nose. "Gross."

Taylor snorts. "I'm surprised Jameela is even entertaining it," she says. "Doesn't she have really bad asthma? Maybe being head girl has literally gone to her head."

"It could be the note," I suggest. "She seemed to take that pretty seriously. Doesn't smoking calm your nerves or something?"

"Eww, no, that's such a myth. Oh, well—sucks for her." Taylor's eyes narrow for a second, but I blink and the expression is gone, as if I imagined it. "Anyway," she chirps, smiling pointedly in my direction, "Cole, tell us all about you. . . ."

A loud, spluttering cough interrupts just as he opens his pretty mouth, and the rooftop falls silent. Jameela is doubled over by the railings, drawing loud, hacking breaths that sound painful, raw.

"For the love of . . ." Marcus breaks away from us and moves over to her, quickly tailed by Taylor.

Cole looks at me in confusion.

"What's happening?"

"I don't know."

We follow the crowd. Jameela is now on her knees, both hands on the ground, trying desperately to calm her breathing, though I can see the fear in her eyes from here. Her friends stand around stupidly, only Emily having the sense to pat her on the back. Jameela weakly pushes her away and tries to get to her feet. I spot Marcus running toward the lounge from the corner of my eye. What's he doing? Getting water?

"For God's sake!" Taylor yells. "The girl has asthma. Does she have an inhaler?"

"Er, yeah, I think so . . . ," Ayesha splutters, looking around with tears in her eyes. "I mean, she should. I think it's in her room; I knew where it was in our dorm last year, but she moved everything, so . . ."

"I've got it." Marcus pushes back through the crowd and shoves a small, pink piece of plastic into Taylor's hand. "It should help; my sister has the same one."

"Jameela?" Taylor's voice is firm but clear, like she's talking to a toddler. Jameela looks up, one hand at her throat, her breath ragged and wheezing. You can hear how sore and inflamed her throat is. The air is almost whistling through it. "Jameela? Take this. Two puffs, OK?"

Jameela grabs the inhaler and forces it into her mouth, pressing the button and taking a deep, rattling breath. Her shoulders relax slightly and she exhales and takes another, the panic clearing from her eyes. She keeps the inhaler in her mouth and takes a noticeably deeper breath, using her free hand to give the crowd a shaky thumbs-up, before dropping the medicine and pulling a face. It clearly tastes awful.

"Good old Taylor," I say, turning back to Cole, who looks as shell-shocked as I feel. "She's always calm in a crisis."

"Jeez." He throws back the rest of his drink. "Think I need another one of these. Come on."

I follow him back to the corner of the rooftop as the crowd at the railing breaks up and the party slowly recovers. We sit cross-legged on a load of cushions that have been piled in the corner, our backs to the wall. "That was crazy," said Cole. "Is it always so eventful at Morton?"

I flash back to the last day of summer term as he grabs another bottle. Taking the boat out that night, the panic as it flipped. Morgan, cold and still while Taylor gave her CPR and I drifted in and out of consciousness. The rest of the newly minted acolytes huddled around, useless, just like tonight. Emily and Ayesha hadn't been able to help their friend then, either. Dr. Patel on the phone, barking orders at the boys, only Marcus actually up and doing something . . .

"No," I say. "Nothing much ever happens here—"

My lie is split by a scream.

"Jameela? JAMEELA!"

For the final time that evening, silence descends on the party as Emily screams her friend's name over and over. Even from here, through a tangle of legs, I can see a body lying on the floor, one hand clasped around her throat. Jameela is still, curled in the fetal position. She doesn't look right.

"Liz? Is she . . ." Cole's voice is tinged with panic.

"No," I nearly whisper. "No, she's just . . . she's just . . ."

I trail off as Frank kneels next to Jameela and takes her pulse, first at her neck, then grabbing her wrist as he tries to time her heartbeats on his watch. After attempting CPR, he places her arm down gently before shaking his head.

Another head girl, dead.

8

WELL.

That was certainly unexpected.

I was happy to let them enjoy the party tonight, but silly little Jameela had to try and be all cool and grown-up, didn't she? I was hoping she'd take the inhaler before bed and pop off quietly, make it look more natural. I can't believe she didn't taste the camphor—she must have been drunk. Getting hold of her inhaler was hardly a challenge, either—I was able to stroll right into her room in plain sight today. But this—well, this was much *more exciting.*

I guess the ads are right: smoking really can kill.

9

"HERE." I DRAPE A GRAY COMFORTER OVER TAYLOR'S SHOUL-
ders and she grabs it gratefully, pulling it down across her bare legs.
"Anything new?"

"No." She's pale. I sit next to her, wedging her body in between
mine and Kat's, as much to stop my own nervous tremors as to
soothe hers. I track their line of sight to the small corner kitchen,
where Dr. Patel is in hushed conversation with a police officer. Most
people have been hustled back downstairs, but a handful of us have
been kept back. A glance around confirms that everyone else in the
room is JB.

"What has Dr. Patel said?" I whisper to Kat. We're all watching
the headmistress now but, as always, she is inscrutable.

"Not a thing," Kat replies. "I mean, not to us, anyway." She turns
to look at me. "Is it a bit weird that there's no ambulance here?"

"I dunno." I shrug. "I guess so. I haven't thought about it."

"Well, there was one when Morgan . . . er, last year?" Kat winces
as soon as the words are out of her mouth. "I'm sorry, you don't
remember, do you?"

"It's fine. But no, I don't remember."

"Tay? Do you think it's weird?" Kat nudges Taylor gently,

but she doesn't look at us. She's away with the fairies. I shake my head.

"Leave her."

We continue to watch Dr. Patel talk to the police officer. Well, I say talk, but it's clear that she's in charge of the situation. He's an old white guy, thick around the middle. Hell of a mustache. Doesn't look like he could catch many hotfooted criminals. Finally, he nods and they shake hands.

Did I just imagine that flash of red and white that passed between Dr. Patel and the officer? I haven't seen many large bills in real life, but that sure looked like one. More than one, in fact.

Bribery?

"Ladies." Dr. Patel turns to us as they walk past our perch on the sofa. "You may go to bed. Thank you."

Taylor stands up, the comforter forgotten, now puddling around her feet. "You don't need me for anything? Questions, or . . ."

Dr. Patel raises a manicured hand and looks pointedly at the police officer. He clears his throat, a rasping sound that makes me feel a bit sick. "Er, no, love. I've got all I need."

"Thank you, Officer Whipsnade." Dr. Patel ushers him down the spiral staircase, pausing only to turn back to us one last time. "Now, girls, I won't tell you again. There is nothing more you can do here, and you need rest. Off to bed. Oh, and Miss Fox? My office, please. Tomorrow. Eight a.m. sharp."

Taylor nods once and we stand in silence, like good girls. I wonder if Kat and Taylor noticed Dr. Patel handing over money too. We follow her orders, though, because that's what Jewel and Bone acolytes do.

The lights are all out in the hallway and there isn't a sound except the soft hiccupping breaths I've been taking to calm myself down. Still, I bet no one's asleep. Light seeps out from beneath each closed door and once Patel's spiky footsteps disappear, a tide of whispering fills each room, the hushed sounds of shock and grief swelling out into the hallway. A couple of muffled sobs make the darkness feel even heavier. I continue to follow my deep-breathing pattern, the one the therapist in the hospital taught me.

Kat snaps the main light off and we climb into bed.

"How the hell am I supposed to sleep?" Taylor says as I wrap myself in blankets. I roll over to face her, my eyes slowly adjusting to the darkness. "I feel like I'm in some kind of horror movie. First Morgan, now Jameela. Am I bad luck? Am I?"

"Shush," I whisper. Kat jumps out of bed again and checks the door handle, twisting the key when she realizes it isn't locked. "You are not bad luck."

"What if the note Jameela got wasn't a joke?" Kat suggests as she burrows back under the covers, her voice quiet in the dark room. "What if someone really did kill them both?"

"But Morton is so safe!" Even as the words leave my mouth, I know that's not true.

"It's not so safe anymore, not after this," Taylor argues, her voice thick with emotion. "And did you see Patel? I'm pretty sure she paid that cop off."

"I did."

"Yep," Kat agrees. "She wasn't particularly discreet, was she?"

"So what now?" I whisper. "Are we saying someone killed them on purpose? Or are we getting carried away?"

"It seems impossible, doesn't it," Taylor says, clearing her throat quietly, as if she's been crying. I wrap the blankets tighter around myself as a shiver travels down my spine. "I mean, I know they weren't . . . well, they weren't the nicest people, but who would do that?"

"Someone who wanted to scare Jameela off, maybe," Kat suggests quietly. "Someone who wanted something she had?"

Taylor's voice is steel-cut. "What exactly does that mean?"

"Oh, no, nothing, Tay. I didn't mean . . ."

"Didn't mean what?" she spits.

I lie still beneath my covers, not daring to breathe. I wasn't expecting an argument tonight, especially not between Kat and Taylor.

"I didn't mean anything," Kat sighs. "I'm tired, I've been traveling all day. I just meant that someone may have been jealous of Jameela being head girl and thought they could scare her off, get her to leave. It could have been anyone—Ayesha, Emily. You know how bitchy that group is. They're like *Mean Girls* without the sassy quotes."

"Was," I correct quietly. "How bitchy that group *was*."

Silence.

"We need to stick together," Kat whispers, "just in case. OK?"

"Yes," I answer. "Taylor?"

"You're right." Taylor's response is muffled by her pillows and I hear the creak as she lifts herself up in the bed. All I can see of her is a silvered silhouette highlighted by the slight glow creeping in from the hallway. "I just can't shake the feeling that I'm bad luck."

"Come on, you're not bad luck," I reassure her as Kat makes soothing noises in agreement. "It's just . . . really unlucky that you were there both times. There's a difference, I promise. Besides, you're kind of a hero, Tay. You tried to save both of them."

Silence. And then the tiniest whisper.

"I clearly didn't try hard enough."

10

MORTON SETTLES BACK INTO A ROUTINE IN THE DAYS AFTER JA-
meela's death. Even so, she is a noticeable absence in classes, especially because everyone is constantly talking about her.

"Can you believe there hasn't been a memorial yet? They did one
for Morgan, so they should do one for her too, right?" Kat quizzes
us on the way down to the main hall.

"It's only Wednesday," I say. It's an early assembly today, with
breakfast served after, so I'm still rubbing my bleary eyes and Taylor
is a literal zombie as Kat bounces along the corridor next to us.
"Maybe there'll be one this morning." I yawn. "I guess we'll find out
any minute." We pause to join the back of a line waiting to go into
the hall. I catch myself searching the crowd for Cole—I haven't seen
him since Monday night—and start to shuffle forward as the large
wooden doors open into the hall. The staff are already on the stage
and we fall into rows automatically—juniors on the left, seniors
on the right—and wait, quietly chattering, until the bell rings and
Dr. Patel stands up.

"I don't see a memorial picture," Kat whispers.

We snap to attention. Dr. Patel goes through the motions of the
assembly, which is like any other—we sing something in Latin that

I know word for word but could not tell you the name of; Mr. Lucas gets up and drones on about football fixtures; and my art teacher briefly mentions an exhibition that seniors can submit work for. I'm ashamed to admit that I daydream about toast through most of it.

"Thank you, and enjoy your day." Dr. Patel ends the assembly, dismissing us. Nothing about Jameela. My stomach rumbles.

"Toast."

"Toast," Taylor agrees. We wait to file out, but thankfully the dining hall is straight across the hall and the crowd melts away quickly. We find a table and dump our bags before heading in separate directions.

"Get me some juice, Tay," I call after her retreating form as she heads over to the cereal bar. It looks like I'm on toast duty. Again. I head over to the big toaster by the doors and grab a pair of silver tongs. I select a slice of bread and drop it onto a little wire conveyor belt, which, while moving at a glacial pace, toasts the bread. I add five more slices, ignoring the huff of a junior behind me—they'll learn. If you have the toaster, you have the toaster. I didn't make the rules.

The first slice drops and slides to the bottom, perfectly crisp and golden brown. I reach for a plate and something outside the open doors catches my eye.

"I can't believe you won't talk to me about this." It's Frank from JB. His face is drawn and his lips are pulled back from his teeth in a snarl. I momentarily forget about the toast and watch.

"I am not doing this here, OK?" The girl in the hallway with him has her back to me; all I can see is dark, shining hair that spills down her back. "Take it to Patel—she'll know what to do."

The figure turns and I see it's Emily, Jameela's friend. Her features are carved into an angry mask as she marches into the dining hall and grabs Ayesha, who is sitting near the door with a group of JB boys.

"Are you done now? Er, hello? I said, are you finished?"

I blink and notice the impatient junior, still waiting. I look down to see I have jammed the toaster.

"Oh, yeah, sorry." I stack the toast on the plate and quickly grab a handful of butter and jam portions. The junior tuts again, but I ignore her.

The whole hall has fallen silent.

"You will talk to me now! Don't you care that your friend is dead?" Frank has followed Emily to her seat and now stands over her, glaring. She stares back at him defiantly as spit bubbles at the corners of his mouth.

"Frank's lost it," Taylor whispers in my ear, appearing from nowhere. She hands me a tiny glass of juice and takes a piece of toast from the top of the stack. We stand, rooted to the spot as Emily jumps up and pushes Frank, both of her hands flat on his chest. He's tall, but skinny and light and he flies back to the doorway, smashing into a junior with a bowl full of cereal. Emily is obviously stronger than she looks.

"How dare you tell me I don't care?" Emily screams at him, tears streaming down her face. "She was my best friend! Not yours. I don't know why you're getting involved!"

"Because it's so obvious!" He gets to his feet, milk dripping from his blazer, and points a shaking hand at Ayesha and her table. "You're telling me that none of you have figured it out? After that note on Monday? And what about you?" He spins to point at me and Taylor, who almost chokes on her dry toast. "You two haven't realized it was a real threat, either? That Jameela was *murdered*? Call yourself Jewel and B—"

"MR. KOWALSKI."

The entire dining hall turns to face the doors, where Dr. Patel stands, her expression furious.

"She looks like she's going to kill him," Taylor whispers. I can't help but agree. Dr. Patel's usually calm exterior is ruffled, betrayed by slightly bulging eyes and pursed lips. There's a red flush to her cheeks that clashes with the forest-green silk shirt she's wearing.

"My office. Now." She doesn't wait for him, instead spinning on a stiletto heel. Her footsteps ring down the corridor. Frank follows, his shoulders slumped now, the fight gone out of him.

"That's the last we'll see of him," Kat bellows as she joins us. The volume level in the room has gone from zero all the way up to ten in a matter of seconds, and my ears ring as we sit back at our table. "He's done for. Reckon she'll suspend him?"

"I really don't know. Have you ever seen Patel so angry?" Taylor asks as she takes another slice from the plate I forgot I was holding. I put it in the middle of the table, along with the jam and butter.

"No, never," I reply. I crane my neck to see Emily, who is still in floods of tears, being comforted by Ayesha while the boys look on awkwardly. A custodian is sorting out the mess left on the floor. When I look back at the plate, there's only one slice of toast left.

"And it's cold," I say aloud.

Kat smiles apologetically. "Sorry, I was hungry. Here." She throws a banana at me and I pull a face. I grab the last slice of toast and smear it with peanut butter, slicing the banana into little circles that I place in a neat pattern on top. I eat, lost in thought, chewing slowly. Frank knows the rules. We never speak about Jewel and Bone—and certainly not in a crowded dining hall. What on earth does he know that caused him to lose control like that?

11

"LIZ? LIZZIE? RISE AND SHINE, SLEEPYHEAD." I FORCE MY EYES open to find Kat's face looming over mine and sit up so fast, I almost headbutt her. "Whoa, sorry! Your alarm was going off, that's all. Were you taking a nap?"

I try my best to refocus, but my head is fuzzy. "Water?"

"Here." Kat thrusts a cold bottle into my hand and I gulp it down gratefully. "Better?"

"Yeah, thanks." Bed. Wednesday evening. Morton. I kick the twisted blanket from my legs and push myself up to sit, rearranging the pillows behind my back. "I thought naps made you feel better. I feel worse than I did before."

"Ah, you need practice, that's all. Naps are the best." Kat joins me on the end of my bed, making a pile of the books and notepads that have surrounded me as I slept. I never, ever nap. I'm usually lucky to fall asleep at all. Kat places my stuff on the floor, kicks off her sneakers, and sits back, cross-legged.

My twin bed is in the corner of our room, pushed up against the wall so you can use it like a sofa. I put the water bottle on my bedside table, a squat, wooden thing with a locking drawer and a cabinet underneath, and lean my head back, looking up at the lone window.

"What time is it?"

"Seven thirty. Good thing we don't have too much prep this week; you won't get away with sleeping all afternoon this year. You did miss dinner, though."

"Please tell me you brought me something?"

Kat grins and produces a little paper bag. "Not exactly gourmet, but the best I could get away with."

"Thanks." I take the bag from her and pull out an apple, a squished bread roll and a little pat of butter. It will do. "So," I say, ripping the paper bag apart and setting my meager dinner out on it, "what did I miss?"

"Not much. People still talking about Frank's outburst. He's all sheepish; Patel must've given him a massive telling-off this morning. No news on another JB meeting, though, so I guess we'll have to wait until the usual one on Monday. Everyone's on edge. The common rooms open on Saturday—we get lunch there this year. Oh, and your hot new friend is eating with the science kids, but Marcus is trying to lure him to the dark side."

I laugh as I tear the bread roll open and paint it with butter, using the foil wrapper to spread it. "He's hardly my friend; I only spoke to him on Monday night." I take a bite and relish the salt. I didn't know real butter was a thing until I got to Morton. "What else?"

"Patel came in to speak to us all, which was weird. I don't think I've ever seen her in the dining hall apart from this morning. She started to talk about Open Evening—it's next Thursday, by the way—and then she finally acknowledged Jameela after, what, two whole days? Said her parents had requested a private ceremony, it was a tragedy, blah, blah, blah, no further action is being taken, but we can go for counseling if we *really* want to."

"Oh, please, as if we have time for therapy. I literally fell asleep under a pile of books this afternoon. So that's it? Nothing's being looked into?"

"That's it. It's one hundred percent suspicious, though."

We are interrupted by a voice coming from the doorway. "Haven't you forgotten something?" Taylor flips her hair, sending a silky curtain off her shoulder so I can see a shiny black shield pinned to her lapel.

I sit up straight. "No. Kat would have said!"

"I wanted the girl herself to tell you," Kat grins. "Go on then, Fox."

"Oh, if I must." Taylor clears her throat and beams at me. "I was officially announced as head girl. Patel told me yesterday morning after, well, you know, and I wasn't allowed to say anything until now."

"Taylor! I can't believe I slept through the whole thing!"

"You'll be there on Monday, when I'm sworn in. That's when it matters. Anyway, guess who's the new deputy?"

"No, not *Emily.*" I groan.

"Yep. She beat me to that robe by a millisecond on initiation night, didn't she?" Kat shrugs, though I can tell she's upset. I reach over to pat her knee.

"She's going to be so—" I start, but Taylor cuts me off.

"Insufferable?"

"I was going to say mean, but insufferable works. I'm sorry, Kat. If you hadn't hung back for me that day, you would have gotten in there before her."

"Hey, don't be. My parents will send me to college anyway, even if it means racking up a lifetime's worth of debt." She shrugs. "Emily might not have that."

"Now who's the nice one?" I grin, pulling a cushion from behind me to throw in her direction.

"Well." Taylor glances down at her lapel, as though she can't believe her luck. "Let's hope this badge isn't cursed or something."

"Third time's the charm?" Kat suggests.

"Nice, Kat." Taylor laughs despite herself as she looks around our cozy dorm room. "I guess I'm moving out, then."

"Not until we pick your university with you!" Kat leaps from the bed and twirls her around, Taylor laughing and spinning like a little plastic doll in a music box.

"Oh, don't you worry." Taylor collapses backward onto her bed, her hair and arms splayed out above her head. "I did that weeks ago."

The rest of the week passed pretty quietly. Well, as quietly as it could when there were whispers of murder and conspiracy in the air. I've only seen Frank once, in classics, and he looked pale, withdrawn. I don't think anyone has spoken to him; they're scared of getting into trouble by association.

"Are you sure we won't get caught?" It's Friday evening and yet again, I seem to be watching Taylor debate about an outfit in the mirror, only this time I'm draped upside down over an armchair in the senior lounge. My head is hanging down from the seat, the ends of my hair just tickling the floor. I'm starting to get pins and needles and my eyes go fuzzy as Taylor traipses to the doorway of her new room. I'm so tired, I could sleep like this, but I promised I'd go to the woods with her—another senior rite of passage for the first week back.

"I don't really care, Lizzie. I just need to *feel* something." I flip myself upright, enjoying the feeling of the blood draining back into my limbs, the tingles dissipating. "How's this?" she asks.

"Perfect, as usual," I say. Her vermilion locks are piled on her head in a huge, messy topknot, tendrils pulled out to frame her face. A pair of tightly belted mom jeans and an off-the-shoulder knitted cream cardigan—that has only been slightly buttoned up—over a lacy crop top complete the look.

"You're sure?"

"Yes, perfectly preppy-casual-gorgeous." I look down at my battered joggers. "Suppose I better get changed, then."

Taylor holds out her hands and I let her grasp mine and pull me from the chair. "Er, yeah. I can't let you talk to Cole in your scruffs."

"Cole is coming?" Hmm, this is starting to almost seem like a good idea.

"Yes, Cole is coming. He's pretty cool." She gives me a sly sideways glance as she drags me into the head girl's bedroom. "Like you haven't noticed."

The corners of my mouth twitch. "Oh, maybe just a little bit . . ."

"Well, you need to borrow something." She starts to burrow through the mountain of clothes on her bed. "God, I love having the space to be messy— Oh, here." She holds out a scrap of fabric and immediately drops it at the look on my face. "Yeah, you're right. Oh! Here—this one will be perfect!"

I take the thin woolen sweater dress from her and hold it up to myself in the mirror. "Do you think I can pull this off?"

"Of course you can! Look." She stretches the material across my shoulders. "The boat neck flatters your hot new bob, and it's a bit fancy but still slouchy and casual. Wear it with your Converse and you'll look effortless."

"Hmmm." I pull my T-shirt off and slide into the dress, shuffling my sweatpants off simultaneously. It's one of those dresses that clings in all the right places but skims over the other bits. The long sleeves are slim, trailing down to a flared cuff, and tiny black metallic stars are stitched all over, catching the light but are otherwise invisible. Taylor was right—the neckline makes my hair look vaguely presentable, though I miss the curtain of blond I used to hide behind.

"You look gorgeous." She grins, holding up a huge eyeshadow palette in the reflection behind me. "But I am totally going to do your makeup."

"No, I—"

"Did I mention Cole?"

I sigh and take a seat on the edge of the bed.

"Fine," I say. "Do your worst."

12

SNEAKING OUT OF THE MAIN BUILDING AT MORTON IS RIDICU-
lously easy. It's almost like they trust us—either that or they don't
care at all. We walk out the back door into the dining hall and
make a run for the bushes behind the huge dumpsters out there.
It's another place I have yet to explore and I feel a little bubble of
anticipation at the thought of a proper party. One that involves
Cole.

It's later than I thought, going on eight thirty, and the sky is all
pink and dusky and gorgeous. Kat is waiting for us in the thicket of
trees behind the dining hall, a couple of other acolytes in tow. She
jumps up and bounces over to us immediately—that girl has way
too much energy—and we all exchange greetings, waving and tap-
ping over our hearts.

"God, we've been here forever. What took so long?" she bellows.
Then Taylor drags me forward and Kat lets out a wolf whistle.

"You can't rush a masterpiece," Taylor brags. I mean, she did do
a good job, I admit. I have that dewy no-makeup, I-woke-up-like-
this vibe going on and she put a couple of messy curls into my
hair so I have what she called a "sexy bedhead," which is not

something I think exists in real life. She curled my hair with her straightener, which I have no idea how to do, and it has brought out natural highlights I wasn't aware I had. She's got such a good eye for this stuff. I'm never confident enough to try anything different. But tonight, I very much look as though my naturally glowing self just threw any old thing on—and yet I look fantastic.

I love it.

"Liz, you hottie!" Kat smiles at me appraisingly and raises an eyebrow in that way everyone wishes they could do. She looks back at Taylor. "Cole?"

Taylor nods. "Cole."

"Right, that's enough, thanks," I say, and aim for the others. "Come on, let's get out of here before we get caught."

"Deal." Kat runs back to the other girls, Beck, a willowy blond who's in JB but is definitely one of the quieter members, and Caroline, who is indeed wearing her favorite V-necked crop top. Kat wiggles her eyebrows at me when she sees that I've noticed and I try to stifle a laugh while we follow them, Taylor's bag clanking as we go.

It's a lot darker in here than I thought, and I think longingly of the flashlight on my iPhone, but it's locked up in Dr. Patel's office with everyone else's—part of the contract when you sign up for Morton. That plus no social media *and* monitored internet time that you have to prebook for weekends only. Safeguarding—something the school prides itself on.

We crunch across the dry forest floor. The grounds around Morton are ridiculous, like acres and acres of forest and fields. If you were out here on your own and something happened, it could be days before you were found. . . .

"Liz? Helllooooo?" I snap back to the present. Taylor is peering at me, her brow slightly furrowed. "You OK? We lost you for a minute."

"Yeah, sorry." I gesture to my head. "Just, you know. I'm fine, though, honest."

"Okaaaay." She draws out the word, as though she thinks it's anything but OK. "If you say so. Look." She points to where the trees are starting to clear a bit and I see a warm yellow flicker. "The boys have started a fire."

"Of course they have." Kat snorts. "So macho."

"Some of us like macho." Taylor smirks just as Marcus's tall, broad frame comes into view. "See you girls later."

I wander around the little enclosure, observing the scene like a mountaineer who's just conquered Everest. I dreamed of evenings like these over the summer, from my horrible single bed in our horrible little apartment. I was stuck in that room, listening to my parents and their shady friends drinking and who knows what else in the living room. Every time I snuck out to use the bathroom, some loser would eye me up and down like I was a piece of meat. My parents didn't notice. I have to pinch myself now that my life is like something out of a TV series about glossy teens whose parents are never around.

But it's real. It's mine. This is life at Morton, especially when you're part of Jewel and Bone. This year is going to be full of chances to go to parties I've never dreamed of, to meet people of real influence and power—people who can help me leave my old life behind.

I just need one donor to see my potential, to sponsor my education. In college, that's when it will really begin. This is just a warm-up.

I wave shyly at faces I recognize and a couple I don't—not particularly well, anyway. All the other acolytes are here, but many of the other seniors are too. Logs have been dragged around a small fire to make seats and a few kids have spread blankets on grass that's scattered with the occasional golden leaf. We're right in the middle of those perfect ember days of summer, the turning weather clinging to memories of warmth.

"Hey." A voice greets me and I turn to face Cole, my breath catching as I remember exactly how gorgeous he is.

"Hey," I echo, somewhat stupidly.

"You sitting down?" He points to an empty log on the far side of the fire. It will fit us both if we sit kind of close. Um, yes, I'm sitting down.

"Sure," I say out loud instead, stretching my face into what I hope is a confident smile, and my feet crunch on tiny twigs underfoot as we head toward it. He gestures for me to sit first, and sure enough, there's only a whisper of air between us when we are both settled.

"Sorry," he says. "Kinda cozy, isn't it. Here." He slides off the log onto the ground. Still close, but I'm grateful for the breathing space. "Better?"

"Yeah, thanks."

We sit in silence for a moment, watching the flames catch on the kindling, small, sharp cracks piercing the quiet shadows. Cole leans forward to poke it with a stick he's found on the ground before throwing it onto the fire.

"Dunno why I did that," he says, slightly sheepish. "There's just something about a fire, isn't there? It's hypnotic."

"I know what you mean." The flames *are* mesmerizing: the way the fire eats away at anything in its path, doing whatever it needs to fulfill its purpose in life.

"Most serial killers begin as arsonists, you know." Kat's voice interrupts and I refocus as she hovers over us with a drinks cooler. "Beer?"

"Thanks." Cole reaches for one and I find myself studying his long, elegant hands again. "Liz? Oh wait, you don't . . ."

"It's fine." I smile as Kat hands me a Diet Coke. "Kat's got me covered."

"Of course. Here." She pulls a drink out for herself and waves a hand at Cole. "Scootch," she says.

He grins apologetically and retakes the seat next to me so Kat can flop into his place, though this time I feel the top of his leg press against mine. I tap my nails against the aluminum can and then pop the tab and take a huge swig to cover my grin, immediately regretting it as the bubbles threaten to make a reappearance.

Thankfully, Cole doesn't notice. "What did you mean? About serial killers being arsonists?"

I start to laugh and cut Kat off before she can get started. "Ignore her. Kat's doing psychology—*everything* is the trait of a serial killer."

"Not everything," she argues, grinning at me, "just, you know, the triad." She places her bottle on the ground between her crossed legs and starts ticking off things on her fingers. "One, arson.

Serial killers generally liked setting fires as kids. Second, wetting the bed."

"Wait." Cole looks uncomfortable. "Wetting the bed means you want to kill people?"

"Why?" Kat eyes him and takes a swig from her drink, replacing the bottle slowly. "You worried?"

"No, I, er—" Cole takes a drink too and I smother a giggle.

"Kat." I mock-chide. "Play nice."

"I am! No, it doesn't, but with some other traits it's a definite red flag."

"Right." He looks relieved and I have to hide another giggle. "So what's the last one? You said triad—that's three, right?"

"Right, so you have arson, bed-wetting, and the last one"—she lowers her voice, the sockets of her eyes hollow in the gloom—"which is where it gets really dark: animal torture."

"Kat, you're not telling the new boy about serial killers, are you?" Taylor's voice sounds from behind me and I lean my head back to face her. She grins down at me, Marcus's arm wrapped around her waist.

"Oh, she is," I say. "We're on to animal torture already."

"Kat!" Taylor admonishes her as Cole looks around in bewilderment.

"Is this normal?" he asks me under his breath as Kat and Taylor rib one another over our heads.

"Afraid so," I say with a laugh, but Kat cuts in.

"Only when I'm vetting my friend's potential boy—"

"Er, thanks, Kat." I quickly interrupt her and feel Cole's eyes burning into me.

"Come on, you weirdo." Taylor ruffles my hair gently as she takes Kat's arm. "Leave these two alone. I'll even let you tell me your Zodiac Killer theory again."

"Well, how can I resist an offer like that?" Kat climbs to her feet, brushing bits of forest floor off her toned legs. "Later, lovebirds," she trills, skipping over to the other side of the clearing. I immediately put my head in my hands.

"Oh my God, I am so sorry," I mutter from between my fingers. "She's just a bit full-on, you know?"

"Hey, I get it. She's your friend, she's looking out for you. I'd probably do the same if I was her and some new guy came in and started talking to the prettiest girl at school."

My hands are glued to my face. *Prettiest girl?* Did he just call me the prettiest girl at school?

"You look nice, tonight, by the way," he continues.

Liz, take your face out of your hands. Slowly, that's it. Good, now look at him.

I look at him.

He's smiling at me.

"I like your hair like that." I realize he's trying to fill the silence because I am acting like a total weirdo, so I go to my default setting of self-deprecation.

"Thanks, it used to be long, though. I hate it like this."

"It did? Why did you cut it if you don't like it?"

I shrug. "No choice. I had an . . . accident last year." I part the waves a bit to show him the tufty bits. "I hit my head. Had to have some pretty gnarly stitches."

"I'm so sorry, I didn't realize. How are you now?"

"Oh, fine." I wave the question off, like I always do. "Apparently I could get seizures or something, but I've been OK so far." I hold up the cola. "But that's why I don't drink."

"Well." Cole holds up his beer and clinks it against my can. "I'm glad you're doing well." He takes a sip and smiles at me. "And, for the record, I like the hair."

13

IT TURNS OUT THAT IT'S EASY TALKING TO COLE—EASIER THAN
talking to anyone, even Taylor and Kat. It's like a clamp in my chest
has released a little, and I realize it's relief. So I keep going, telling
him about my miserable time over the holidays, a summer of painkillers and wasted days watching the sky from a dirty window. I
leave out some details, of course. It's hard to discuss things without
giving away JB, sometimes.

"Jeez." He opens a second beer. "That must've been a lot to deal
with. I'm sorry."

"Thanks." I feel I should be honest, so I say, "We weren't friends,
exactly, but"—I gesture around the clearing—"Morton's pretty
small. You can't help but get to know each other."

"In that case, fill me in. Give me a rundown of everyone here."
He leans back and nods toward the others in the clearing. I'm grateful for the change of topic and scan the crowd.

"Well, you kind of know Marcus and Taylor. King and queen of
Morton." I smile. "You've met Kat . . . Oh, here we go." I point to a
tall, slim white boy with a shock of dark hair. "That's Frank."

"Oh, yeah. He's the dude who was shouting about Jameela in
the dining hall, right?"

"Right." I wince. "That was pretty bad. He's in my classics class. I always thought he was really quiet, but obviously not. He's here for English. Some kind of writing scholar—Kat says his stuff is amazing but it's super dark. He can be very . . . intense, I guess. Oh, and he has these really striking blue eyes, but whatever you do, don't mention it to him or you'll never hear the end of it. He loves to talk about them." Cole snorts as I scan the crowd, my eyes landing on a short girl with sad eyes. "That's Emily, I dunno if you remember her from the pajama party?"

"She was Jameela's friend. The one Frank was yelling at."

"Yeah. She and Jameela were both besties with Morgan last year; there were four of them in this clique—Morgan, Jameela, Emily, and Ayesha. I know you're not supposed to speak ill of the dead, but they were kind of the mean girls of the junior class."

"She doesn't look mean," Cole observes. I take in Emily's hunched frame and vacant stare. No, she doesn't look mean.

"I guess losing friends changes you," I say. "Emily's here for math, like Jameela was; she does classics with me too, though. Can't remember what her other subject is. She used to do this trick last year where you'd fire massive numbers at her and she'd just multiply them right away, do it in her head. I don't think she ever got one wrong."

"That's a pretty cool party trick. You got one?" He's smiling.

"Of course." I go to flick my hair before remembering it's gone. Ugh. "I can recite all the kings and queens of England since William the Conqueror. In order. With the dates they ruled."

"Serious?"

"Of course. What about you?"

"Periodic table. I can tell you the order and letters for every

element. Could probably do it backward too. Never tried, though."
He looks stricken for a moment. "I just realized that makes me a
huge geek, doesn't it?"

"Welcome to the club." I smile, gesturing around. "We are literally the biggest geeks in the country. It's wonderful."

Cole beams at me. "Agreed. Carry on. Who's next?"

"Er, let's see." I nod my head toward the girl Emily is with.
"That's Ayesha, the final of the foursome." She's subdued too, sitting close to Emily and Frank. Presumably they've made up after what
happened on Wednesday. She's nervously fiddling with her gauzy
blue headscarf, undoing and retying it over and over again as they
speak in hushed tones. I wonder if they're still dwelling on the note.
"Fluent in about five languages but zero common sense."

"Hey, there's nothing wrong with that." Cole nudges me gently.
"We're not all blessed with practicality, you know."

"Oh, no, really?" I tease, turning to catch his eye. "Then I'm
afraid we can't be friends."

"Don't say that." Cole brushes his hand on the side of my leg
and I hold in a little hiccup of breath, forcing myself to focus on the
others while simultaneously letting my hand drift to my lap and rest
next to his. I have to clear my throat before I can carry on.

"Those two are Joe and Ethan." I point to a short, stocky boy
with tight black curls and a skinny kid with cut-glass cheekbones
and skin even paler than mine. "They're both here for computer science. Ethan was Morgan's boyfriend . . ." I trail off, realizing every
single person I've mentioned is a Jewel and Bone acolyte.

Which means that every one of them is a potential suspect—at
least according to Frank.

"What about those two?" Cole points over to where Kat is now holding court in the clearing, minus her T-shirt, taking shots out of two people's belly buttons.

"Oh, God." I groan, but I can't help laughing. "That's Beck and Caroline. They do English with Kat and are, er, easily influenced." Cole's eyes are wide as they resume their seats on the floor with three boys from the languages department, cross-legged, each holding a fanned-out hand of cards. Caroline's lipstick is smudged and her crop top is askew. One of the boys, Luke, another acolyte, is pulling a tight black T-shirt over his head, a finely carved set of abs peeking through. "Strip/dare poker. Kat made it up last year—strip poker meets truth or dare. I can't tell you *how* many items of clothing she has lost this way."

Cole laughs before peeling his eyes away and I feel the tiniest little tug of jealousy under my ribs. "Good to know that even us geeks know how to have fun, I guess. Though I don't know if I'm ready for that much fun." He lowers his voice. "Your friend Kat kind of scares me."

"Yeah," I agree, "she scares most people. She's the best, though. These are the things that happen when you can't get on the internet, I guess." I sit up straight, realizing I've been doing most of the talking. "What about you? Glad to be here, at Morton?"

"Hell, yeah. I was lucky to get in. It was like a dream, you know? Like winning the lottery or something."

"I know what you mean. How did your parents take it?"

"They were thrilled." He smiles. "Mom's from Taiwan and always dreamed her son would get a top-notch education—she never did. I had a scholarship at the local grammar school. I thought she was proud then, but when my tutor called us in over the summer to meet Dr. Patel and she offered me a place here, I thought Mom was going to have a heart attack. She practically packed my bags that night." He smiles at the memory and I find myself obsessing over a teeny freckle on his cheek. "I hadn't even heard of it before then—but I feel very lucky. Anyway, what about you?" He sips at his beer. "Were your parents the same? I mean, you got in here last year; you must be super clever. Not like us wait-list dweebs. I bet they were proud."

"Yeah." I think of the day I sat in my head teacher's office with Dr. Patel. Dad had stayed in bed and Mom was pacing back and forth outside, one of her so-called friend's dramas playing out on the phone she held in one hand as she took long puffs off a cigarette with the other. We watched her from the window and I realized she wasn't even slightly aware that she was late for our meeting.

"Yeah," I repeat. "They were thrilled too. Anyway!" I force brightness into my voice. "How's your first week been? Is science here everything you dreamed it would be?"

"Absolutely. The equipment in the lab is insane, like, university-standard. There are machines worth at least a quarter mil. It's like I've died and come to geek heaven." He winces. "Sorry, poor choice of words, given . . . everything. You know what I mean, though, right?"

"Of course I do," I reassure him. "I thought about this place all summer. I couldn't wait to get back. Has Marcus been looking after you?"

"Yeah, he's pretty chill, seems like a good guy. Taylor's been great too. You guys are tight, right?"

"She's my best friend. Not sure what I'd do without her."

"That's nice." He slips me a glance from beneath his brow. "Everyone needs someone they feel like that about."

My cheeks flame again and I take a sip of my drink, realize it's empty, and style it out the best I can.

"Yeah." I force myself to catch his eye and let a shy smile stretch my lips as his warm fingers start to close around my cool ones. "Yeah, they do."

"Er, sorry to interrupt." I tear my eyes away from Cole's and look up to see Frank standing there. The fire is smoldering behind him and Emily and Ayesha are throwing fistfuls of dirt on the dying cinders. "The juniors have called to say Patel's on the rampage. We need to get back to the dorms ASAP."

"Great," I mutter, watching his retreating form. I get to my feet and look around for anything that might have been left behind—mainly, items of Kat's clothing.

"What does that mean?" Cole says.

"It means we are going to be in big trouble if we don't get out of here now."

I always forget how quickly night can fall, even when you're expecting it. Everyone has scattered and the woods seem huge and empty.

Eerie.

"Hey," Cole whispers from behind me, "how did someone call Frank to tell him Patel was coming? I thought we weren't allowed phones. Oh, and his eyes are really blue, aren't they? He totally wears contacts."

"Oh, sweet summer child." I smile, hoping he gets the *Game of Thrones* reference. "We all have these." I pause and lean down to pull a tiny phone from the collar of my high-tops, where it fits snugly behind my anklebone. "There's always a couple of first-years on Dr. Patel watch. They keep a lookout and call whoever the designated senior is when there's a party going on. It's weird; we have nothing much to do with them apart from that, but it's like a tradition—I think Morgan and Jameela did it last year, when we were the juniors. Frank must have been the designated senior tonight."

"But burner phones, Cersei?" I knew he'd get it. "Seriously?"

"Yep." I tuck it back down and start walking again, weaving beneath the trees and keeping my eyes open for a flash of light that might indicate someone looking for us. "They're old Nokias—you can only text and call on them, but the battery lasts forever. And they have this addictive snake game on them too." I pause, a twig snapping somewhere up ahead. "Wait there," I whisper to Cole. I sneak forward and hear it again. "Quiet, I think there's someone there," I hiss, turning back to him. "We need to go back."

But I'm alone.

"Cole?" I try, a little louder. I squint through the darkness and feel the scar along my head start to itch, the way it does when anxiety makes my skin prickle. "Cole?"

Nothing.

I stand still and shut my eyes, listening carefully. I'm not sure how much time passes, but finally I hear another crunch underfoot and my eyes fly open, searching the gloom in the direction of the sound.

"Cole?"

My voice sounds small but too loud at the same time, echoing through the inky dark. I will my feet forward and start to walk, panting as though I've just run laps. Sweat trickles down the nape of my neck and I realize I'm terrified.

Of what?

It's funny, isn't it, how your body knows when something's not right. My feet don't want to walk this way and my adrenaline is pumping so hard I feel sick. There's such a sudden sense of wrongness in the air, it's almost tangible. I can feel it.

"Cole?"

"Liz." A voice croaks in response this time and I speed up at the sound of it, rounding a tight knot of trees in the dark. I fumble for my tiny phone, knowing the light will be pathetic, but it will be something, so when I stumble on the scene, I see only sepia-toned snatches of it. "He . . . I think he's . . ."

He doesn't finish his sentence, but I see it all. Cole, kneeling in the leaves. The sticky, viscous red on a jagged rock.

A pale, dead hand, curled around a plastic inhaler.

14

I DID NOT SET OUT WITH MURDEROUS INTENTIONS TONIGHT, *but that boy caught me by surprise. I should have expected it, after his outburst earlier this week. I should have known that someone would be watching. I mean, that's what I do. I should have seen it coming.*

It was his own fault. He didn't have to get involved. I thought he had been scared off. He wasn't part of the original plan. Cornering me like that in the woods, shoving the inhaler under my nose. Said he knew I'd poisoned it; he'd figured it out. Please. As if he could have known what I was planning. He probably ended the party early on purpose, so he could try to get me on my own in the dark. Intimidate me.

Well, that didn't work out too well for him, did it?

He didn't let go of the damn inhaler, though. I'll need to figure out how to get that back at some point, just in case it can be traced to me.

Yes—it was his fault. He should have left it alone. The rock I found in my hand was just right. Heavier than I thought it would be, but not too heavy.

No, it was the perfect weight to smash his meddling little head in.

15

"COLE?" MY EYES DART BETWEEN THE BLOODY ROCK AND Frank's limp body. He's facedown and I move the light away from the matted mess that was his head so I don't have to look at it anymore. "What happened?"

"I was going to ask you the same thing. I just . . . found him." He chokes the words out, his features bone-white in the gloom. "I tripped over this." He holds the rock out, away from himself, searching for somewhere to put it down.

"OK, let's put that down. It's OK." I start to edge over to him, around the body, when I stop.

I don't know him. How can I trust him?

"Liz, I didn't . . . Oh God, please don't think . . ." He breaks off as he retches, bringing up the contents of his stomach on the forest floor. I kneel down next to him.

"Hey, shush, it's OK. Here, give me that." I pry the rock from his hand gingerly. I can just about make out blood and hair on it, try not to get my fingers in it. My own dinner threatens to make a reappearance.

"Lizzie?" A familiar voice hisses through the darkness and

a figure emerges. "What are you . . . OH MY GOD! Is that . . . Frank?" Kat's voice shoots up several octaves and I jump up, pulling her down to floor level, though I don't know who—or what—we're hiding from.

"We just found him, and—"

"Lizzie." Kat's voice is calm and measured, which is how I know she's freaking out. "You're holding a really big rock. With lots of blood on it." I look down at my hand and the rock falls from my fingers in slow motion. Kat continues to talk, but my ears are muffled, like someone stuck cotton balls into them, or I'm underwater. I hear her say, "Is he alive?"

"What?" Cole's head snaps up.

"Frank, is he alive?"

It never even occurred to me. Between the rock and the bloody mess of his head, I just assumed he wasn't. Kat goes into full crisis mode, snapping orders at Cole to help her roll Frank onto his side so she can check his pulse.

Nothing.

"I'm going to start CPR," Kat says, rolling him unceremoniously onto his back, the pink inhaler bouncing away from his hand. I wince as his body thuds back to the ground, little eddies of dry soil dancing around him.

"I'm not sure if that's a good idea, Ms. Paphitis." My head snaps up as the figure of Dr. Patel emerges from the trees with the groundskeeper trailing behind her. "We can take over from here."

"But he might be alive," she says, her voice small as she follows the beam of light from the groundskeeper's flashlight to Frank's lifeless eyes.

She drops him as though his cold, dead skin has burned her fingers.

Dr. Patel waves the groundskeeper forward and he begins to cover the body—Frank—with a dark plastic sheet.

"I need to know what happened here tonight. But first, go back to the school."

The headmistress ushers us away and I climb to my feet slowly, my eyes on a faint pink gleam in the grass. Jameela's inhaler.

I don't know what makes me do it, but I inch my hand over and pick it up, sliding it into my long, flared sleeve as I stand.

"Listen very carefully. I want you three to go back to the main building." Dr. Patel looks at Cole and takes in the dark stain on his T-shirt. "Straight to my office, do you understand? Don't speak to anyone or stop to clean up. I will radio Nurse Templeton to meet you there and we will take care of"—she waves a hand vaguely behind her—"this. I will be along very shortly. Do I make myself clear?"

"Yes, Dr. Patel," we mutter together. Is it weird that this seems . . . normal? Is this what shock feels like?

We shuffle along in silence, not bothering to sneak back in, just walking right in the front doors of the school. The brightly lit hallways smell of citrus and beeswax, and the usually soft lights pluck at my eyes. I notice that Kat's top is inside out.

I think I'm getting a migraine.

"Come on," I say to Cole. His face is ashen and there is a smear of blood on his cheek, where he has tried to wipe away the dirt and tears. Now all three decorate his face like some kind of macabre war paint. "The office is this way."

The school is silent. It must be after ten now and lights-out is at half past, so anyone with any sense is in bed.

When did I start shaking so hard?

We stop outside the door, a huge, wooden slab with a shining plaque on it. DR. PATEL, HEADMISTRESS.

"Do you think we should go in?" Kat whispers. Her hand is shaking too as she reaches for the polished brass handle. "Did she say wait inside?"

"I can't remember." My teeth are chattering now and I'm freezing, trembling in my borrowed dress. "Cole?"

He stares blankly at the wall.

"Let's just go in," Kat says decisively. The handle turns easily and the door swings inward with no sound. Patel's office is fairly stark, no family photos or anything personal. There are some certificates on the wall behind her desk, which is carved from another monstrous piece of wood. Three low-slung armchairs line this side and we stumble toward them. A tall, wing-backed chair stands watch on the opposite side, waiting for Dr. Patel to come back.

"Do you want some water?" Kat asks. I sink into one of the green leather guest chairs as Kat helps herself to a drink. I shake my head, but she fills two more paper cups and brings them over for me and Cole anyway. I take mine gratefully, forgetting all about the inhaler wedged into my sleeve. It falls out, bouncing off the floor.

"What's this?" She grabs it with her too-fast reflexes.

"Frank was holding it." Cole's voice is quiet, his eyes firmly on the lip of his paper cup. "When I found him."

Kat sinks into an empty seat and studies the little pink inhaler. A faint red lipstick mark still decorates the mouthpiece and she turns it over and over in her hands as I watch, mesmerized.

"What was Frank doing with Jameela's inhaler?" she mumbles, more to herself than either of us.

"I don't know," I say. My voice cracks. "It doesn't make any sense."

I switch my gaze between her and the white institutional clock on the wall. Where do you even buy those? I'm sure every school and hospital has the same ones. I saw a bunch over the summer.

"Ah, you're here. Thank you." We all jump at Dr. Patel's voice—those hinges really are well-oiled. Kat slides the inhaler under her leg as Dr. Patel strides to her chair and sits down. Her camel-colored blazer is immaculate, even though she's just been dealing with a dead body in the woods, and she's not the slightest bit out of breath. "Now." She folds her fingers together and places her hands on the desk. "Tell me what happened."

We all stare at her for a second. She gives a little sigh. "Cole, please."

"I don't know." He looks like he's about to cry. "We were walking, and—"

"Walking where?"

Cole shrugs miserably and Dr. Patel switches her gaze to me. "Elizabeth?"

Full name. Yikes. I let out a long breath.

"We were at a senior party," I admit, feeling Kat's eyes boring into me. The nicest girl at Morton strikes again. "It was just a few of us in the woods. We were on our way back when—well, when we got split up in the woods, and . . ." I trail off, fully aware of how pathetic this sounds.

"And?"

"I found Frank," Cole admits. "I was looking for Liz and then I tripped on a rock and fell. I picked it up and then I saw . . . him. And his head was all . . ." He stops, patting the back of his own head and wincing.

"You didn't touch the body?"

"No. Well, except when Kat came. She wanted to see if he was still alive." Kat nods in agreement.

Dr. Patel's gaze flicks to me. "Where were you while this was going on, Elizabeth?"

"With Cole, well, mostly. I got turned all around in the woods and lost him for a few minutes. When I finally found him, he was with the . . . with Frank."

"And Frank was already dead?"

I nod. The image of Cole holding the bloody rock flashes before my eyes.

Dr. Patel nods. "All right. Well, that's quite enough for tonight. Get some rest. This is a police matter now."

"Like Jameela?" Kat mutters.

"Excuse me?" Dr. Patel's voice could freeze the water in my cup.

"Nothing, sorry, Dr. Patel."

"Indeed." A knock on the door saves Kat from whatever Dr. Patel is about to say next. "Yes?"

"You asked for me?"

"Come in, nurse." The door swings open as Nurse Templeton, a short, matronly woman, steps into the office. A green first aid kit dangles from her hand. "My apologies, I don't think we need you after all. We don't seem to actually have any injuries here." She looks at each of us in turn. "Do we?"

We shake our heads in silence.

"Oh." There's an edge of annoyance in Nurse Templeton's voice. I look at her closely and see the collar of her nightgown poking out from beneath her uniform. We've dragged her out of bed. "I might as well check them over, now that I'm here."

"No need," Dr. Patel says. The two women stare at one another until Nurse Templeton drops her gaze to the floor.

"Very well." She admits defeat, but not before glancing at us once more. "Make sure you come and see me if you need to, please."

"I'm sure they will." Dr. Patel doesn't give us the chance to respond. "Good night."

The door clicks behind the nurse's retreating figure.

"Now." Dr. Patel stands up, pushing back the large chair and pointing us toward the door. I stand up in a trance and follow the others. "Take yourselves off to bed. I would rather you didn't discuss this with anyone for now, not until we find out what happened. Chances are Frank merely tripped and fell in the dark. An unfortunate accident." Dr. Patel opens the door. "Try not to worry about it too much. Good night."

The door shuts silently behind us as we emerge into the hall and stare at one another. There's a fire in Cole's eyes.

"An *accident*?" he hisses.

"It could be . . . ," I try, but the words sound wrong.

Kat is looking at the inhaler in her hand.

"I think Cole's right. Listen, what if . . ." She pauses, looking from the inhaler to the closed door and then back to Cole. To me.

"What if what?" I press.

"What if Frank figured out Morgan and Jameela were murdered? And that's why he was killed."

16

I TAKE MY TIME WALKING DOWN THE LONG, CURVING STAIR-case and pause for a second at the bottom, letting the sunlight that washes through the long windows warm me. I managed to sleep for a couple of hours but I feel drained, hollowed out.

I've only just stopped shaking.

I pick up the pace again and follow the corridor over to the West Wing, passing through the entrance hall and past the office of Mr. Lucas, the second master. Morton is quiet—it's early for a Saturday morning, just before nine. Most kids take today as a rest day and work through Sundays instead.

"Hey." Cole is leaning against the honey-colored wall next to a huge pair of glass-paneled doors. He straightens up as I approach.

"Hey." Eloquent, Liz. "Ready for your official tour?"

Cole jams his hands deep into the pockets of his gray sweat-pants. "Tour? I thought that was Taylor's job, you know, as head girl and whatever."

"I made her trade with me. She was happy to." I gesture to the shining prefect badge that I've pinned to my plain black T-shirt. "I'm authorized to do them too." I study his face. "Disappointed?"

"No," he says softly, taking his hands out of his pockets again and tugging at the toggle at the end of the zipper on his hoodie. "Not at all. I just . . . didn't sleep much, did you?"

"No," I admit. Did Cole stay awake seeing Frank's body too? I think of the bloody rock in his hand. "That's why I asked Taylor to swap. I mean, that was one of the reasons. I thought we could talk about it." I'm sure his face just grew a little paler. "You know, if you wanted to."

"Maybe later," he says slowly. "After the tour? I think I need to take my mind off it for a bit."

"Sure, later. Listen, we can skip the tour if you want. It's only because you didn't get to come to Open Evening, that's all."

"Are you kidding? I've been looking forward to this. I've only really seen the science lab and my room this week. It's been a bit of a whirlwind." A smile tickles the corners of his mouth. "Even more now that you're here."

I flush. "No pressure, then." I gesture to the doors and hope he can't see how embarrassed I am. "After you."

"Wait a second, I've always wanted to do this . . ." He grabs one polished doorknob in each hand and counts under his breath before pushing both doors open in unison and they swing inward. "You may enter . . . Oh, wow."

"I know, right?"

Morton's library is what I'd dreamed libraries should look like when I was a little kid: nothing like the shabby bookshelves at my underfunded elementary school. Three walls are decorated with floor-to-ceiling windows. Each wall has a "reading nook" built in and they are punctuated throughout with bookshelves that soar up to the high ceiling. The ceiling is a work of art in itself, all original beams and plaster ceiling roses. They even have those massive ladders on wheels so you can get to the books at the very top—I swear I will have my *Beauty and the Beast* moment before I leave.

Cole starts to cross the polished black-and-white tiles, pausing to brush a hand over the study benches in the center of the room and finally stopping to snap the lamp switch on and off.

"It's like something out of a film," he whispers loudly, his library voice. I smile.

"I know, that's what I thought when I first saw it too. The little green lights and everything."

"Yeah. I feel like I'm in the New York Public Library or something. It's so cool." He wanders farther into the room and I can't help feeling a little pride that it's me showing him this. "Hey." He stops at a squat glass cabinet in the center of the room. "What's all this?"

"Those are Morton's 'curiosities,'" I tell him, coming closer. "Things that the founder had in his collection when he started the school. Old white guys love to collect stuff on their adventures. Some of it's a bit politically incorrect, I guess, but it's all pretty fascinating."

"There's more?"

"Yeah, look." I gesture around the room to the cabinets at the end of every study bench and in front of each reading nook. "It'll take ages to see everything, but can I show you some of my favorites?"

"Yeah, sure."

"This one"—I point at a small black disk—"is made from obsidian. See how shiny it is? Apparently it was used by magicians to scry the future. You know, see visions and stuff."

He laughs. "Visions? Bet they made them all up. I mean, it's just an extrusive rock. It's made from cooled lava."

"Maybe they did." I stare at the glassy surface. "I wonder if it ever really worked."

"Probably not," Cole says with a laugh and I straighten up. "I'm a scientist, remember? Come on, what else have we got?"

"Let's go over here." I lead him to the cabinet that's farthest from the double doors, at the opposite side of the room below a huge stained-glass window. "I love this one." I point to what looks like an open book, made of wood—only, there are no pages inside it. Instead, there are little drawers. "This was owned by the Poisoner of Dusseldorf, back in the 1780s. See these hidden drawers? They had plants in them, like belladonna. He used to take a lover and kill them slowly, then move on to another and another. . . . Grim, right?" Cole nods, his lips tight. "Guess what the outside of the book looks like."

"Please don't tell me it's the Bible."

"Got it in one. They think it was shipped over from Germany in the late 1800s, along with Old Josef."

"Who's Old Josef?"

Oops.

"One of those guys." I think quickly, pointing to a nearby cabinet full of phrenology heads, which I know are *definitely* problematic. "The psychology kids name them all."

"Weirdos." He smiles at me. "You do classics, but what else? I know we're not studying the same subjects. I didn't see you all week."

"Yeah, classics. I love it. I study modern history and art too.

Anything old tickles my geek weak point, and I love to be creative. I find it really soothing. A bit different from science—I'm just good at 'interpreting' stuff. You are actually a clever person."

"Guilty." He laughs and holds a hand up. "I find natural poisons pretty fascinating, you know? It's like, nature's own defense system."

"I guess so."

"How about one more and then we hit the dining room for breakfast, right? That has to be on the tour. I'm starved."

"Deal," I say. I glance around, trying to decide, but Cole chooses first. He walks over to a cabinet with just one item in it and calls, "What's this one?"

"You've chosen my all-time favorite." I smile as I stop in front of the glass case. Inside is a terra-cotta sculpture, a tiny, glorious angel, its face worn and blank, the skeleton of its wire wings poking through, poised to take flight. Ancient pieces of clay have crumbled from the innards and the whole effect is morbidly beautiful. "It's a Bernini."

"Bernini was a sculptor, right?"

I smile and nod, delighted he has heard of him. "He was. Most of his work is in the Vatican, but this little one was an early study for the angels on the Ponte Sant'Angelo in Rome. You ever been?" He shakes his head. "Me neither," I admit, "but I dream about it. Bernini sculpted these beautiful angels, all of them perfect, flawless. They're stunning. I prefer this, though, his early prototype. You can see the raw ideas and it's so moving—broken, flawed, but still so beautiful." I stop, embarrassed, feeling Cole's eyes on me. "Sorry. Told you—history nerd."

"Don't apologize. You just look pretty when you're so animated, that's all." He stops. "Sorry, I'm making it weird."

"No, you're not." I smile up at him as a slice of sunlight cuts through the room and lands perfectly on the sculpture. "All right, then," I say, smiling even wider. "Breakfast?"

I point out the common rooms as we leave, directly across from the entrance to the library, and promise to bring him back later; they're officially open to us today. The dining hall is over at the opposite end of school and we walk there in silence, but it's a nice silence. Comfortable. We follow the smell of toast into the hall, which is predictably jammed full of students, and join the line for breakfast. When I try to look through fresh eyes, like Cole must be doing, I see it's all so Morton. Long tables with uniformed kitchen staff serving behind them. Crisp white tablecloths and piles of food in baskets and on silver serving dishes.

He grins. "This is a bit different from during the week! Look at all this. It's like a hotel breakfast, isn't it?"

"It is?" I've never had a hotel breakfast. "They do this every Saturday and Sunday. Beats the DIY cereal stations we usually have."

"Does it ever!" Cole starts piling stuff onto his plate as we reach the front of the line and I watch as he charms the serving staff into giving him double of everything. I select my own food carefully, avoiding anything that might trigger a headache, and pour myself a glass of orange juice.

"Want one?" I ask Cole, who nods without tearing his eyes away from the pastry stand. I pour a second and balance both little glasses in one hand. "Come on, then."

He reluctantly follows me away from the food as I weave through the dining hall, heading for our table. All the seats are cafeteria-style—long wooden counters lined with long wooden benches. I reach the corner where Taylor, Kat, and Marcus are already huddled and gesture for Cole to grab his glass from me. I put my own breakfast down and climb into the seat next to Kat as Cole settles himself across from me, next to Marcus.

"Morning, sunshine." Taylor smiles at me over a half-eaten yogurt, but the smile doesn't reach her eyes. "How're you feeling?"

"OK," I say, and study the top of my own raspberry yogurt before peeling the foil lid back and scraping the thick, creamy gloop off with my spoon. "How're you, Kat? Sleep much?"

"Not really," she mumbles from behind a steaming cup of coffee, "hence the caffeine. This week has been something else, hasn't it? I'm half afraid to go to sleep in case . . . oh, I don't know. In case something else happens, I guess." She lifts her cup and wrinkles her nose at the smell. "I don't even like this stuff, but I need to hit the gym this morning."

"Me too," says Marcus. "I'll come with if you don't wanna be on your own. I'll test you on your personal best while you quiz me on covalent bonds."

Kat smiles wickedly. She loves being underestimated. "Bring it on."

"You wanna come, Cole?" Marcus mops up the remains of his breakfast with a piece of toast as he talks and I wonder how they have such big appetites after last night. I look down at the red flecks in my pink yogurt and feel my stomach turn. I push it away.

"No, thanks, maybe tomorrow. Liz here is giving me the big Morton tour today," Cole answers. I'm grateful he wants to stick with me; I need the distraction after what happened last night. I can't deal with it yet.

"We've just seen the library," I explain. "I thought we'd do the whole loop and meet you guys back in the common room for lunch?"

"Sounds good to me," Kat says, downing the dregs of her coffee and stretching. "I need a few hours of normal before everyone starts asking us about last night." She shakes her head. "Did you see the cop car parked out front this morning? I think we might get hauled in for questioning at some point. I still can't believe it happened."

"What?" I didn't see a car this morning. It must have arrived after I met Cole and I was too busy chatting with him on the way back to notice.

The buzz in the air suddenly becomes more noticeable. People are talking about last night.

"Yeah," says Kat. "I don't think anyone has been told yet, but it won't be long. It's not every day that there's a police presence at school. I'm going to try to enjoy the normal while it lasts."

"You're right," I agree softly. "A few hours of normal would be nice." I sip my orange juice, but it's bitter and pulpy, so I push that away too. I'll fill up my water bottle on the way out. "What're you doing today, Tay?"

She sighs. "Homework. No Saturday's off for me this year, even with everything that's going on. You'd think Patel would give me the day off after last night, but Open Evening is approaching and my head girl duties are tomorrow, so I have to get it all finished today. I'll still meet you guys for lunch, though. I'll need the brain food. Say oneish?"

I look at the clock over the doorway—ten fifteen—and nod. "Sounds good to me, gives us plenty of time. That OK with you, Cole?"

He looks up through a forkful of scrambled egg and nods, swallowing.

"You think I've got time for seconds?"

17

"I THOUGHT WE'D START OUT HERE ON THE GROUNDS AND then finish with the rest of the house on the way back for lunch?"

"Sure." Cole follows me out the main doors and I pause to inhale the smell of the rose and lavender gardens on either side, my favorite scents. They soothe my soul and I open my eyes, ready to begin.

"This way." I walk down the path to the large circular drive in front of the house. It's like one of those driveways you see on films about royalty, where they bring the car right up to the front door. There's even a fountain in the middle.

The police vehicle looks out of place in front of it.

"No way. You think they'll want to talk to us today?"

"Probably. We were at the crime scene."

We walk past the car in silence. It's empty of people, but the seats are littered with food wrappers, the floor on the passenger side full of paper coffee cups. The officers must be inside the school. I shiver.

"I still can't get over how wild this place is," Cole says after a few seconds, as if to break the tension. Our feet crunch on the gravel as we veer off to the right and circle back around the side of the building. The columns that form a kind of veranda all the way around Morton line one side and the library peers out at us. Cole nods, recognizing where he is, getting his bearings.

On the other side, tall hedges loom above, twice the size of me.

"This place is ridiculous," Cole murmurs.

"I know what you mean. How the other half live, right?" I stop in front of a tall iron fence that punctures the row of bushes. "I'll show you out here and then we can go around the back of the house."

To the lake. But I don't say that out loud.

The gate is open, as usual, and Cole follows me beyond the hedges and on to a short, manicured lawn. We follow the path and stop in front of a parking lot. It's full of boring cars, apart from Mr. Lucas's convertible BMW. He's definitely having a midlife crisis.

"Nothing too exciting on this side, but worth knowing about. Teachers' parking lot here, and that"—I point to a large building that was once a barn or an outhouse of some kind—"is the teachers' living quarters."

"They all live here too?"

"Not all of them, but yeah, some. Most of the staff who have families live in Prescott. It's the nearest town with decent schools and transportation, but it's almost an hour away, so some choose to live on-site. Dr. Patel does, and she has her own entrance and quarters, as far as I know." We weave through the parked cars and follow a short road that leads to yet more gates. "This is the staff entrance, for deliveries to the kitchen and stuff." I pause and point over to the far side, away from the house. "The stables are there if you like horses. I tried riding last year, and, er, let's say it wasn't one of the things I'm good at."

Cole grins. "I am clearly going to need you to tell me this story."

"Another time." I laugh, remembering the horse bolting while I clung on for dear life. "Not enough time has passed for it to be funny yet. Anyway," I continue, ignoring his sexy little smirk, "there's a paddock and a plot of land—the school is really big on organic, homegrown fruit and veggies—and Creepy Billy's place is over there too."

"Wait—I'm sorry. Creepy who, now?"

I give Cole my best wicked grin and lower my voice. "Creepy Billy, the groundskeeper. You met him last night." He squints nervously past the greenhouses as though he can magic him up by staring. "He always skulks around, carrying this long-handled fork." I drop my voice to a whisper. "They say he sharpens it every night, on the corner of an old gravestone."

"Awesome," Cole breathes, and I can't help it, I start to giggle. "Wait, are you trying to trick me?"

"Kind of," I admit. "I mean, I have heard those stories, but he just seems like a nice old guy. He avoids us mostly—I don't blame him."

"Yeah, that's sad. Let's be nice if we see him."

"Deal." He is so sweet, I just can't. "So let's go see the fun stuff."

"Lead the way." He holds an arm out and I take us back through the gate in the hedge and continue around the back of the school building. We don't stop chatting the whole way—he tells me about home, how he lives with his mom and younger sister. I don't ask about his dad and he doesn't volunteer the information, but there's pain behind his eyes when he talks about his family.

We walk behind the school and I point out the common rooms

and the kitchens, then the dining hall. We finally reach another gate, a mirror image of the last one, and beyond it I see a sparkle of blue water. The lake is out this way.

I take a deep breath and step through.

"Hey." Cole puts a gentle hand on my shoulder. "Are you OK? You don't look so good."

"Of course." I try to force a note of brightness into my voice, but it falls flat. "So, this is the lake." We look out at the large expanse of water. A path surrounds the whole thing, and from here we can see a few people jogging around the far side. "The running club," I point out. "You like to run?"

"Nah, I get bored." Cole smiles. "Football is my thing." I roll my eyes. "Hey, it's the sport of royalty—twenty-two kings playing on a field of gold."

"Oh, please." I'm only half listening to him, though. My eyes keep drifting back to the little pier halfway between us and the far side of the lake, where a bunch of kayaks and canoes are moored. Cole follows my gaze.

"What is it?"

I take a deep breath. "Do you know why you got a place in second year? I mean, aside from you being super clever, which you must be."

"Yeah, I heard a kid died. Morgan, the old head girl? I felt a bit weird about it, to be honest. Like I was taking her place. The first thing I did when I got the offer was google Morton, so I already knew that much."

"Well, yeah. Morgan died out here, on the lake." I swallow hard, the words sticking in my throat. "*We* were out here."

"We? What, like you and her? God, Liz, I'm so sorry. I did

wonder when you said you'd banged your head in an accident, but I didn't want to pry. What happened?"

I can almost see that night playing out in front of me, a faded film reel projecting onto the still water. "It was a . . . dare. To take the boats out at night." An *initiation* was what Morgan called it. "It was the last day of the school year. We'd been drinking and Morgan was showing off." My voice trails away and my fingers automatically find the scar in my hair.

"Hey, stop. You don't have to tell me." Cole's hand is on my shoulder again and I feel the heat of his skin seep through my T-shirt.

I glance up at him. "I don't really remember much more, anyway." I lower my head and part my hair so he can see the scar properly and I hear his sharp intake of breath. I flick my hair back and smile weakly. "The boat flipped. I got this and she . . . didn't make it back."

"I'm so sorry." His hand is still on my shoulder and he lets it slide down my arm, his warm fingers wrapping around my own. "You were pretty lucky, then."

"Yeah." I squeeze his hand and drop it gently, embarrassed. He is too sweet. "Come on, let's check out the sports fields."

Cole is way too into the football field, enthusing about the pitch and the stands and going on about goalposts and penalty boxes. I let him talk, though, enjoying the feeling of release that has settled over me. I'd been holding that night in all summer and finally confronting it, seeing the lake again, has made me feel lighter than I have in weeks.

We walk around the cages that enclose the hockey, net ball, and tennis courts and loop back toward the lake path. "One more stop," I tell him, pointing at a low building that sits behind the net ball court, "and then we can head back for lunch."

"Perfect. This must be the gym, then, right? Marcus told me it was out here."

"Yeah." We head into the foyer. It's pretty busy in there, mainly boys sitting around between sets, but over in the far corner, by the water cooler, are Marcus and Kat.

"Jeez, she can bench more than me!" Cole splutters. I grin. Kat is lying on a bench, her feet firmly planted on the floor, pushing a weighted iron bar into the air. Huge black disks hang on each side and I see Cole mentally adding up the weight. He nods in awe. "*Definitely* more than me."

"Hey, guys!" I wave as Marcus helps Kat place the barbell in its rest. She slides out and waves, grabbing her bottle of water off the floor before heading over to us.

"That was pretty impressive," Cole says to her.

"What, for a girl?"

"Hell no, for anyone. I'm impressed."

"She still hasn't beaten my PB, though," Marcus says, sidling up behind her. Kat rolls her eyes. I swear if she had a towel, she would whip him with it.

"Give me time." She drains her bottle. "Speaking of time, is it almost lunch yet?"

"Almost twelve. We're heading back now and collapsing in the common room. Coming?"

Kat holds the damp fabric of her gray top away from her skin and shakes her head. "I need a shower, but we'll see you there."

"Yeah, same. Meet you in the common room." Marcus agrees.

He and Kat head over to the showers, ribbing each other good-naturedly on the way.

Cole and I leave the gym and start back on the path to the lake. The early autumn sun casts golden rays across the water and I relish its warmth as we stroll along in comfortable silence.

"Do they have a bit of a thing going on or what?" Cole interrupts my moment of zen.

"Who? What—Marcus and Kat?" I start laughing. "God, no. Marcus and Taylor are practically married. He would never. He and Kat are more like brother and sister than anything. And Kat is . . ."

"Is she gay? Or bi?"

"What, because she can lift weights?" I tease him.

"I'm no misogynist." Good to know. "I saw her kissing that girl in the crop top last night, the one she'd been drinking shots . . . er, from . . ."

"Ha! Typical Kat." I can't help smiling. "She's . . . not really into relationships." I shrug. "She likes who she likes—and she hates labels."

"Fair enough." He gives me a sidelong glance. "What about you? Are you into relationships? Or, to be even more blunt—is there someone I should be worried about?"

I duck my head, allowing a short curtain of hair to hide my face. "No, no one special."

"Cool." His fingers fold around mine again.

This time I don't let go.

18

THE COMMON ROOM IS ALREADY PACKED WHEN WE GET BACK to the main building, and I watch as Cole's eyes widen at the lunch spread. It's not too dissimilar from breakfast this morning, but it's a huge senior privilege—the juniors eat in the dining room, as we usually do.

"Yes" is all he says.

I've got to admit, I'm feeling pretty hungry myself after our walk around the grounds this morning. I didn't get much exercise over the holidays—our apartment complex isn't exactly one you'd want to walk around alone in—and I can feel the muscles in my legs already starting to ache. Maybe I should take Kat up on her gym offer after all. Eww—I feel sweaty just thinking about it.

"What's the plan?" Cole asks, his eyes still firmly on the covered silver platters.

"Come on," I say. "Let's find somewhere to sit."

The common room is long and slender. Windows pierce the long wall, just like in the library, but the light doesn't streak in the same way. Instead we can see the tall hedges that separate us from the staff parking lot—the path Cole and I took earlier. The decor is similar to the lounge upstairs—essentially Morton: wood-paneled walls, highly polished surfaces, and battered but comfy leather chairs. The space is filled with sofas and seating areas where low-slung armchairs are arranged around old leather chests and wooden boxes that double as coffee tables. It's pretty similar to the juniors' common room, though that one has hardly any windows.

A huge stone fireplace dominates the wall in the center of the room and three worn green sofas are wrapped around it. It immediately marks itself as the most coveted spot in the room and I grin when I spot Taylor's red hair streaming over the arm of one of the couches.

"Amazing," I say as we join her, and she grins up from her prostrate position. "How long have you been here?"

"Ages," she says, pulling herself upright. "I came in as soon as I saw them open the doors from the library and pretended to be asleep so no one would join me. Gotta mark out my territory now that I'm head girl, right?"

"Legend." Cole smiles. I take a seat on the sofa opposite Taylor, and even though there's a third one facing the fireplace, he sits next to me. Taylor raises an eyebrow and I shoot her a warning look.

"Good tour, was it?" she asks innocently.

"Yeah, this place is amazing, I love it. And my tour guide wasn't bad, either, so thanks for that." Taylor's grin is in danger of straining a cheek muscle as Cole gets to his feet. "The food is out! I'm gonna go grab something. Liz, you want anything?"

I shake my head. "No. I'll go up in a bit, thanks."

"Taylor?"

"No, we'll keep the seats. You go ahead."

We follow his tall frame as Marcus and Kat come in through the double doors, both scrubbed and clean-looking. Marcus joins Cole in the food line, slapping his back, while Kat comes over to us, swinging her gym bag onto the floor and sprawling on the spare sofa.

"Well, well, well." Taylor fixes her gaze on me like the proverbial cat that caught the canary. "Sounds like Liz had a nice morning with the new boy."

"Yes, thank you," I say primly. They look at me expectantly. "He's great. Too good for me, though," I confess.

"What!" Kat squeals, drawing glances as she leans forward. She doesn't lower her voice, though; that's not her style. "Lizzie, you're the best. You deserve the best. And, well." She leers in the direction where Cole and Marcus are piling food onto their plates. "He is pretty damn close."

I bite my lip. The idea that such a handsome, kind, funny new boy would like *me,* right off the bat . . . it doesn't feel possible, somehow. Things like that just don't happen to me.

"Kat!" I can't help laughing as she wiggles her eyebrows. "Stop being such a deviant. But, yeah, I like him." I put a hand to my head. "He's really calming to talk to," I say at last.

"And he is capital *H* Hot," Taylor says, and Kat nods her agreement. I let my gaze drift and see Cole walking back over. He flashes me a smile and I return it.

After lunch, the chest that masquerades as a table is littered with the remnants and I watch, mesmerized, as Taylor methodically scrapes leftovers onto one plate before piling them all up and placing the cutlery on top. "Once a waitress," she mutters as Marcus grabs the stack from her and carries them back to the staff at the other end of the room. Cole nudges me and whispers in my ear.

"You were right," he says, "they are totally a married couple."

The room is quieter now, as most people have gone off to hang out on the lawn in the sunshine, but I'm comfy. I feel myself getting sleepy—I could doze off right here, with Cole's arm resting gently behind me. I sink lower in my seat, eyes heavy, and it feels natural when Cole slips his arm down around my shoulder. I hesitate for a second, but then I relax into him just a little.

Marcus sits back down next to Taylor and lowers his voice. "Does anyone else know about Frank yet?"

"I don't know," I say. I look around at the other students, eating and chatting. "It all feels a bit surreal. Like, if you two hadn't been with me, I'd think I dreamed it."

"Yeah, I know what you mean," Cole agrees, withdrawing his arm, much to my disappointment. He mimics Marcus's pose, closing our little group. "No one has mentioned it *at all*. You would think it's big news, but nothing. When Jameela . . . died . . . it was all anyone could talk about in class, right?" We nod in agreement.

"I guess we've barely seen anyone this morning, though," I say. "Tay, was there any chatter in the library?"

"I don't think so." She flicks her eyes up to the ceiling, thinking. "I saw his roommates in the library, but they didn't seem too concerned. After his outburst earlier this week, maybe they think he was finally sent home."

"Wouldn't they be worried?" Kat asks. "If one of you didn't come back one night, I'd worry, especially if there were police around."

Cole shrugs. "Maybe they've been in with Patel all morning. I guess the police could be here for anything. And the whole not coming home thing—the guys might not think much of it. They might think he . . . well, stayed out late or something." He flushes, and I realize that "or something" means "hooked up."

Taylor is frowning. "Patel has covered it up, hasn't she? Three student deaths in less than eight weeks can't look great for the school."

There's a murmur of agreement as we all sit and contemplate what a bad reputation for Morton might mean for our futures. We're quiet for a moment, and then I think of something. "Kat?" I ask, my voice low. "Do you still have the inhaler?"

"Inhaler?" Taylor repeats. "What inhaler?"

"Jameela's inhaler," Kat says. She riffles through her gym bag and pulls out a plastic sandwich bag. Sealed inside is Jameela's pink inhaler. "These guys found it in Frank's hand. I wanted to preserve the evidence." She says it so seriously that none of us even think to laugh. "It's all a bit intense, isn't it? I mean, first Jameela . . ."

"Are we saying that Jameela's death wasn't an accident?" Taylor says. "But surely—I mean, she was smoking . . . it was just one of those things. . . ."

"Why did Frank have it, then?" Kat asks, placing the bag on the table. We all stare at it. "Patel said he must have fallen and hit his head. Do we believe that?"

"Well, I certainly don't." Another voice crashes our private conversation.

I swear, our heads all whip around at the exact same moment, as though some unseen puppet master has just tugged at our strings. We turn as a figure behind us gets to her feet.

"You know, it's rude to eavesdrop," Taylor snarls as Emily walks around and stands in the gap between the sofas.

"Oh, please—like Kat knows anything about discretion. Do you want to hear what I've got to say or not?"

Kat shrugs, apparently taking no offense at practically being called a loudmouth, and gestures to the empty seat next to her.

The rest of us aren't as laid-back—Cole stiffens next to my bouncing knee, Taylor looks like she might throw up, and tension is emanating from Marcus across the table. We could really do without our little Agatha Christie act getting back to the headmistress. Emily doesn't seem to notice any of it as she perches on the edge of the seat, her watery eyes fixed on the inhaler. She's lost her two best friends in a matter of weeks. It would be like losing Taylor and Kat. I shiver.

"What do you want to say?" I ask gently. "Go ahead." There's a wobble in my voice and Cole takes my hand again.

"Jameela's *accidental* death. First off, how come there was no memorial, like there was for Morgan? People aren't even talking about it. Well, it's all bull, isn't it? All cloak-and-dagger."

"People are talking about her, of course they are," Marcus says uncertainly.

"No one *official* has said anything, though, have they? No formal assembly, no mention of her at all apart from Patel saying her family wanted to keep it all private. Do you know what I think?" Emily asks.

We all stare at her.

"Jameela's parents adored her, but they had nothing. That's why she was so desperate to be head girl. They'd want some kind of compensation."

"You're saying Patel . . . paid them not to ask questions?" Marcus says.

"Yeah. It's like she just disappeared. Like she was never even here." Emily nods at the inhaler. "Jameela knew she shouldn't smoke—she knew her asthma could get really bad. But the inhaler should have helped her. I've seen her use it so many times, and it always helped, so the fact that she . . . that she . . ."

We all sit in silence, not sure what to do or say. I stare down at the worn rug beneath the coffee chest, tracing its faded patterns with my eyes until I feel dizzy. I remember Jameela taking deep breaths with the inhaler. *It should have helped her.*

Emily blinks back tears. "Now you're saying that Frank is dead? And he had this with him?"

I risk a glance up. Every face is somber, and there are tears streaking down Emily's cheeks. No one speaks.

"Well?" she demands quietly. "Is it true? Is Frank dead too?"

"Yes," I croak. I clear my voice and try again. "Yes. We found him last night, on the way back from the party."

"Who did?" Emily asks sharply. "You?"

I nod.

"Actually, it was me," Cole says, his voice small. "I found him. He was already . . . his head." Cole swallows and closes his eyes. I squeeze his fingers.

"And me." Kat picks up the plastic bag. "And it's true, he was holding this. So the question is why? Why did Frank have Jameela's inhaler?"

Emily laughs, a hollow, humorless sound. "Isn't it obvious?" She looks around at us, stares into the faces of each of my friends. "So much for the brightest and the best." She slows her speech down, like she's talking to a group of small children. "There's something wrong with that inhaler and Frank knew it. Someone poisoned my friend and he found out. Then whoever it was killed him too."

None of us say anything for a moment.

"I knew it!" Kat hisses. "Something is going on and we have to do something about it. Oh, God. What do we do?"

"Wait a second." Marcus holds up a hand, the voice of reason. "We don't know if any of this is true. Maybe Jameela *just* had an asthma attack and Frank *just* fell in the woods. It's sad and, yeah, unusual, but that's all it is. There's no evidence we have a *killer* here."

"Prove it, then." Emily folds her arms defiantly.

"Prove what?" he says, bewildered. "That it's unusual?"

"No, you idiot," Emily responds coldly. "Prove the inhaler isn't poisoned."

"How am I supposed to do that?"

"You're a scientist, aren't you?" She says it accusingly, like it's a bad thing. "Then test the inhaler. Test it and prove my best friend wasn't murdered."

19

"TELL ME AGAIN WHAT WE'RE ACTUALLY DOING HERE." I SQUIRM on the hard wooden stool, trying for the seventeenth time to get comfortable.

"Don't bother." Marcus looks up from the cupboard he's rummaging in. "I think they're made to be uncomfortable on purpose. Ah." He straightens up and shuts the door with one foot. "Here, put these on."

"You've got to be kidding." I stare at the clear plastic safety goggles he puts in my hand.

"Nope, science lab rules—safety first."

I throw a sidelong glance at Cole, who shrugs and puts on his own scratched-up pair. "Man's right. Come on, get them on." I give Kat one last, hopeful look of rebellion, but she's already wearing hers and vogueing into the reflection of a glass cabinet. I bet Taylor wouldn't wear them if she was here.

"Come on, Lizzie, suit up!" she demands. I sigh and slide the glasses over the bridge of my nose, where they give me an immediate headache.

"Fine," I grumble. "Now answer my question. What are we doing?"

"Gas chromatography-mass spectroscopy," Marcus replies. Cole nods, his eyes lighting up. Kat plays with the gas taps mounted on the center of the table and Marcus slaps her hands away playfully. She frowns.

"Which is what?"

"A way of seeing if there's anything in that inhaler that shouldn't be."

"Right," I reply, casting my mind back to high-school science. "So you need to separate the components somehow? How do we do that?"

Kat looks up, her hands on the gas taps again. "Please tell me it's the thing with the Bunsen burners where you set stuff on fire and it turns different colors."

"Er, not quite, and if you keep messing with those, you're going to end up with no eyebrows." Marcus places the plastic bag containing Jameela's inhaler on the table and gestures to the canister through the plastic. "Everything in here should be a liquid. It's kept in a compressed chamber, so when the pump is activated, it lets out a small, measured amount that becomes a gas at body temp. We need to make sure that everything in there *should* be in there. I asked Mr. Lucas if we could have access to the gas chromatography machine this afternoon, and—"

Kat cuts him off. "What? You told a teacher about this?"

"No, of course not!" Marcus cuts *her* off. For a moment, I think I see real anger on his face, but the look is gone so quickly, I might have imagined it. "No, Cole and I told him we wanted to up our game a bit, for university applications." He points at a hulking white machine in the corner. "Most high schools don't even have these, but you know Morton. No expense spared. Just another bonus point on our applications." He picks up the bag. "Cole, give me a hand?"

"Sure." Cole eases his long legs from the stool and I watch him approach the machine.

"Not that Mr. Head Boy needs the points," Kat whispers in my ear. "Anyway, I thought that was the photocopier." I stifle a laugh, ignoring the barbed comment. That's not like Kat; it's just the stress of the whole situation.

"Me too," I admit. "Come on, let's see what they're doing."

Kat and I stand back slightly as we watch the boys work. "Can you believe Taylor knows how to do all this stuff too?" she says in awe. "Girl's a total knockout *and* a genius. Makes me proud."

"Me too." I smile, nodding toward the boys. "How come all the science kids are hotties? My classics class is severely lacking. . . ." I stop suddenly, realizing there'll be two empty seats there tomorrow morning. First Jameela and now Frank, gone.

"Hey." Kat squeezes my hand. It's like she can read my mind. "This is why we're here, to try and help. To get some evidence."

"Who would we even show it to?" I say in a small voice.

"We'll show it to someone," Kat says firmly, and I nod. We turn our attention back to Marcus and Cole. Marcus gingerly takes the inhaler from the bag and twists the silver cylinder, separating it from the plastic casing. A familiar smell drifts through the air, something menthol, but I can't quite place it. "Can you smell that?" I ask Kat.

"What? Oh." She pauses to take a sniff of her Fleetwood Mac T-shirt. "This?" I inhale the fabric.

"Yeah. I thought it was from the inhaler for a sec."

"No, it's me. Tiger Balm," she explains, lowering her voice.

"Lifting those weights with Marcus did me in, but don't tell him, will you? I'm in agony, think I pulled a lat."

I nod sympathetically, even though I can't remember what a lat is. "Your secret's safe with me."

"Thanks." Kat addresses the boys. "How long will this take?"

"About an hour, I think," Cole replies, his eyes on the syringe in Marcus's hand. Marcus nods his agreement and narrows his dark eyes, inserting the sharp needle into the tiny opening at the bottom of the cylinder.

"Hold still," he murmurs, and we watch in rapt silence. When he's sure it's all in place, he starts to pull back the end of the syringe slowly, filling the small chamber with a tiny amount of liquid. Satisfied, he removes the needle. "Is there enough in there for a second try if this doesn't work?"

Cole holds the canister up to his ear and shakes it. Guess we're past worrying about fingerprints. "Yeah, sounds like there is."

"Good." Marcus walks back to the machine and starts to press buttons. A low whirring sound fills the room and he begins making checks with Cole. "Carrier gas ready?"

Cole checks a section at the end and nods. "Yep."

"OK, I'm going to put this into the injector port." Marcus glances up at us, kicking into teacher mode. "Once this goes in, it'll travel around the column, which is like a long, twisty glass tube, and then the components will start to separate. The chemicals with the highest boiling points will eluate—sorry, come out—first, and once it's done, we should have the results of what's in here."

"All right, then." I nod and we watch as he once again inserts the syringe needle, this time into a port on the top of the machine.

"What do we do while we wait?" I ask.

Kat sighs and looks back at her heavy bag. "Homework."

"What was that?" A short series of beeps sounds and I tear my eyes away from a book about the Parthenon that's been keeping me distracted.

"The results." Cole looks me in the eye. "They're ready."

A cold, hollow feeling starts to spread in the pit of my stomach. It's the moment of truth. I say a silent prayer to whichever gods might be listening. I want the results to show that nothing unusual was in the inhaler. Just a tragic accident, that's all. Then things could get back to normal.

But I'm not sure they ever will.

"Let's all go look together," Kat says. Marcus nods and stands up, the metal legs of his stool scraping across the hard floor.

We walk over to the machine hesitantly. There's a computer screen linked up to the apparatus and it is flashing, telling us it's ready to reveal its secrets. I take a deep breath as Cole's hand closes around mine on one side and Kat's does the same on the other, forming a human chain, and I relax slightly. Marcus drags a stool in front of the monitor and quickly taps on the keyboard.

Over his shoulder I can see a line graph full of little peaks, like I imagine a lie detector must look like, or a Richter scale. Three large ones stand out from the others.

Marcus points at the screen. "OK, so these peaks represent the ions present in the liquid from the inhaler. We can ignore the smaller ones—they're just trace elements from the air and whatever.

We want to focus on the big ones, then we interpret and try to identify them."

"So what's in there?" I ask.

"I'm not sure." He runs a large hand over the back of his head, scratching at the short bristles there. "I can't tell you the generic names without looking them up—I'm not so hot on those. I can tell you the pharmaceutical names, though."

Cole drops my hand to retrieve the inhaler, now reassembled and back in the bag. He twists the canister through the plastic and peers at the label. "Right, you tell me what you think they are."

"OK, so . . . first one is beclomethasone dipropionate," Marcus reads from the screen.

"Yep, got that." Cole nods as he squints at the tiny writing. "Next?"

"Formoterol fumarate?" My gaze flits between the two boys, like I'm watching a tennis match. Beside me, Kat does the same.

"Er, wait a sec . . . Oh, yeah, it's here. Got it."

"You want the third?"

"Yeah." Cole peels apart the seal on the bag and removes the inhaler. "Sorry, can't see it through the bag. Go ahead."

"OK, so the third is . . . trimethylbicyclo heptan."

I hold my breath, waiting for Cole to confirm that it's an ingredient in the inhaler.

"Jeez," Kat whispers.

Cole reads the label carefully. Then he looks up slowly and shakes his head.

"No." His voice is hoarse, and he drops the inhaler back into the bag. "No. There are only two ingredients on here. That's definitely not one of them."

"I don't believe it." Marcus turns on his stool, his shoulders sagging. "You know what this means?"

I nod, swallowing hard. The very words I'm thinking spill out of Kat's mouth.

"It means there was something in Jameela's inhaler that shouldn't have been there. It means that Emily was right." Kat looks at me, fear barely hidden in her thickly lashed eyes. "Someone killed Jameela, and Frank knew it, so someone killed him too."

"It's worse than that," Marcus says softly. "It means it was one of us."

20

"WHAT DID HE MEAN, *ONE OF US?*"

Taylor's snuggled in her old dorm bed, catching up on our news. Outside the door we can hear sobs, the patter of feet from one room to another. Frank's death is common knowledge now—another tragic accident at Morton Academy. Taylor looks tired, her face washed clean of makeup, so her brows and lashes are pale. There's a red, inflamed mark on her cheekbone.

"Not one of *us* exactly, but someone here, at Morton." Kat responds between sit-ups, her feet hooked under my bed.

"Well, duh. Who else is it going to be? Bless him—he's not always the fastest on the uptake, is he? Maybe we should go and see Patel, tell her what we know. I mean, I'm head girl, we're all Jewel and Bone acolytes. There's got to be some level of trust there. She'll have our backs, surely?"

"I don't know anything anymore." I sigh. I'm holding a bag of candy, but I've lost my appetite. "We think she bribed that police officer after all."

"She might just be protecting the school; I bet the school board was a nightmare after Morgan's death was in the papers last July."

"Maybe." I shrug.

"Well, I'm out of big ideas. Here, pass me some of those, will you?" I throw Taylor a mini bag of Haribo. She nods at Kat. "Why does watching her exercise just make me crave sugar?"

"Wait a sec," I say, "haven't you spoken to Marcus today?"

"No, can you believe it?" Taylor slides a jelly ring onto her finger and starts to nibble at it. "Patel kept me busy with head girl stuff all day. It wasn't even fun Jewel and Bone party stuff, just Open Evening nonsense. There's going to be prospective donors there or something, so I had to draw up a timetable for the tours."

"I forgot Opening Day was so soon."

I think back to the day I landed on the doorstep at Morton. It took my breath away—I'd never seen anything like it. I'd taken a handful of my exams early and Dr. Patel had come to interview me at my high school. She offered me a place on the spot, and I came on my own to see if it was real.

I had been saving up the money I got washing hair at my secret Saturday job, so I used it for the train ticket and didn't tell anyone. It was love at first sight and I couldn't get here fast enough after that. My parents have never seen it, not that they'd be interested, anyway. They signed the paperwork, which made things less difficult, but if they knew what it was really like, they'd just say I thought I was better than them or something.

"Do you have to do the tours and stuff?" I ask now.

"Yeah, I think we all do, actually." Taylor rips the head off a small bear with her perfect white teeth and puts on a big, fake smile as Kat collapses back on the carpet. "Hi, hello," Taylor chirps, "welcome to

Morton Academy, the exclusive, scholarship-only school for super-clever students, where people are dropping like flies!" Her voice breaks on the last word as she sniffs back a sob.

"Oh, hon. We can't panic, not now," Kat says from the floor, her cropped tee showing off enviable abs. "We just have to put a brave face on, for a little while."

"Kat's right," I agree, carefully folding my little plastic packet. "We have to keep our heads down, at least until we know who we can and can't trust."

"God, is this for real?" Taylor burrows down under the comforter. "How did we end up in this mess? I mean, first Morgan, then Jameela, and now poor Frank—I mean, he was a bit weird and all, but he didn't deserve to die."

"No, of course he didn't," Kat says soothingly as she climbs into her own bed. "No one deserves that. I just have so many questions."

I scooch back in my bed. "Like what?" I ask, feeling a slight stirring of interest under all my worry. Kat is smart, after all.

"OK." Kat begins to count on her fingers. "First off, why didn't whoever poisoned Jameela take the inhaler after? Second. How did Frank get it in the first place? *He* could have done it, for all we know. Third—or is it fourth?—did Patel really bribe that cop? Fifth—why hasn't there been a memorial for Jameela?"

"That's obvious," I say. "Dr. Patel doesn't want anyone to know things aren't normal."

"That's what I mean, though. She should be trying to pretend everything is normal. But surely it would be *more* normal for her to have some kind of event, like for Morgan?"

"I really don't know," I admit. I put my face in my hands. "Ugh, it's all too much effort. Today has been a lot."

"Have you taken your meds?" Kat asks as she snuggles down.

"Yes, Mom." I smile. "Have you?"

She furrows a brow. "What do you mean?"

"Your shoulder. Or"—I point at the offending area—"your lat or whatever it was. Feeling better?"

"Oh. Yeah, thanks." She looks uncomfortable and changes the subject. "You sleeping here again tonight, Tay?"

"Yeah." Her voice is muffled from behind the comforter. "If that's OK?"

"Of course it is," I say. "It's still your bed, even though you do have the fancy room upstairs."

The comforter shudders.

"I can't sleep up there. It was hard enough being up there on my own after Jameela, but since Friday, since Frank . . ."

"Hey, hey. I told you, it's still your bed, right, Kat?"

"Right," she agrees. That menthol smell drifts across the room as she discreetly rubs Tiger Balm into her shoulder.

"I'm gonna go brush my teeth." I stand and slide into flip-flops. The worn rubber is cool against my skin and I suppress a little shiver. "You coming, Tay?" She mumbles something unintelligible as I tug at the bottom of her cover.

"Yes, fine," she groans as she throws the comforter off and swaps it for a fluffy robe.

We pad down the hallway to the shared bathroom, where our feet slap against the tiles. It's a cavernlike, stainless-steel room, the walls lined with squat, white porcelain tiles that echo with every step.

I'm glad Taylor is here—it's definitely not my favorite part of school to be alone in. We brush our teeth quickly, the silence between us secure, comfortable. I notice again how tired she looks—she really hasn't been sleeping. Second-year stress must be taking it out of her. I wonder if her face hurts.

We tiptoe back, aware of how quiet it is in the other rooms. I check my watch and realize it's almost an hour past lights-out. Homework really does take longer this year; I mean, we all heard the seniors say that, but I just thought they were being dramatic.

We reach our dorm room and gently close the door behind us. Kat is flaked out already, good sleep being a side effect of exercise, or something ridiculous like that.

"Night, hon." Taylor gives me a hug and a kiss on the cheek, which I return, our nightly little routine. I never got a kiss before bedtime when I was growing up and my heart always swells a little, grateful that I found such a good friend.

"Night." I climb into bed and make myself comfortable, tucking my toes under the bottom of the comforter so the monsters don't get me, before reaching one arm out to switch off my lamp. Sleep doesn't come quickly to me in general, but no smartphone means no music, no reading fanfic under the covers, and definitely no podcasts. Instead I let my eyes drift shut and do the deep-breathing exercises the doctor taught me. I place my hands on my stomach, breathing in through my nose until I feel my belly swell—then I let it out slowly, puffing my cheeks, expelling my breath through the small O of my mouth. I try it a few more times and allow my mind to drift back to the good things that came out of this weekend—namely, Cole. Cole's fingers twining through my own as we walked around the lake, the way it felt to snuggle into the crook of his arm, however briefly that was. A sleepy smile twitches at the corners of my mouth as my mind unravels.

Until something scratches at the edges of my consciousness.

I can't quite put my finger on whatever it is, my mind half surrendered to sleep. Something someone said today, maybe? It's just out of my grasp, and I'm too far gone, so I have no choice but to relinquish it to oblivion.

Monday morning dawns way too early, but there's no chance of sleeping in when Kat is bouncing around your room. "Rise and shiiiine," she booms, yanking the blanket off me. My feet curl involuntarily as I crack one eye and see that she's already up and showered.

"Please tell me you haven't been to the gym already." I yawn, arching my back and stretching my arms out wide.

"Of course not." She grins. "Just a quick jog around the lake. You should come with me next time."

"Er, yeah. Maybe." I glance over at Taylor's empty bed, the comforter rumpled. "Where's Tay?" Taylor is normally harder to wake up than me.

"Dunno." Kat shrugs as she starts to comb through her wild brown hair. "She was already gone when I got back from my run. Come on, you better get up. I'm starving, going to head straight down."

"OK, OK." I grab my shower bag and pull a towel from the hamper. "Save me a seat, I won't be long." I walk back down to the bathroom, the sounds of hair dryers and morning chatter filtering through the doors. Like the night before, though, there's just one thing on my mind, only now I remember what it is.

How come Taylor couldn't sleep thinking about Frank on Friday, when she didn't find out until Saturday morning?

21

FOR PEOPLE WHO ARE MEANT TO BE SO INTELLIGENT, THAT IN-
*haler wasn't hidden particularly well. I waited until the early morning,
while they were still asleep, and searched the room on silent feet. And
there it was, in a plastic bag, under the bed. I mean, come on.*

UNDER THE BED.

*I'll feel better once I get rid of it. Stupid, stupid Frank. He had to
get himself involved, didn't he? Now they're all sniffing around like the
bloody Scooby gang.*

*I really didn't think it would have to go this far. Now it's like I don't
have a choice anymore. The dice have been rolled for me.*

*If I want to succeed, there will have to be more accidents. It's as
simple as that.*

22

THE DINING ROOM IS FULL WHEN I ARRIVE AND BACK TO NOR-
mal after the lavish weekend, which means self-service cereal or
fruit. I grab some cornflakes with a splash of oat milk—dairy really
messes with my head these days—and an apple, then go to find
the others.

"Hey." I slide onto the bench across from Marcus and Cole. Cole
gives me a shy smile, which makes me feel warm inside. "Where are
the others?"

"Gone already," Marcus says. "Kat has some early-morning study
group in the library and Taylor was leaving when we got here." He
shakes his head. "Girl is working way too hard."

"Yeah," I murmur, "but she's got a lot to live up to this year."
Shouts and laughter echo around the dining hall and for a second, I
can almost believe that everything is . . . normal. "Right?"

"Yeah, she does." He stirs a spoon of sugar into his mug. "You
see the picture of Frank in the hallway? Seems Patel wants some
kind of a memorial this time."

"Yeah." I spotted it coming down the stairs. The same easel that
Morgan's photo had been propped up on, the same black fabric

skimming the floor. "I still can't believe it. I know Frank could be intense, but he was pretty funny sometimes too, you know. And that boy knew his ancient civilizations."

"Yeah, I did a bit of head-deputy stuff with him last week, before he . . . well, you know." Marcus clears his throat as Cole and I exchange glances. "Anyway, I'd better take off too." Marcus stands up and points at us both in turn. "Let you two catch up." He wiggles his eyebrows to break the tension and grabs his tray, dropping it back at the serving hatch before striding out the door.

"Smooth," Cole says with a laugh.

"Cringe," I agree.

I lift a jug from the table and pour it into a glass, tiny ghosts of ice cubes flowing out with the water. I reach into my pocket for my pills and hesitate—do I want Cole to see me take these? Well, it's that or take them later without food, and that makes me feel queasy. I don't want to feel like I did the last time that happened. I pull out the blister packet and pop two pills from the silver foil, drop them into my mouth, and wash them down with a swig of water. Cole doesn't bat an eyelid. I think he's actually perfect.

"You got a class first thing?" he asks as he wipes his hands on a linen napkin. No paper here—it might be a standard breakfast on a weekday, but it's still Morton.

"I do." I check my watch. "Not until nine, though, so I've got half an hour. You?"

"Same," he says, leaning back in his chair and stretching his long arms over his head. His white shirt is crisp and starched and just the tiniest bit too tight. His top button is undone, allowing a glimpse of his neck.

He says something and I have to shake myself to attention.

"Sorry, what?"

Cole gives me a grin that turns my stomach inside out. "I said, do you want to go for a walk?"

"I have a better idea." I place the uneaten apple into my bag for later, throw the strap over one shoulder and climb across the bench. My tartan skirt rides up and I'm sure I catch him looking. "You wanna see the secret way upstairs?"

"The secret way?" He stands too and shrugs on his blazer, which looks twice the size of mine. The pop of acid-green piping does something wonderful to his eyes.

"Yeah." We both lift our trays and head back to the serving hatch, sliding them onto waiting carts. "It's the old servants' stairs, from when this was a manor house. You know, so the rich people wouldn't see the servants coming and going. We're not really supposed to use them, but everyone does."

We head out and stop in front of a solid wooden door. "Storeroom?" Cole asks.

"Yep." I glance around furtively and grab the handle. "Come on." We slip inside and close the door behind us. I fumble for the light switch, flipping the old-fashioned lever. Ancient fluorescent lights flicker and groan overhead as we walk through the large pantry. I see Cole eyeing a shelf of biscuits and catch his hand.

"Don't even think about it," I warn him. "The cook has, like, psychic abilities when it comes to stock levels. Marcus got his ass handed to him for stealing some cookies last year, and I think he's still scared of her."

"Consider me warned. So where's this staircase?"

"Back here." I walk to the rear of the room and lay my hand on a door. It's nothing like the one we came in through, though it's just as old. The timber is splintered at the bottom, where it has caught on the stone step over the years, and the handle is just a piece of rope that has been looped through a roughly hewn hole in the wood. It's not a door meant for noble eyes. I pull the rope handle toward me and a cold draft hits us both as it swings out. I shiver. "No heating in there," I tell him. "No lights either, so be careful."

"OK." The door groans shut and we're plunged into darkness as Cole starts to climb the steps behind me. Something brushes my hand and I give a little yelp. "Sorry, it's just me." He grabs my hand, more firmly than he has so far, and I relish the heat that seeps from his skin as he joins me on the same step.

"I can't see anything. Maybe we should wait a minute, let our eyes adjust," he says, his voice low. I can just make out his shape in the darkness and feel as though I'm being drawn toward him. "Are you cold?"

"A little." My voice is low and husky too, and the roof of my mouth is suddenly desertlike. Cole takes a step closer and his body brushes against mine. I move back automatically, the cold stone of the wall pressing into my back, even though all I want to do is lean into him.

"Sorry," he whispers again.

"Don't be."

He takes another step forward and then our bodies are pressing together and all I can feel is the heat of him. "Without sounding like a total creep, I've wanted to do this since the first time I saw you," he whispers as he slips his hands beneath my blazer and wraps them around my waist. I'm fairly sure I've stopped breathing and I can actually hear the blood pounding around my body. I mirror him automatically, my arms sliding beneath the scratchy gray tweed of his jacket. My pulse quickens; he's so warm. My head lifts toward his all on its own, and his lips find mine in the darkness.

The kiss is slow at first—soft, hesitant, his lips pillowing my own—but gradually it becomes something deeper, more urgent, and our bodies are leaning into each other and his hands are wrapped in my hair and I don't even care about my scar, and . . .

"Was that the bell?" Cole whispers the words between kisses on the base of my neck and it takes me a second to come around, remember where I am. He slides his hands back down to my waist and I take a deep, shaking breath.

"The . . . the what?"

He laughs and drops another kiss onto my lips, which quickly turns into another.

"The five-minute bell," he repeats, resting his forehead against my own.

"What? No, you can't be serious!" He releases me and my whole body feels in danger of collapse as I try to focus. "Ugh, we need to go, now." I pick up my bag from the floor, even though I have precisely no recollection of how it got there, and start to take the steps two at a time. A sliver of light comes into view as we reach the second floor and I push open a door that's the twin of the one downstairs. We emerge into a small cleaning closet, stacked with mops and sprays and stinking of bleach. I go to open the next door when he pulls me back.

"Wait." His grin is crooked, mischievous, as he whirls me around.

For a second I think he's going to kiss me again and, you know what, it won't make a difference if I'm late for one class, and . . .

"Here." He runs his hands over my hair and I realize that if I look as disheveled as he does, I might as well be wearing a shirt emblazoned with JUST IN FROM AN EARLY-MORNING MAKE-OUT SESH on it.

His hands fix my collar and I return the favor, neatening the knot of his tie and smoothing his hair back into place where I must have smooshed it with overeager hands.

"Better?" I ask.

"Perfect," he replies, leaning down for one more kiss. It's soft and lingering and over way too soon. We give ourselves one final shake and emerge to see people filtering into classrooms. There are more than a few raised eyebrows and I *should* be embarrassed, but we just grin at each other. I kind of wish I had that T-shirt now.

"See you at lunch?"

"Definitely." He squeezes my hand before heading in the direction of the science lab and I practically float to my classics class. I'm feeling disgustingly happy when I'm brought back to earth with a bump.

"Well?" Emily stands guard in front of the classroom, arms folded. She looks awful. The smile slides from my face.

"Not here," I whisper, trying to sound reassuring. "There are teachers around. We can talk later, after JB tonight."

"Fine." She steps aside, leaving the doorway clear so I can pass. "But I'm holding you to it."

23

AS IT TURNS OUT, I DON'T SEE COLE AT LUNCH. AFTER CLASSICS, with its two empty desks and Emily glaring at the back of my head all morning, I have the worst headache coming on. I go back to the dorm for some painkillers—even though what I actually want to do is climb into bed and cry for three hours straight. What was I doing, thinking I could be happy when everything is so scary and confusing?

The corridor is empty—we're not really supposed to come back until later—and kind of spooky, but if I don't address this now, I'll just be really sick this afternoon.

I unlock the door to our room only to see a figure sitting at our dressing table.

"Taylor! What are you doing up here?"

"I could ask you the same question." She turns around on the stool so I can see the concealer stick in her hand. "I'm trying to cover this up." She gestures to the raised area of skin on her cheek. I frown and move closer. It looks much worse than it did last night.

"Is that from the other night?"

"Yeah, the stupid loose nail in my blusher brush. It seemed to be fine, but today it's just . . ." She stops and makes an exploding motion with her free hand.

"Ugh, I'm sorry. It looks sore. Here." I head to my bedside table and pull open the drawer, or the medicine cabinet, as we call it—I'm the one with all the Tylenol, ointments, and Band-Aids. "Put some of this on it."

"Thanks." Taylor takes the little tub of antibacterial ointment and smears some directly onto the scratch, dabbing it in with a pinkie finger. "What are you doing up here, anyway?"

"Headache." I grimace, holding up a packet of ibuprofen and plopping onto my bed. Should I tell her about Emily? I watch as she dabs concealer onto the scratch and I swallow hard. "Er, Tay? Can I ask you something?"

"Sure." She doesn't turn to face me, but her eyes watch me in the mirror. "What is it?"

"I was just wondering, I mean, I wanted to ask you . . . you said something last night that . . ." The words spill out on top of one another and I pause to gather them back together into a more coherent sentence. "Last night you said you couldn't sleep alone on Friday because of Frank. But you couldn't have known he was dead on Friday—you were already asleep when we got back—so how did you know?"

"Oh, God, is that all?" She dabs blusher onto the apples of her cheeks and I admire how deftly she hides the scratch. "I thought you were going to ask me to move out of the dorm or something! I know it's not really fair that I have the head girl room and never use it. . . ."

"No, of course not! I was just wondering how, well, how you knew. That's all."

She doesn't answer for a minute, concentrating on her makeup. "Marcus told me," she says at last.

I take a breath. "But you wouldn't have seen Marcus," I said.

"Well, he texted me on my burner. Said Frank had been found in the woods. It gave me the creeps."

"Oh." I guess that makes sense. So why do I feel so uneasy?

"What?" She turns to face me now and there's a glimmer of something—anger?—in her eyes. "Don't you believe me?"

"Jeez, Tay, of course I do! But I'm freaking out here—first Morgan, then Jameela, and Frank . . . That inhaler had something in it that should NOT have been there, and I . . . I . . . ." My breath is coming in hiccupping gulps now and tears burn the inner corners of my eyes. I try my best to push it back and take deep breaths, let my mind go blank, block everything out. I don't want to have a fight, not now.

"Hey, hey." There's a warm hand on my back as the bed dips beside me, taking Taylor's weight. "Deep breaths. I know, it's insane, I don't know what's going on, but . . . wait." She stops dead. "*Morgan?* You actually think Morgan was murdered?"

"No. Yes. Oh, I don't know!" My breathing is still shaky and I suck in some shallow gulps of air. "But remember the note? *'Morgan's death was not an accident. I killed her. And you're next.'* That's what it said. Jameela read it out last Monday at the meeting and the next thing we know, she's dead. Frank thought there was something wrong with her inhaler and he's found dead. Are you telling me this didn't start with Morgan?"

There's a silence. All I can hear is my own ragged breathing.

"You're saying that Jameela and Frank were killed because they got involved," says Taylor slowly.

I nod. "Yeah. I think they were asking too many questions, just like . . ."

"Just like us," Taylor finishes. Her eyes meet mine, wide and scared. "Oh God."

"Yep," I agree.

"Right." She hops to her feet and checks her watch. "We haven't had this conversation. I want you to carry on playing dumb—well, you know, not *dumb*, but act like you don't know anything about what was found in the inhaler."

"Er, that might be a problem. Emily ambushed me today before classics."

Taylor holds up a hand. "Leave her to me. She's going to be sworn in as deputy head girl tonight, so she will have to listen to me, OK?"

"OK." If Taylor's right—if Emily has a trace of self-preservation, she'll keep her mouth shut tonight, at least until after we have spoken to her. Unfortunately, despite Morton being full of some of the most intelligent people I've ever met, common sense can be pretty thin on the ground.

"Come on, we'd better go." Taylor leans down to glance in the mirror one last time, pulls a brush through her hair, and stands up straight. "What do you have this afternoon?"

"Art."

"Nice. Wish I could draw," she says, holding the door open for me, "but I am strictly a stick-people kinda gal."

"Yeah, it's a nice class." We head down the corridor to the main staircase, but Taylor looks distracted.

"Hey, what's up?" I ask.

"Nothing." She keeps walking, but I grab hold of her arm and we stop in the middle of the hallway. "Oh, I'm fine. I just keep thinking about something, that's all."

"What? Come on, you can tell me."

"I know, I guess I just don't want to say it out loud." I wait, not saying anything, a trick I learned from my doctor in the hospital over the summer. Give her time and she will talk, if she really wants to. "It's just . . . well, if what you said about Morgan is right, if she was, you know . . . *killed* . . . then you know what that means, don't you?"

I stay quiet as she gains the energy to voice her fears aloud.

"It means one of us really *did* do it, as in someone from Jewel and Bone. There was no one else there that night on the lake; it was just us who took the boats out. . . . That ridiculous initiation, we should never have agreed to it . . . then Patel and Creepy Billy were there, and . . ." Her words fade out as she keeps on talking.

Another thought has taken hold, one I can't ignore.

Taylor said that Marcus told her about Frank. But Marcus wasn't with us when we found Frank. He was back in his dorm, asleep.

So how the hell did he know what had happened?

24

ART CLASS IS ALWAYS JUST WHAT I NEED. IT REALLY DOES CALM me down, especially with so much pressure on this year. When the lesson comes to an end, I linger behind, tidying up slowly, packing away pieces of charcoal and taking my time washing my hands in the large porcelain sink, the kind you see in old farmhouses. I watch the soot rinse from my fingers, gray swirls disappearing down the drain.

"Hey," a voice calls from the other side of the room, and I turn to see Cole poking his head around the doorframe. "Taylor said I might find you here. Do you mind?"

"No, not at all!" I take a wedge of paper towels and dry my hands quickly, then grab my portfolio and put it away on the rack. Cole does not need to see the inner workings of my brain—not yet, anyway. "I'm sorry I didn't see you at lunch."

"Hey, don't worry." He's hovering in the doorway, hands jammed deep into his pockets now. "As long as you're not avoiding me, you know, after this morning?"

"No!" Oh God, I practically just shouted that right in his face. "No, sorry, I just had a headache." I join him at the door. "Emily was hounding me earlier."

"Oh. Yikes."

"Yeah." I don't want to go into too much detail, especially after slipping up and almost telling him about JB when I mentioned Old Josef the other day. Can you imagine his reaction if I told him I was part of a secret society that stands around the bones of a dead guy in velvet robes, all so a top university will consider me? I change the subject quickly. "What are you up to now?"

"Homework, or prep, as you guys call it. Want to join me?"

"Actually, yeah, that sounds perfect. I have some modern history stuff I need to look up. Library?"

"Sounds like a plan. Can we stop for cake in the common room first, though? Marcus said we get afternoon tea every day now."

My stomach rumbles. "Of course," I reply. "I am always down for cake."

The common room is crammed, as usual—cake, scones, and tea come out at four and by then everyone is ravenous after a day of classes. I select a scone—no raisins, thank you very much—with butter, some of Creepy Billy's homemade jam, which is, quite frankly, amazing, and a cup of steaming hot Earl Grey tea. We join the others in what I already think of as "our" seats, and I notice that Cole's plateful of Victoria sponge cake is rivaled only by Marcus's. There's a happy, crumb-filled silence and when I've inhaled my scone, I curl up onto the seat, satiated by the sugar. I hold a shallow white cup between my hands, and I relish the heat seeping into my bones. But I miss mugs.

"You miss what?" Kat asks between mouthfuls of lemon drizzle.

"Er, mugs." I really do need to watch what I say aloud—how embarrassing. Mugs. I cringe inwardly.

"I get it," Cole chimes in, delicately picking up his cup, the handle between his thumb and forefinger. "These things have, like, a thimbleful of tea in them. Give me a chipped mug with strong tea in it any day."

"Agreed!" I laugh. I do like the Earl Grey, but he doesn't have to know that. "So, what's everyone doing before dinner?"

A chorus of "Prep" goes up and Cole gives me a wry smile. Looks like we'll have company. We return our plates to the cart and wander over to the library, the five of us talking quietly as we enter. The desk by my Bernini is empty and I make a beeline to it, drop my bag as the others settle on the benches, and head straight to the circular central desk, where the computers are. I settle myself in front of one and get started.

"How does this thing work, then, if there's no internet?" I swear I feel the whisper of a kiss on the back of my neck as Cole appears behind me and I almost full-on swoon.

"Oh, there is internet, just not on these. You need to book internet time on one of the laptops, so it can be monitored. This is easy, though—you just type in your class and there's usually a list of recommended reading, like this." I point to the screen, where my modern history reading list is displayed. "I have a paper due on small-town legends. So I click here." I press the touch screen and a title is highlighted with a blue bar. I repeat the process. "Then here and here"—two more blue bars—"then hit Submit."

The small printer whirrs and spits out a piece of paper. At the top is my name, the date and time, and the list of books I've requested.

"Then we take it to the librarian. She's really good; she can usually recommend a couple of extras that aren't on the list, if you tell her what you're doing." I point at the screen. "Your turn."

When we both have our lists, we follow the curve of the desk around to the opposite side, where Ms. Somerville, the librarian, is stacking books onto a cart.

"Liz, how lovely to see you! And Cole, is it? You're the new student." It's more of a statement than a question—Ms. Somerville knows everyone—and she quickly moves on. "What can I get you today?"

We put our papers on the highly polished wooden desk and she studies them. "Chemistry, botanics, very good. Actually, I know an excellent book that looks at the chemistry of plants; it will link up these topics for you. I'll bring it out. And, Liz, urban legends—now, that is interesting. I have some original sources in the archives I think you'll enjoy."

"Thank you." She lifts the counter and bustles off to the shelves, deftly selecting books. "Come on," I say to Cole. "She'll bring them over."

He follows me back to the desk. "OK, so urban legends? That's pretty cool."

"Yeah, I love how something gets so twisted by retellings. For this essay I'm doing, I have to choose one and unpack it, laying out the facts and trying to identify the historical basis—there is usually at least one. Every place has its own urban legends; you just have to ask around. I'm surprised there aren't more about Morton, to be honest."

"I bet there are," he says enthusiastically. "We just have to ask the right people."

"True. I've only heard the usual—saying 'Bloody Mary' into the mirror in the second-floor bathrooms, the white lady in the woods, that sort of stuff."

"Ever done it? The Bloody Mary thing?"

"God, no. I'm not stupid, Cole." I bump him with my hip as he follows me back to the table and we sit, smiling at each other. I wonder if he's been constantly reliving this morning too. Kat is already hidden behind a graphic novel of *The Tempest,* and Taylor and Marcus have their heads bowed together over a very detailed drawing of the human anatomy. Cole raises his eyebrows and I stifle a giggle.

"Here we go." Ms. Somerville appears as if by magic and Taylor slams the cover of her book shut. Ms. Somerville just smiles and deposits a pile of books in front of Cole before placing a mixture of books and brown envelopes on my desk. "Now, Liz, these are originals, so please take great care with them. Put them back into the envelopes when you are finished."

"I will. Thanks, Ms. Somerville." I pick up the envelope on top, which has two small circles on the flap with a short length of string wrapped around them in a figure eight to keep the envelope sealed. I carefully unravel it and slide out the pamphlet I find inside.

It doesn't look too old—maybe the 1990s or so. It's a brochure for some kind of spooky walking tour at a place called Gallow Ford. I read through the legends and put it to one side, thinking it might be useful later, and open the second envelope, which contains a small booklet.

This one is more local to the school, and I recognize some of the stories from the ones the seniors tried to frighten us with last year. I flip through the booklet and take notes about any tales I haven't heard of. Then I stop on one particular page.

"Hey, guys," I whisper, and four pairs of eyes swivel in my direction. "Look at this."

I spin the booklet around so they can see and point at a short article entitled "Club or Cult?"

"Have you guys ever heard of this? A cult from around here in the late nineties?"

"A cult?" Kat's eyes sparkle with undisguised morbid glee. She loves this sort of thing. "Oooh, I listened to so many podcasts about cults over the summer! But no, I didn't know there was one around here." She pauses to skim the article, occasionally shaking her head as we all stare at her, our resident murderino. "OK, this is grim."

"Why grim?" Marcus asks, half listening and half taking notes for his homework.

"Because they killed people. This guy—Bradley Harrison—he convinced his followers to murder others. Like Charles Manson." Kat looks up to see a pool of blank faces. "Oh, you're kidding! You've never heard of Charlie Manson?"

"Nooooo," Taylor says as we shake our heads.

"Ridiculous. OK—so Manson had a cult in the sixties. His followers committed a bunch of murders because he told them to and he didn't lift a finger." She taps the article. "Sounds like this guy did the same thing in the late nineties. Got his followers to kill on his behalf."

"Jeez," Taylor whispers. "And it wasn't that long ago?"

"Well, before we were born," I explain.

"Ugh, that's awful," murmurs Taylor. "And around here? The nearest town is Prescott. That's tiny! I wonder where this stuff happened?"

"Kind of all over. Looks like he had links to Prescott, or close by, anyway, but some of the murders were in Oxford, Boston, London . . ." I trail off as I read the others. Cambridge, New York.

"University towns?" Cole reads my thoughts.

"Yeah, I guess. They had a pretty huge reach for a cult, though. That's scary. He was transatlantic."

"Does it say how they died?" Kat asks, her eyes on the page.

"Here, take it." I push the article over to her and Kat starts to read out loud. For some reason, my heart has started beating hard.

"Drowning," she says. "Poisoning . . ."

"And let me guess," Cole interrupts, "being beaten with a rock?"

Kat looks up. "Amongst other things, yes."

My mind spins until all I can see is the blur of faces around me. My brain is working overtime.

"Wait, so how did the leader"—I lean over and consult the article—"this Bradley Harrison . . . get his followers to *kill* people for him?" I ask, taking the paper back and reading to the end so I can answer my own question.

"Cult leaders are very charismatic," Kat says. "And it sounds like he promised them success, financial security, all that stuff."

I shudder. "Who would want to do something like that?"

Kat's eyes are shining. "The Transcendental Faithful, by the looks of it. That was the name of the cult. I mean, he would have been totally sociopathic, no empathy for others. He just wanted to get to the top of the pile and everyone else be damned. He got other people to do his dirty work for him." She is silent, biting her lip. "Wait. Are we saying . . ."

"Spit it out," Taylor says with a laugh, but her voice is quiet. Nervous.

We all know what Kat's going to say.

"Are they . . . back? The cult? What if that explains what has been going on? This is the perfect spot for a cult to take root and commit a load of murders." She prods the paper with a bitten fingernail. "I mean, look around."

"At what?" Marcus says, trying for a joke. "We're totally isolated."

"Exactly. The school is secluded," I murmur in agreement. "The closest bus stop is a twenty-minute walk away, and then it's another forty-five minutes to get into Prescott, if you're lucky. Which means . . ."

"Which means we're sitting ducks," Kat says.

25

THE SMOKY SMELL OF MELTING WAX BURROWS INTO MY NOSE as I follow Taylor down the steps in the old chapel. I shrug on the velvet cape, just as I did a week earlier, our Monday ritual. So much has happened since.

"You think Patel will initiate more acolytes? You know, to replace Jameela and Frank?" I hiss to Taylor as she tucks her red hair beneath her hood.

"I dunno." Her voice is so low, I have to strain to hear. "They didn't replace Morgan, did they? Even though they had all summer. I reckon we'll be getting ready to start meeting and greeting Jewel and Bone donors, soon, looking for sponsors. But who knows?"

We follow the procession of silent, black-clad figures gliding around the circle, over the stagnant water. It has been a warm week, and the smell is unmistakable but bearable. Just.

Dr. Patel starts her intonation and invites the new head girl up to the center. I watch it all like it's happening to someone else—watch as Taylor goes through the motions, watch as Emily is called up to take the place of deputy head. For the first time at one of these meetings, my mind begins to drift—it's hard to think that a week ago I was bursting with excitement. I wonder if I'll ever get that feeling back.

I peer out to the side from beneath my hood and count the figures standing around me. Four empty plinths. I start a list in my head: Taylor and Emily, that's two; Morgan and Jameela make four. But there's no empty place where Frank should be. Have they filled the spot? A new deputy head boy?

Interesting.

I look back in time to see Taylor and Emily lay their bloodied hands on Old Josef. I recite the words with the others.

"Excellent. I sincerely hope that this is the final time we must initiate a new head girl this academic year." Patel's voice is cold and businesslike. "However, before we come to our usual business, we must induct one new member. Acolyte, please approach."

I was right. There's a murmur from a few of the members who must not have noticed the extra body in the room. A figure breaks away from their podium and strides forward confidently, ripples of velvet drifting in their wake. This person is tall, taller than me because the bottom of their cloak doesn't drag through the water beneath, like mine does. The person reaches the center and Patel instructs them to remove their hood.

They do.

"Cole," I breathe.

My heart tightens a little. Yes, there's a sliver of relief, I guess, that I can talk to him about this stuff now, I don't have to hide it from him, but it's overshadowed by anxiety. Will he stop whatever is going on between us because I didn't tell him about this? Will he think I'm a liar, trust me less?

He is initiated into the fold in a blur and before I know it, hoods are removed and a round of applause goes up to welcome our newest deputy. I join in and smile when he catches my eye, but in the pit of my stomach, I feel something like dread.

"Here he is!"

Cole appears at the glass balcony doors of the girls' senior lounge and Marcus jumps to his feet, whooping and cheering. Cole smiles back, but there's a red flush to his cheeks as he enters. Except for us, the room is empty.

The weather is balmy and beautiful for a September evening, but since Jameela's death last week, no one has ventured outside to the roof garden, or up here at all, really, unless it's to leave cards, candles, or bunches of wildflowers. The flowers are decaying now, their petals turning to brown mulch, but no one has moved them.

"Hey." Cole joins us quietly and slides into the empty seat next to me. He smiles. "So, I really am part of the gang now, right?"

"I'm sorry we didn't tell you," I say, and the others murmur in half-hearted agreement, "but, you know, secret society and all that."

"Yeah, I get it." He stares off into the distance.

"So," Marcus interrupts loudly, "how does it feel to have almost beaten my time in the hunt?"

Cole scratches the back of his head and grins, this shy smile that's the most endearing thing I've ever seen. "It feels good. Though I'll tell you what, when I got that note stabbed onto my pillow with a skull badge, inviting me to 'the hunt,' I wondered what the hell I'd got myself into."

"It seems scary," I reassure him, "but it's just a good old scavenger hunt. You must have made good time on it to take the deputy place, though?"

"Yeah. In fact, you helped with that."

"I did? How?"

"When you showed me around the library, remember when you showed me that poison Bible?" I nod. The others have stopped paying attention. Marcus and Taylor are whispering together and Kat is texting, grinning down at the little screen on her burner phone. I take advantage of this and lean in even closer to Cole. "Well, when I got to the last riddle, the one about a *holy disguise,* I went to look at it again. It's right by that massive window, the one with the picture of a chapel in it. When the sun shone on it . . ."

". . . it practically pointed the way," I finish for him.

"Yeah," he grins, before touching a kiss to the tip of my nose. "So, thank you."

"You are so welcome." How long is the acceptable amount of time for staring into someone's eyes at such close range? I can't tear my gaze away from him. I let out a deep sigh, not realizing the others can hear me. The cackle of our friends bursting into laughter kind of breaks the spell. I pull myself away from Cole a little.

"Well," Kat says loudly, breaking our awkward silence as she rearranges herself on her armchair, folding her legs beneath her and pulling her long sleeves down over her hands. "If the lovebirds have quite finished, we have more important stuff to tend to. Who wants to know what I found out today?"

"How gruesome is it?" asks Taylor. "I'm gonna need to know if it's gross or not first." She's curled up with Marcus on a cuddle chair, her legs stretched over his lap as he lazily draws circles on her bare knees. Taylor touches her cheek gingerly, a raised line now visible beneath her makeup. "I don't know if I can take more murder cult stuff."

"Nothing gruesome. Well, not really." Kat leans forward. "It's about Creepy Billy."

"Creepy Billy? Wait." Cole looks at me. "That's the grounds-keeper you told me about, right?"

"Right."

"Yep. So," Kat continues, "I saw him just before we left for JB tonight, pushing that ancient little wheelbarrow of his around. Seriously, as if Morton won't get him a new one. It's basically an antique. Anyway, I saw him talking to a student. . . ." She trails off dramatically.

"Right," I prompt her. "What's so weird about that?"

"Well." Kat pauses, enjoying our undivided attention. "*Said student* handed him something and Billy handed something back. Something wrapped in brown paper."

"Someone was buying off him?" Marcus asks.

"*Buying off him?*" Kat snorts. "What are you, some kind of drug lord?"

Marcus's jaw tightens. "I saw a thing or two growing up."

Taylor strokes his cheek and diverts Kat's attention. "What was in the brown paper?" she asks.

"I dunno." Kat shrugs. "But who knows what he grows out there on that plot of land. It could have been anything."

"You think it was *drugs*, then?" I whisper the word, even though we're the only ones up here. "You think he's growing something and selling it to students? That's a serious accusation to make."

"That's what it looked like." Kat holds her hands palm up. "Just saying it like I saw it. There is one really important question you have failed to ask me, though."

"I was just about to." Taylor yawns. "Sorry about that. So, Kat, just who did you see meeting with our very own creepy grounds-keeper in such a nefarious manner?"

Kat leans back in her seat, her eyes twinkling as she answers.

"Emily."

26

THERE WAS MUCH DISCUSSION ABOUT *EXACTLY* WHAT EMILY
had been buying from Creepy Billy before we sloped off to bed last
night. Now, in the bright light of a Tuesday morning, it's as clear
as mud.

I get dressed slowly. Outside, the sun is shining and the leaves
are beginning to turn. Taylor and Kat are already gone. I head out
into the corridor, looking cautiously around—I don't want to run
into Emily on my own. I decide I'll dash down to the dining hall for
an apple and then go the secret way to class. My lips twitch into a
smile as I think about what happened when I went that way to class
yesterday. . . .

"Liz." Emily emerges from the shadows by her dorm room and
I curse inwardly.

"Hey, Emily." I make a show of looking at my battered leather
wristwatch and yawning. "Can't stop, I slept in and class starts in ten
minutes, so . . ."

"Don't give me that." Her voice is cold, monotone, and the hairs
on the back of my neck stand up. For a person who usually looks
so perfectly groomed, she couldn't look much worse. There are dark

circles under her eyes and her skin is washed-out, pasty-looking. Her hair is down but in need of a wash, grease parting the roots. She looks like the poster girl for smoking things you shouldn't. I wonder if Creepy Billy really is dealing stuff on the side? "I've been waiting to talk to you."

"Now?"

"Yes, *now*. Why are you all avoiding me?" Emily's dull eyes bore into mine and I'm suddenly hyperaware that we're alone. No one would hear us up here if anything happened.

"I'm not," I say weakly. "*We're* not. We're all just . . . busy."

"Seriously?" Emily tucks her dull locks behind her ears and her eyelid flickers in a twitch I haven't noticed before. "That's all you can come up with? I ask you to help me find out who killed my best friend and you're *busy*?"

"Emily, listen. I'm sorry, I really am. But you know that we will get into so much trouble if we're late for class, and—" She holds up a dismissive hand to cut me off.

"Liz, I just want you to help me. Something weird is going on and I'm . . . I'm running out of people I can trust." Her face crumples and for the first time, I see below her cold exterior. "I can't sleep, Ayesha is useless, and my other friends are d-d-dead." The last word comes out in a huge, hiccupping gulp, and I can see she's on the verge of a panic attack.

"OK, OK." I gently grab hold of her forearms and look her in the eye as sobs rack her chest. "I'll help you, of course I will." I glance at the watch on my outstretched arm and nod to it. "But look, we really will be late for class. I don't know about you, but I don't want to be on a watch list right at the start of the year, do you?"

"Fine." She pulls away, and just like that, her stony expression returns. "I'll be at the library later, for prep. Make sure you come and find me. There's something I want to show you."

"OK." I breathe a sigh of relief. "Of course, I'll be there."

"I mean it, Liz." She starts to walk away, but hesitates. Emily turns back on her heel and points a shaking finger at me. "I'm deputy head girl now. Make sure you're there or your first Jewel and Bone sponsor meeting won't happen. Understand?" She storms off then, leaving my shocked gaze trailing behind her as she stalks down the corridor.

I guess I don't have a choice.

The rest of Tuesday passes in a blur of classes. At the end of the day, I catch sight of Kat on the balcony that surrounds the central staircase. I sharpen my elbows and push through the throng until I get to her. "Hey, Kat!"

"Liz!" She pauses, waiting for me to catch up, and I feel the little thrill I often get from being up so high. It's quite a drop from here to the bottom of the stairs. "Good day?"

"Not bad." I fall into step with her and we follow the crowd down the stone staircase. "Need to talk to you guys, though."

"Oh? About you-know-who?"

"Yeah, not here, though." We traipse to the bottom in silence.

She nods. "OK, tell you what. Let's grab the others—and some cake—and discuss." I nod in relieved agreement.

The late-afternoon sun follows us down the corridor as we pass the library on our way to the common room. I make myself as small as possible, in case Emily is already in there, ready to pounce.

Our table is empty, so I sink gratefully into the cool leather and close my eyes. Kat heads to the tea table as I mentally run through that day's prep—carry on researching the local history essay, start some still-life studies for a new art project, and pull together a presentation on the French Revolution. Unfortunately, none of it is as interesting as what I *really* want to look up—that local cult.

"Hey, honey." I pry open my tired eyes as Taylor and Marcus flop onto the sofa across the table. "Good day?"

"Not bad," I repeat. I study Taylor's cheek—it seems to be even more swollen today, more visible beneath her makeup. Maybe I should tell her to get it looked at, but I don't want to freak her out any more right now. For someone who wants to be a doctor, she's got a weird thing about needles. "You?"

Taylor shrugs. "Same. Busy."

We sit in comfortable silence as Kat approaches with a plateful of goodies and a cup of Earl Grey for me. "Thank you." I take the tiny white cup and blow across the rim, watching the steam float away, the string from the tea bag dancing. I grab the tab and swirl it around before lifting it out and placing it onto the matching saucer, where the liquid pools. "Listen, I need to talk to you guys, but I want to wait till Cole gets here. Where is he, anyway? Didn't you guys have a class with him last thing?"

"Yeah." Marcus sprays crumbs when he speaks and Taylor squeals and slaps his thigh. "Sorry." He swallows and grins at us. "He went back to his room for something, said he'd meet us here," Marcus says.

"Oh, OK." I settle back and take a tiny sip of tea. I yelp—it's *way* too hot. "Shit!" I put the cup down, my tongue on fire.

"Lizzie! Wash your mouth out!" Kat is laughing incredulously, her face stretched into exaggerated shock.

"What do you mean?"

"You, swearing! I don't think I've ever heard a naughty word from your mouth before. You've changed."

"It was hot," I say innocently. She chuckles and I shrug, turning my attention to whether I want a chocolate-chip cookie or a scone, when just then, Cole appears, breathing hard.

"Hey." He drops down next to me and plants a kiss on my cheek like it's the most natural thing in the world. I avoid the ridiculous grins and Kat's shaking head and focus on Cole instead.

"Hi. Everything OK?"

"Yep. Just had to go and grab something." He reaches into his bag and rummages for a second. "Close your eyes."

"I— What?"

"Close your eyes," he repeats. I hesitate, but he looks so earnest, I can't help obliging. I sigh and squeeze my lids shut.

"Fine. But if you play any kind of trick on me . . ."

"As if I would. Now hold out your hands."

"Oh, come on, Cole, I don't like surprises."

"Trust me," he says, taking hold of my hands and placing them faceup on my lap. My mind flashes to all the things he could put in there—something gross, a spider or a bug . . . "Ready?"

I nod hesitantly.

"OK," he says, and I feel the weight of a cool, smooth object in my hands. It feels familiar, and as I wrap a hand around it, I feel the handle and a "C" carved into the side. I open my eyes and stare at it.

"It's a mug," Cole explains.

"A mug?" I repeat stupidly as Taylor squeals from across the table.

"Yeah, you know, the other day, you said you missed mugs. And I had this one that my mom gave me, but I don't really drink tea, so . . ." He trails off. "I'm sorry, it's stupid, isn't it?"

"No!" I twirl the mug in my hands and smile up at him. "It's so thoughtful to bring it down."

"Really?"

"Really." I lean forward and kiss him softly on the lips. "Thanks for letting me borrow it."

"Oh, no, it's yours." He smiles. "I want you to keep it. Like, a present. Is that OK?"

"Oh my GOD," Kat bellows over. "You two are ADORABLE. It's disgusting."

I grin down at the mug and back up at Cole. "Completely disgusting," I agree happily.

"We'll grab a table and keep an eye out for Emily and you guys go and see what you can find." Taylor steers Marcus and Cole across the library to an empty seat as Kat and I head to the computers. No one seemed particularly surprised that Emily had ambushed me this morning, and we've agreed to tell her what we found out about the inhaler. But we also need to find out more about this cult.

"We want anything from late 1999 to early 2000, right?" Kat drops her bag on the floor next to mine as we start to navigate the system.

"Yeah, but where do we start? There's not exactly a section on 'murder cults,' is there?" I notice a tall wooden cabinet in front of the far wall, between two windows. It's crammed full of tiny wooden drawers, and I recognize it from something similar in my old school's library, where they hadn't fully computerized everything. "Look—there's a card catalog. If that's organized by date, it could be easier to search."

"OK." Kat collects our bags, and I'm already five steps ahead of her. The closer we get to the card catalog, the more anticipation that builds in my stomach. I have a good feeling about this.

That lasts for about three seconds.

"Well, they're not in date order," I say. The little drawers are arranged alphabetically, of course, and the small, typed labels all blur into one. Besides, my stomach hurts. I must have eaten too much.

"No," Kat agrees, "but at least they're arranged by subject. Hmmmm." She trails a finger along some drawers to the left. "A, B, C . . ."

"I doubt there's a section on cults, Kat." I sigh. My hand lowers to the waistband of my skirt and I tug at it a little, suddenly feeling bloated.

"Don't know if you don't try," she responds. "Wait, are you all right?"

A wave of cramps seizes me and I double over. It passes and I wave Kat off. "Ooof, just cramps. My period must be due. Come on, let's keep looking."

I'm right, though; there is nothing on cults. I try the "S" section as I rub my stomach. Nothing on secret societies, either.

"What about newspapers?" I say at last. "That article we saw was a clipping, wasn't it?"

"Yeah, a photocopy, I think. But you're right, there must be old papers or something in the archives."

"There's no drawer labeled 'newspapers,'" I muse, the cogs in my brain not feeling particularly well-oiled today. God, my stomach hurts. "Do we know the names of any local papers? I have literally never seen one."

"The clipping was from the local paper—the *Prescott Times,* I think. Anything like that?"

I scour the drawers and gasp. "Yes!" I say, drawing glances from people actually trying to study, then lower my voice. "Whoops. But yes, look." I tug at a small brass handle and the wooden drawer releases with a groan. "Ugh, it's so stiff! Here." I remove the first card, a plain rectangle, slightly yellowed with age. Some kind of code is typed on it. "NC-03-12-99. Any ideas?"

Kat thinks for a moment. "NC—newspaper clipping? Newspaper cutting?"

"Ooh, good, yes, you genius. What about the rest? A date?"

"Possibly." Kat reads it again as I fight another wave of cramps. I glance around and then surreptitiously undo the button on the back of my skirt. Ahh, that's better. "The third of the twelfth—so that's the third of December—1999?"

"That sounds more like it." I flick through the next few cards and the dates start to go backward rather than forward. "They just get older—99, 98, 97. Is there another drawer?" I push that one shut and look at the one beneath.

"Doesn't seem like it."

"Great." This was turning out to be a waste of time. "Why would they stop there? I mean, why remove anything more recent than the end of the last millennium?"

"I dunno." Kat's attention is waning. "Everything after 2000 might be in the digital archive. Listen, if it's not here, maybe we should leave it for now. I have so much prep to do and it's been so hard to concentrate recently. . . ."

"I guess." It doesn't sit right with me, though—why just stop collecting newspapers after 1999? It seems like a very un-library thing to do. "I'm going to ask the librarian. Maybe they're some-where else. You go and get on with whatever you need to do while you're in the mood for it. I know it's been hard to focus the last few days."

"Thanks, hon. Meet you back at the table."

"Sure." I make sure the drawer is shut properly and head over to the central desk, where Ms. Somerville is tidying away large books onto a cart, presumably to put back into storage.

"Hello again, Liz. Just a second." She hefts one more book onto the pile and turns to face me, her hand already outstretched for a ticket. "What will it be today?"

"I don't have a slip," I explain, holding up my empty hands. "I was hoping you could tell me if we have any newspaper clippings in the archives."

"Of course we do." She points to the card catalog Kat and I were just looking through. "You'll find most in there, though there are a few in the computer system. Most newspapers are automatically archived these days, though. Is it something in particular, dear?"

"Erm, yes, kind of. Do you remember the book you gave me yesterday, with all the local clippings in it?"

"I do." Her expression is unreadable.

"There was something in there I'd like to know more about," I say, "for an essay."

"And what was that?"

"The, er, cult. The murder one."

"Oh, yes, the Transcendent Faithful, they called themselves." She lowers her voice and winces. "Oh, dear, no, I'm afraid you won't find anything else about that in here. It was a terribly messy affair. In fact, I'm surprised it's still in that book at all—shows how long it's been since somebody reserved that, I suppose."

"Why won't I be able to find out any more?"

"The records were removed, I'm afraid. When Morton employed a certain new headmistress, there was somewhat of a cull on the more . . . unsavory aspects of the library. Unsavory in Dr. Patel's eyes, at least."

"I see," I mumble, but inside I'm fizzing. How dare she! How dare Dr. Patel get rid of information, like she's running some sort of fascist state rather than a school.

"Although . . ." Ms. Somerville glances around and lowers her voice. "I have heard tell that someone"—she tips her head toward the window and I follow it to see she's gesturing over at the plot of land tended by the groundskeeper—"has created their own kind of . . . clandestine archive."

"Really? Creepy Billy—er, Mr. Loomis?"

Ms. Somerville straightens up. "I'm not sure I know what you mean," she responds, though her eyes are twinkling and she nods ever so slightly. "Now, can I get you anything else?"

27

"WHY WOULD PATEL REMOVE ARTICLES ABOUT THAT CULT IN PAR-ticular, though?" Taylor mutters, her eyes on a complicated-looking molecular diagram. "Unless she had something to do with it?"

"Nah," Marcus chimes in, his brow furrowed. "I mean, yeah, she can be a stone-cold *beeyatch,* but that doesn't mean she was involved in some kind of murder cult. Or does it?"

"No," Kat says firmly, "it doesn't." She rolls her eyes. "I swear, it's the twenty-first century, and if a woman still doesn't smile and make pretty for the men, she must have something wrong with her."

"Hey!" Marcus points the eraser end of his pencil at Kat. "I did not say that."

"But what if she *was* involved?" I ask, trying to connect the dots. "What if she was part of that cult all those years ago and now she's doing the same thing? Killing off students for some kind of power, control . . ."

"She already has that as headmistress," Kat argues. "We do what-ever she says. Especially as acolytes—she's the one who will match us with donors who might turn into sponsors. She can make or break us."

There's a mumble of agreement around the table.

"What if she wants more?" Cole says slowly. "What if she wants to be more than a headmistress?"

"That's a good point," says Taylor. "She was head girl when she went to Morton. She would have had the pick of any college, any career she wanted. Do you think she loved Morton so much, she wanted to come back and run the place?"

"Maybe." Kat taps a pen against her chin. "I mean, *we* do, don't we? Love it here, I mean."

"I do love it," Marcus says, "but I can't wait to see what else is out there, you know? And no offense to the teachers, but I know I'm getting a full ride to study science at MIT—there's no chance I want to come back here as anything other than a future sponsor, to help some other kid out."

"Agreed," Taylor says. "I'm working too hard to let all this go. We might have sponsorship, but if you don't get the grades, you don't get the support."

Cole looks at me and voices what we're all thinking. "So what happened to Patel?"

"This is why we need to find out about this cult," says Kat.

I clear my throat. "I'm just going to ask him. Creepy Billy."

Cole levels a serious look across the table. "Are you serious? You just want to march up and knock on his door?"

"Er . . . yes?"

"Well, I'm going with you, then."

"Fine. Good, I mean." I try a smile. "It'll be fine, I promise."

"Great. One more thing." Kat shuts the book she's studying, finally giving in to our conversation. "What if Emily *wasn't* buying drugs off him?"

"She looked pretty off this morning. . . ," I say, thinking back to Emily's dirty hair, her sobs. "Definitely not her usual perfect self."

"OK, fair point," Kat says, "but what if . . ."

"Guys, I love you, but I'm going to need you all to pipe the eff down." Taylor is taking notes so furiously, I almost expect to see steam coming from her pen. "This is just not sinking in."

"Here, let me help. . . ." Marcus attempts to look at the page and I jump a foot in the air as Taylor snatches the book from him and thumps the heavy cover shut, drawing glances from all sides. My stomach twinges at the sudden movement.

"I'm—I'm sorry," she stutters. "I didn't mean to . . ." Marcus's face is stony and she sighs, gathering up her things. "I'll be in my room."

I watch her leave the library, my mouth slightly agape. Taylor never loses her composure, ever, no matter what. I wonder what's going on.

"I guess I'd better check on her," Marcus mumbles, shoving his own notes into his bag, throwing the strap over one shoulder, and standing up. "She's really feeling this workload. See you later, guys." He strides out the door, taking a right as he follows Taylor's path.

"Is that a normal thing for them?" Cole asks as he stares at the doorway.

"No," I admit, leaning back in my chair to rub my stomach. "I've never seen her lose it with Marcus before," I say, bewildered. A twinge of pain shoots through my stomach.

"Me either," agrees Kat. "But it is the final year. I don't know about you, but stuff is getting more complicated."

I eye the pile of textbooks about French political history I have yet to open and then look at Cole. "Complicated" seems like the right word.

"At least Emily hasn't shown up, right?" Kat says. "Although it would be interesting to talk to her. She was best friends with two of the victims."

"Yeah, it would— Ouch!" I break off and clutch my stomach.

Kat points at my midsection. "Make sure you get some antacid on the way back up, won't you?"

"I have some upstairs." I take a deep breath to ease the pain. "I wonder what Emily is doing if she's not here, though." I shake my head. "She was so intense this morning about wanting to show me something today."

"I was in the restroom at lunch and heard one of the languages kids say she was sick in French," Kat says, her head back down in a collection of sonnets. "Maybe there's something going around."

"And you've only thought to tell me this now? I've spent the whole day dodging her!"

"Yeah, sorry. Slipped my mind. I thought she'd drag herself here no matter what after what you said, though. I hope she hasn't given you anything."

"Yeah, me too."

We sit in silence for a few minutes and I pretend to read, but it's no good. "I can't focus," I say, closing the book. "We need a plan." Cole and Kat follow suit and the three of us sit there for a second, thinking. "What are you both doing tomorrow afternoon?"

"Hockey," Kat says, while Cole shrugs. Wednesday afternoons are usually for clubs and extracurriculars. I turn to Cole.

"If you're not signed up for anything yet, why don't we both go and see Creepy Billy tomorrow?"

"And say what?" Cole looks far from convinced, as if he regrets saying he'd come with me.

"I dunno, we can tell him we're doing an essay or something. I can show him my urban studies notes. It's only partly a lie."

"Listen, I know I said I'd go with you, but I'm not so sure it's a good idea. I mean, Kat just saw him trading something with Emily, right? How do we know he's not involved in all this? I mean, why has he kept all that junk? And if it's not cult-related, he could still be dealing bad stuff to vulnerable people. Plus, his name has the word 'creepy' in it. I'm hardly eager to go knocking on his door."

"Although," Kat says, her eyes still on her Shakespeare, "he could have been giving her *anything*."

"Like . . . information?" I say.

Kat nods. "I bet Creepy Billy sees and hears everything, you know."

Cole shakes his head and lets out a low groan. "Is this what it's always like being surrounded by smart people? You don't get a second to breathe?"

"Pretty much." Kat shrugs, going back to her books.

"So, Cole," I say, tilting my head at him in what I hope is an irresistible way, "are you in?"

"Fine," he says, kissing me while Kat makes a yakking sound, "but only because it's for you."

28

THE MAIN CORRIDORS ARE QUIET ON A WEDNESDAY AFTER-noon. I nod and smile at the random student wandering past in full-on Morton sports regalia, but the building seems deserted apart from that. Most people are off doing enrichment activities. It's required in first year, but as seniors we can use the time to study if we want to, which is a blessing for someone who despises sports as much as I do. I relish the peace, having crawled through this morning's classes after another night of tossing and turning.

My feet tap on the polished tiles of the entryway as I pace back and forth, my black patent-leather shoes making a swishing sound every time I stop and turn on the ball of my foot. I pause, arch my neck, and look up, the stairs empty for once, not full of chattering teenagers. As ever, I'm taken aback by the grandeur of the entrance hall, the beautiful sweeping staircases that billow out and meet back again on the first floor below the huge stained-glass window. At Christmastime they put a twenty-foot-tall tree in the middle and decorate it with ornaments that are bigger than my head. It's like something out of a fairy tale.

"OK, there, daydreamer?" I blink at Cole's voice behind me and spin around.

"Hey! I was worried you'd forgotten about me." I catch his hand and point at the currently empty space. "Just looking forward to when they put the Christmas tree up, that's all. Wait till you see it, it's amazing."

"Cool." He loosens his tie slightly with his free hand. "How're you feeling?" I furrow my brow and tip my head as he rushes to explain. "You know, your, er, cramps. Feeling better?"

He's so thoughtful. "Yeah, all fine." I beam at him as he runs a finger around the inside of his shirt collar. The cramps eased last night, thankfully.

"God, it's boiling today—do we still have to wear our uniform this afternoon?"

"Technically, yes," I say, dropping his hand, "but I think you can get away with being a bit more casual." I look him in the eye and slowly, deliberately, untuck my shirt. "See?"

"Oh, you maverick!" Cole cries as he makes a big deal of shrugging off his blazer. "I don't know if I can handle the heady rebellion of it all!" I squeal and he lunges for me, nipping my waist with both hands. "See? The mere glimpse of an untucked shirt has made me wild!"

"Stop," I try between peals of laughter that leave me doubled over and breathless. I squirm away and dissolve into giggles again. "I hate being tickled."

"Really?" He grins wickedly, picking up his blazer from the floor. "I couldn't tell."

"Liar." I smile back as he offers me his hand again and I fold my fingers into his. They're cool and strong and send a glorious little chill up my arm.

"Are you sure you want to do this?"

"I am." I nod. I hold up my reporter's notepad and pen and give him my best perky smile. "Hi there, Mr. Loomis, I was hoping to ask you some questions for a school project, would you mind?"

"Well, I'd answer your questions"—Cole drops a soft kiss on my cheek—"but I'm biased."

"Come on. The quicker we do this, the better. I thought we could finish the tour of the back staircase once we're done."

Cole snaps to attention immediately. "Well, why didn't you say so?" He sweeps his free hand before us, gesturing to the double doors. "After you."

Even though I've seen Creepy Billy's—*Mr. Loomis's*, I remind myself— house from a distance before, I always imagine it as run-down and derelict. However, the closer we get to it, I can see that it is immaculately kept. Hanging baskets decorate the redbrick walls, so that late-summer flowers trail down either side of a painted black door that bears the hand-carved sign that says GROUNDSKEEPER'S LODGE, and there are window boxes full of tall, fragrant purple flowers with bleeding yellow hearts.

"Irises," Cole comments. The surprise must be evident on my face. "They're my mom's favorite. You don't usually see them in autumn."

Oh, my heart.

"Hopefully he's home." I square my shoulders and paste on a smile, my hand poised to knock.

The door opens before my knuckles touch the wood.

"Wondered when one of you would show up," Creepy Billy

grunts in the gloom of the cottage, "and now there's two of you. Well, come on in, then, I suppose." He pauses to point at the irises. "Rebloomers. Come back before you go home for the holidays," he says to Cole, "and I'll give you a cutting for your mother."

I turn to Cole as Mr. Loomis shuffles away. His mouth is hanging open.

"Didn't expect that," he says.

"Neither did I." I glance at the open door.

"Come on, then," Billy shouts from inside, "I haven't got all day."

I take a deep breath and step over the threshold, Cole on my heels. The cottage is small but clean, and the stone floor is well-swept. A small log fire smolders in the corner of the little living room, making it stuffy and smoky but undeniably cozy.

Billy appears from behind another door with a pot of tea and three old tin mugs. "Sit down, then," he grumbles, setting them on the small wooden table before disappearing back into what I can only assume is the kitchen. Cole and I sit on the low, brown tweed sofa, a relic from the eighties, by the looks of it.

Billy returns with a small carton of milk and some cubes of sugar. "Help yourselves, will you?" He sits slowly in a worn, low-slung armchair, the way older people whose joints are stiff and painful do, and grabs a poker from beside the fire.

"What do you need?" He doesn't look at us; instead, he focuses on moving the coals around slowly, methodically.

"Erm, thanks for having us, Mr. Loomis," I start, nodding at Cole to start pouring tea. "I was hoping to ask you some questions if that's OK? For a—"

"'Bout that blasted cult, is it?" he interrupts, and Cole's hand falters, spilling hot tea onto the wood. "Here." He pulls a rag from the pocket of his overalls and throws it at Cole. "Mop that up."

"How did you know that's what we'd ask about?" I ask, my curiosity getting the better of me. No point in keeping up a charade if I don't have to.

"You finished?" Billy asks Cole, who nods and hands me a cup of steaming black tea. Billy leans forward, close enough that I can see the grizzled gray of his stubble and the stains on his teeth. He grabs the teapot and fills his mug, his grime-encrusted nails closing around two sugar cubes that he drops in with a splash. He follows with an unholy amount of milk, doesn't bother to stir, and leans back.

This time he fixes his eyes on me. "Was about time someone started digging around, if you ask me. Clever bunch of kids are bound to be curious, and that nosy mare in the library let slip that she'd given someone that booklet with the clipping in. So." He stops to take a sip from his mug. "What exactly do you want to know?"

"I'm not really sure," I answer honestly. "We . . ." Cole shoots me a look. "Well, *I* was hoping to get a look at your, er, collection?"

"You mean the newspaper clippings?"

"Yes! Do you really have them?"

Billy nods, scratching his chin, his nails scraping on the bristles there. "I do. They're not in any kind of order, though; you'll have to do that yourself."

"That's fine!" I fail to keep the excitement out of my voice. "Can I ask—why did you keep them?"

"Hate seeing history thrown away," he explains, slurping from his mug. "Been here longer than any of you. People want to come in and change the history of this place to suit themselves, and it just don't work like that. You got to know your history if you don't want to repeat it, 'specially the bad stuff. This headmistress isn't the first one to do it, so I keep whatever they chuck and return it all when a new head takes over." He drains his cup as his words sink in. Creepy Billy, unofficial archivist of Morton Academy. "You ready, then? Leave them cups here, don't want you spilling on anything."

"Of course." I set down my untouched mug and stand, Cole following suit, though I can see that he politely drank his tea, too.

Billy pushes himself up into a standing position. "I'm working on the plot this afternoon, just out there." He points a gnarled finger back toward the front door. "So you can stay for a bit. Just stay out of the other room, that's mine. No need to be going in there anyway."

"Of course," Cole says. "We'll respect your privacy." Billy appraises him and nods.

"Good. You got an hour, then I'm back in for another cup of tea and a rest, so I expect you to be done by then."

"Of course, thanks, Cr— Mr. Loomis."

"Call me Billy." He smiles, though it's full of browning teeth rather than humor. "Just drop the 'Creepy,' will you?"

"Uh, thank you, Billy," I say. Cole and I exchange wide-eyed looks as we follow him through a narrow hallway and into the kitchen. Like the small front room, it's bright and clean, well-scrubbed but simple. There are three doors in here—the one on the back wall is propped open and leads to a small, pretty garden, which must be Billy's private space. The others are to the left, side by side on the whitewashed stone wall. We follow Billy to one and he pulls it open before walking off without another word.

"Holy . . . ," Cole breathes, before dissolving into a loud cough.

I couldn't have said it better myself.

The tiny box room is in stark contrast to the rest of the house. The small space is cramped and dusty, brown file boxes piled haphazardly on top of one another, most of them towering over me. By the look of things, there was an awful lot of stuff Patel wanted to get rid of when she was put in charge.

"Ready to dive in?" I ask.

"Let's do it," Cole responds, before immediately sneezing three times in a row.

29

"YOU KNOW, YOU'D THINK ALL THAT SNIFFLING WOULD GET annoying, but you still look very cute."

Cole glares at me over his open box of newspaper clippings. The air is hot, humid, and thick with dust motes; his eyes are red-rimmed and streaming with allergy tears. "I'm fine," he says defensively, sniffing loudly. "We'll be done soon, right?"

"I hope so." I thump the lid down on my own box and heft it out of the way, causing another wave of dust to fill the little room. "Oops, sorry!" I squeak as Cole lets off another volley of sneezes.

"I hope so too." He uses the sleeve of his shirt to wipe his forehead and he comes away with a trail of gray dirt on his previously white sleeve.

"Here, one second—let me grab you a tissue."

"No," he sniffles, "I'm fine, honestly—" He's cut off by a barrage of sneezes and sighs. "OK. Thank you."

"One minute," I promise him. I stand and wipe my own sweaty, dust-laden palms on my checked skirt, the dirt blending in with the tweedy fabric. I'm sure I saw a door in the little hallway between the front room and the kitchen—that has to be the bathroom.

I sneak back through the kitchen, half afraid Billy will come back and think I'm snooping. I'm right, though—there's a small bathroom off the hallway, barely large enough to swing a cat in, though thankfully as clean as the rest of the cottage.

I wash my hands in cool, soapy water, my eyes drifting around the room. It's pretty spare except for a small ledge of plants on the windowsill above the sink, all in terra-cotta pots with little lollipop sticks stuck into the soil. I grab a piece of tissue to dry my hands and lean a little closer to see if I can make out the writing, but it's all smudged where the wood has swollen over timeless waterings and the letters are not familiar enough to recognize.

"Belladonna, camphor, and castor." Billy's gruff voice invades my thoughts and I jump, realizing the door is still wide open.

"You scared me!" I put a still damp hand to my heart, which is racing. "I'm sorry, I was just washing my hands," I say, my words spilling out over each other. "It's dusty in there."

"Humph," he says, "long as you're not snooping." He nods to the plants. "Hard to grow those, and they're poisonous. Don't touch 'em."

"I won't." I look back at the plants for a second. "Why do you grow them, if they're poisonous?"

"I like a challenge," he says. "Now, if you don't mind . . ." I stand awkwardly before I realize he probably wants to use his own bathroom.

"Oh! Sorry." I grab some more tissue and hold it up. "For Cole. He has allergies. All the dust, you know."

"Humph," Billy says again as I hurry past him. "You got twenty minutes," he calls after me.

"What was all that?" Cole asks as I reenter the room and gently close the door. His eyes are practically swollen shut now, and I feel awful that he's sat through all this to help me, especially when he could have been off signing up for football.

"Here, that's enough." I clear a space by the window, open it wide and guide him to it. "I just saw Billy, he said we've got twenty minutes, so I'll just speed-read anything that's left while you sit here. He's growing some crazy plants in his bathroom. . . ." Cole raises an eyebrow and I laugh. "No, not that kind. Though I wouldn't mind a closer look at his plot of land one night . . ."

"Don't you dare. Crazy like how?"

"Poisonous stuff, like belladonna. A couple of others too—castor and camphor, maybe?" I search in my bag and produce an almost-empty bottle of water, pouring a little onto some of the tissues. "Here. Lean against the wall and put these on your eyes." He doesn't argue, just does as I say. A low moan escapes his lips.

"Ohhh, that's better," he murmurs.

"Good." I leave him sitting by the window and start on the boxes we have yet to root through. I'm about a third of the way into one of the last boxes when I see something interesting. "Hey, I think I've got something."

"You do?" Cole lifts the pads of tissue from his eyes and uses them to wipe the little bits of black dust gunk that have gathered in the corners. "Yuck. I need to wash my face."

"Five more minutes." I set the book aside and go through the rest of the box. Nothing. A quick check of the remaining two storage boxes doesn't turn up anything else. "I think that's it."

"Really? Thank God." He starts to climb to his feet, the dissolving tissue now useless in his hand.

"Wait a sec, let me see if I'm right." I pick up the thick, leather-bound volume that I set aside. It's one of those old photo albums, the pages inside sticky and covered in plastic. But instead of pictures, the book is crammed with newspaper clippings—specifically the *Prescott Times, 1999–2000.*

"Here." Cole picks up his blazer and bag from the floor and opens the flap that covers the top of his satchel. "Let's borrow it." He takes it from me without another word and slides it into his bag, throwing his blazer across the top.

"Cole!" Is he serious? "We can't, it's stealing!"

"No, it's not," he argues, "it's borrowing. We'll give it back when we're done; it's not like he'll notice."

"I don't know. . . ."

"Well, I do. Come on, Goody Two-shoes." He leaves the room and I have no real choice but to follow him. We leave the cottage and pass Billy grafting plants on the land in front, tending to the berries that I realize he must use to make his famous jam. The long, sharp garden fork in his hand gleams in the sunlight.

"Thank you." I wave. He nods and grunts and that's it. Poor Billy. He's less creepy and more lonely, I think.

I gasp as we enter the cool space of the entrance hall. "I can't believe we just did that," I say. It's still early and the school sports don't finish for another hour at least.

"Sorry I couldn't survive much longer in that room," Cole says, looking down at his shirt. "Jeez, I'm filthy." He draws a finger across my forehead and pulls it away, coated in dust. "And so are you."

"Ewww! Right, let's go and get cleaned up. Why don't we go for a shower. . . ."

"*We?*" He grins and I poke him in the chest.

"*Separate* showers, obviously, and then meet in the girls' lounge upstairs? No one goes in there anymore. . . ."

"OK," he says more somberly. "Give me twenty minutes." We climb the stairs together and pause under the huge window, its rainbow lights dancing on the stone steps. "See you soon."

"See you soon." He waves before walking to the stairs that lead up to the boys' dorms. I head the other way, dreaming of a hot shower. I hear him sneezing the whole time.

30

I DON'T REALIZE HOW FILTHY I AM UNTIL I WATCH THE SCUMMY gray foam slope down my feet and into the shower drain. Yuck.

I close my eyes and enjoy the solitude for a second, tilting my head forward so the water trickles down my back. I have the whole bathroom to myself, so the water is actually hot and there are no unidentified hairs here before me, which is both nice and unusual. Sharing a bathroom with so many girls isn't ideal, but I'm used to it—I never had much privacy at home, either. I think of the private bathroom upstairs in the head girl's room. Lucky Taylor!

I crank the handle into the Off position and shiver as the cold air immediately hits. I grab the huge, fluffy white towel from the hook on the door. I shroud myself in it and emerge in a cloud of steam, my feet sliding around in my flip-flops as I carry my little shower bag over to the bank of mirrors.

I catch sight of myself through the mist and do a double take. I lean in, wiping away the steam, letting my fingers trail along the mirror and push wet strands of hair away from my face. I look . . . healthy. Healthier than I've looked in ages. My eyes are bright and my cheeks are flushed and I watch a huge smile spread across my face as I think of why, or, more accurately, *who* is responsible for the change.

I reflect on the last few days. Despite the truly awful things that have happened, despite the fear and worry and heartbreak . . . I am actually *happy.* I'm back at Morton, something I worried all summer might not happen.

And then there's Cole. I watch as my smile gets even brighter.

I pull my comb out of the shower bag and brush my hair back before parting it along the center as fat drops of water roll down my shoulders. I grab another towel from the fresh pile on the counter and tip my head forward, starting to rough-dry my hair. Just then, I hear the main bathroom door open and shut.

"Hi," I call to let whoever it is know that someone's in here. "I'm almost done." I blot my hair some more, until it stops dripping on me, pack up my things into my bag, including a little pot of Kat's Tiger Balm that has somehow made its way into my stuff, and head to the door.

The air is still steamy—I may have gone a little overboard with the temperature in the shower earlier—and I can't see anyone else in the room. Did I imagine the sound of the door just before? Or did it close in the wind or something?

"Hello?" I try again, feeling ridiculous. Nothing.

I start toward the door again and realize I've left my shower bag behind. Christ—I forget the simplest things these days. If it's not written down, whether it's homework or taking my meds, it doesn't happen. I turn back to the mirrors, clutching my towel around me, the steam clearing slightly. My bag comes into focus, right where I left it. And then so does the mirror.

Alongside the clear patch I wiped in the glass, there are words written in the steam—enormous, dripping words that run from the top of the mirror to the bottom. I squint, reading them, then I grab my bag, spin on my heel, and run. But not before the message is seared into my brain, one I know I won't forget.

DEAD
GIRLS
CAN'T
WIN

"Hey." Cole is already waiting for me as I run up the spiral staircase to the seniors' lounge.

"Hey," he repeats, his voice laced with concern. "What's up? Did something happen?"

I don't answer. Instead I run over and throw my arms around him, pressing my face into his chest. He pulls me away. "Whoa, you're soaking! Liz, tell me what happened."

I blurt out the whole story. By the time I'm done, I'm out of breath. "It was just . . . freaky. Like, it appeared out of nowhere. I thought I was on my own, but . . ." I trail off. "You don't believe me, do you?"

"Believe what?" Kat's cheerful voice echoes across from the staircase. "What have you been up to, Lizzie?" She grins, wagging a finger. Then she gets a good look at my face. "What happened?"

I fill her in, starting to shiver. I'd raced back to my room and pulled on the nearest things I could find, and I now realize my thin T-shirt is soaking wet.

"I'll go and have a look," she says, heading back down the stairs. "Liz, change into this." She chucks an oversized hoodie in my direction and disappears. I shiver again.

"Go on, then, do what you need to do." Cole makes a big show of covering his eyes. "I won't peek, promise."

"Er, I'll just go into Taylor's room." I am suddenly very aware that my T-shirt is now incredibly see-through and hold the hoodie across myself as I dart to the room. Thankfully, it's open. "Hello?" I try, just in case, but the room is empty, as it has been all week.

I shrug out of the wet tee. Taylor's hair dryer has made it up here, so I give my now-damp bra a good blast on the hot setting before sliding Kat's hoodie over my head. The thick fleece inside feels like velvet on my bare skin, so different from my thin, cheapo one. Not that there's anything wrong with mine, I remind myself—I can just tell this one is more expensive. It comes down past my thighs and I push the sleeves up to my elbows, noticing that the coral color brightens up my face. I start to blow-dry my hair, my bones warming too. Then I flip my hair and use Taylor's paddle brush.

"Hey, that's better!" Cole smiles as I emerge, opening his arms for another hug. "Mmm, much better," he mumbles into my warm hair. I close my eyes and allow myself to settle for a moment, but it doesn't last long. I can hear the sound of feet on metal steps ringing around the room.

"Hey." Kat emerges, and I can tell by the look on her face that I'm not going to want to hear what she has to say. "Feeling better?"

I ignore the question. "Did you see it?" I break away from Cole and start to fiddle with my sleeves, dragging them down past my knuckles. My thumbs find little holes made to poke through, so I do, relishing the feeling of safety it provides.

"Come on," Kat says kindly, her eyes darting over my head to look at Cole. "Let's sit down."

"What? No." I look between the two of them. "I'm not a child. Just tell me."

"Well, there was nothing there." Kat's face is apologetic, but I can't help it—I start to laugh. It's hollow, though, strange and flat.

"It was written in steam, Kat! Someone could have wiped it away, or the cleaners came in, or—or it just—I don't know, evaporated or something. You know . . ."—I make a poofing gesture with both hands—"science!"

She's quiet, her head down, not quite avoiding my eyes, but not meeting them, either.

I turn to Cole. "You believe me, don't you?"

"Of course I do." He says it with such conviction, I feel buoyed for a second.

"Thank you," I whisper.

"Lizzie, I believe you too," Kat says, her voice quiet. "I'm just . . . scared. I don't know if this thing is over. . . ."

"Or if it's only just beginning? I know," I whisper. I hold my hand out to her. She comes over and takes it. "I'm sorry. Come on, you're right, we need to sit down."

We choose the leather sofas closest to Taylor's room and sink into them. It's only then that I realize Cole has his schoolbag with him.

"I almost forgot," I say. "Do you have it?"

"Have what?" Kat asks, stretching her legs out, taking up an entire two-seater as she flips her sneakers off and props her feet on the arm. She's got a different hoodie on now, this one creamy against her olive skin. "Should I text the others, tell them what happened? Where we are?"

"Yeah, good idea." Cole tugs the book from his bag and I notice that his initials are carved into the leather. "A parting gift," he explains, following my gaze, "from my mom. To say congrats. You know what moms are like."

"That's so cute," I say, trying to think of the last thing my mom gave me, apart from a hard time.

"They're on their way." Kat's little silver flip phone disappears into a pocket and she sits up. "Come on, let's forget about threatening messages and talk about murder cults." Her voice holds only a trace of sarcasm. "What have you two been up to?"

I explain as Cole pulls a packet of antibacterial wipes from his bag and starts wiping the dust from the cover. "Poor Cole was allergic to everything." I smile at him, his eyes still faintly red. "But he soldiered on and then, uh, borrowed this book. Billy didn't give us much time, so I haven't looked properly, but the dates are right."

"Dates are right for what?" Taylor and Marcus appear at the top of the stairs, both dressed in baggy pants and hoodies, though Taylor's hoodie is cropped, so it shows off her tanned stomach. They look ridiculously cute and matchy. I realize this means Marcus has not even bothered sneaking over the wall this time—he's come up the stairs through the girls' dorms. It looks like they've stopped caring if they're caught or not.

"For the murder cult," I explain, beckoning them over. Cole pushes the now clean book into the center of the low coffee table and I slide off my seat, scooting onto the floor and settling myself between his legs. I pat the space next to me and Taylor shuffles close, Marcus taking the seat behind her. A curtain of red hair hangs over her cheek. "Hey," I say quietly, "how's the scratch?"

"Rank," she sighs, pushing the hair behind her ear. The scratch is more of a wound now, the edges crusting beneath the heavy foundation she's tried to hide it with. It looks painful.

"Oh, honey," I sympathize, "have you been to see the nurse? I bet she could give you something for it."

"No, I've been too busy, but I will. So." She changes the subject swiftly as Kat and I exchange worried glances. "Fill us in."

At this rate, Taylor is going to burn out. Still, maybe being head girl requires this sort of dedication. I tip my head backward to look at Cole. "Your turn."

Cole repeats the events of the afternoon. I'm itching to start looking through the clippings. "There might not be anything in there," Cole finishes, "but it was the only thing that looked promising, so . . ."

"So let's look at it, my God, I am dying of suspense!" Kat blurts out and flips the cover open, which breaks the tension I had not quite realized was there.

"OK." I laugh. "Let's look."

Kat scoots around the table to my left side and we start to flip through, the five of us scouring each page. They're all local newspaper clippings about Morton—mostly what you'd expect. Outstanding exam results, local community work, Oxbridge acceptances, that sort of thing. Some alumni stuff too, soirees where Morton alumni came back to showcase their success and donate toward the future of the school. Every one of them would have been through Jewel and Bone, I think. It is one of these pieces, dated September 1999 and accompanied with a smudged black-and-white photograph, that makes Kat grab my hand so I don't turn the page.

"Look at the caption," she whispers.

"*'Nikhita Patel,'*" Marcus reads aloud, "*'Head Girl of Morton Academy, greets Old Boy Bradley Harrison, CEO of Transcendental Health Enterprises.'*"

31

"WAIT," MARCUS SAYS EXCITEDLY, LEANING OVER TAYLOR AGAIN, both hands on her shoulders. "That was the name of that guy, the cult guy!"

We all peer at him. "Babe," Taylor says with a sigh, patting him on the knee, "for someone so smart, you can be a total himbo."

"Sexist," Marcus grumbles, leaning back. "It's him, though, right?"

"Definitely," I agree, "and *that*"—I point to the smiling girl shaking his hand—"is Dr. Patel."

"I don't believe it," Kat breathes, looking up at the list of past head girls on the wall. Jameela's photograph is up there now too. I hadn't realized. Her smile is wide, proud. She looks as though she has the world at her feet.

My stomach flips. That's it. *That's* Jameela's legacy: a photo on a wall in a school that hardly anyone will see.

"There she is." I point Dr. Patel out to Cole. Her hair is long, dark, and parted to one side, her cheeks flushed and fresh, her brown eyes smiling. There's a small golden plaque beneath the frame engraved with her name and the date: 1999–2000. She looks pretty much the same apart from the fact that the girl in the picture looks happy.

"Dr. Patel never smiles these days," I murmur.

"Maybe it's Botox," Taylor says. "Plus I reckon she's had some fillers—her lips looked suspiciously thinner when she was eighteen, don't you think?"

"She can't be more than forty," Cole says, looking at the date of the photo. "Pretty young to be a headmistress, then?"

"I suppose so."

"Come on, are there any more?" Taylor nudges me impatiently. I flip through the pages carefully, scanning the clippings. They are brittle, starting to crack with age. You can tell they haven't been looked after properly.

"Bor-ing," Marcus groans.

"Wait!" I stop toward the end of the book, another pixelated photo of Bradley Harrison gazing out from the page. He's wearing a tuxedo and holding a brandy glass in one hand. The background makes it clear that this picture was also taken here, at Morton. He was clearly a donor. I wonder if he was a Jewel and Bone sponsor too. Even though he's in a sea of people, some kind of event happening around him, his eyes have managed to find the camera. Stubble covers his cheeks and lower jaw. You can see that he must have been good-looking at some point, but this picture looks more like a mug shot, his eyes dark and penetrating, and his mouth twisted into a privileged white-boy smirk.

"God, I hate his face," Kat murmurs.

"*'Bradley Harrison,'*" I read aloud, "*'CEO of Transcendental Health Enterprises, is being sought for questioning by local police after a spate of suspicious deaths last month.'"* I check the date on the top of the clipping—October 13, 1999. *"'The former Morton Academy head boy has been linked to the alleged murders, amongst rumors of cult-related activities. This is the most recent photograph of the suspect, taken at an event at Morton Academy last month. Police advise that you should not approach him directly, but instead call the hotline number below.'"*

"Jeez," Kat whispers. "That's horrible." But her eyes are glittering. "Keep going."

Though I flip the page, Bradley Harrison's face remains etched into my eyelids. I see his sneer every time I blink. "Look." I point at two small, formal-looking clippings on the next page. "Obituaries."

They're worded similarly, both lamenting the passing of someone young. People who have left Morton and gone on to great things, only for their lives to be "snuffed out." A couple more of these phrases jump out, most notably "unexpected and sudden death" and "ongoing investigation."

"Come on, then, resident true-crime guru," I say to Kat. "Are we talking murder?"

"Oh, def murdered," she says, brushing her unruly hair behind one ear and leaning closer. Her damp hair is starting to curl and wave, the exact opposite of my limp spaghetti strings from earlier. "If there's an investigation into a death, that's never a good thing."

I flip to the next page. We're nearing the end of the book now, and I'm starting to worry that this is all we'll find out.

But I'm wrong.

"Bingo," I say quietly.

Every single body around me leans in as we absorb the

double-page spread. This one is dated June 2000 and clearly taken from a tabloid rather than the local paper. "MURDER CULT LEADER FOUND GUILTY" screams the headline, and another photo of Bradley Harrison is splashed across the page. This time he looks gaunt and unkempt, flanked by police officers, hands cuffed firmly behind his back.

"Just— Wait a second." Taylor puts a hand on the page, as though she wants to unsee the article. "What are we doing? Things have been tragic enough around here recently. Let's just take this to . . ." She stops.

"To who?" I press. "Dr. Patel? The police?"

"I don't like this," whimpers Taylor. We ignore her; this is too important.

"In true crime, there are no coincidences," Kat says. "Look." She points at the article and begins to read aloud. *"'Though Harrison was not found guilty of murder himself, he was charged with coercion and conspiracy to murder. The surviving members of the cult have stated that Harrison was the driving force behind the slayings, telling followers that if they sacrificed another human being, they would reap the benefits in power and wealth.'"*

"That is twisted," Cole murmurs. "What about *him,* though? What was *he* going to get out of all this?"

"His rivals out of the way, maybe?" Kat replies. "These psychos are always way too clever. They pull the strings and watch the fallout. Revel in it, even. I told you, it's like Charles Manson. He made people do all sorts of terrible stuff, but never got his own hands dirty." She taps the newsprint. "Sounds like our boy Bradley did the same thing, and listen to this." She points to a line and reads aloud.

"'Harrison was sentenced to life imprisonment. However, he will potentially be eligible for parole in 2019.'"

"You're kidding," I breathe. "That means he could be out now. Like, around here?"

"Yep." Kat stands and stretches, making her way back to the empty sofa. "And even worse," she says as she sits, "look at the way those poor people died."

I glance back at the article and see a small box in the corner. It lists names, ages, and manners of death—for easy reading, I think in disgust. Tabloids are gross.

"'Drowning, poison, bludgeoning, and . . . stabbing,'" I read out. "'Harrison's followers believed that the more traumatic the death, the greater their reward would be.'"

"That is so messed up," Taylor mutters, moving to sit on Marcus's lap, curling into a ball as though he can protect her from the idea. "Why would people believe him?"

"Cult leaders prey on the vulnerable," Kat explains. "Harrison would have told them everything they wanted to hear. Things they'd ached to hear their whole lives. Told them they were special, important, beloved . . ."

"I kind of get it," Cole says quietly. "I mean, who doesn't want to be told they're worth something? That something they do will be remembered, their sacrifices worthwhile?"

Silence descends upon us like a thick layer of snow. We *all* get it, to a point. After all, that's why we're here, at Morton.

"Anyway," Kat breaks the silence, "we can't deny that there's an awful lot of similarity between these crimes and the events of the last few days. And weeks, if we count Morgan."

"Let's not get carried away just yet," Marcus says. "I still need to check what that was in Jameela's inhaler before we can say for certain. I can't do it until we get internet access this weekend—I haven't been able to find the right books anywhere."

No one says anything. We all know it was poison.

"He could be out now," I say, and my voice sounds very small. "He could be anywhere, even here. They could be working together."

"Bradley Harrison on the loose," Kat sighs. "Yet another thing we need the internet for. Stupid burner phones. God, I miss the twenty-first century sometimes."

"Guys," Cole says. "You've missed the last line. Listen: '*The prosecution hinged on the words of one surviving member of the cult, another former student of Morton Academy. Rikesh Patel explained how Harrison had brainwashed him into attempting to kill his own sister so that he could achieve the success that had evaded him since he left the school.*'"

"His *sister?*" Kat sits up, her gaze traveling to the wall of headshots.

"Yep." Cole nods. "His sister, head girl at Morton Academy. Nikhita Patel."

32

"WELL," KAT SAYS, LETTING OUT A BREATH. "YOU GUYS CER-tainly brought us some serious information."

"Hmm." I'm not fully listening. I trail my fingers over the final page in the book. It's empty, but the plastic overlay is crinkled and there are traces of newsprint on the sticky surface beneath.

"You think there was something in here?" Cole says, his gaze alert.

"Maybe." I frown, trying to think. "Emily said she had some-thing to show us. . . ."

"And do you think it's whatever was here?"

"What if we've been thinking about this all wrong?" I say. I flip back a couple of pages and tap the photo of Patel with Harrison. "This proves they at least met, and he doesn't seem to be much older than her, really. What if Dr. Patel was involved in the cult, rather than just being a victim of it? What if . . ." I take a deep breath and close my eyes. "What if the cult *was* the school? What if it was Jewel and Bone, just under another name?"

I open my eyes and their expressions are wide and shocked but not disbelieving.

"No," Taylor murmurs.

"Dr. Patel got rid of this stuff," I say. "We know she was head girl at the time of the Transcendent Faithful and that she was at least aware of Harrison before that. We know he was a head boy and he came back to Morton for events—like sponsorship dinners—so he must have been part of Jewel and Bone, right? All Morton successes belonged to it—still do."

"Yeah, they do," Kat says around a mouthful of nail-bitten fingers. "I mean, that's why we're all in it, right?"

Five heads nod around the table.

"It's why I am," I say, thinking about my parents' tiny apartment. "I need to get out of the cesspool I grew up in." Cole squeezes my shoulder and I lean back, feeling safe for a second.

"Me too," Marcus agrees. "I want to be a doctor, help people. There was no chance that would happen for me at home."

"Babe, don't worry about the past." Taylor kisses him on the cheek. "You'll be the world's hottest doctor. I wanted out too. We all did."

"How exactly does this society set you on the path to success? Or is this something I should have asked before starting the hunt?" Cole asks. I keep forgetting he's the new boy.

"The school was founded—" I'm interrupted by the corner of a cushion landing in my open mouth along with a series of groans.

"History lesson alert," Kat yells, dodging the pillow as I stand up and toss it back to her.

"As I was saying," I carry on, moving around to the other sofa and sitting down opposite Cole, "Patrick Morton founded the academy in 1906. It was a pretty common thing to do back then; philanthropy was a big deal to the rich folk who had nothing better to spend their fortunes on. Anyway, he realized he could do more than educate the clever kids he was bankrolling—he could ensure lifelong success if he put them in touch with the right people—successful people. So he decided to set up an offshoot of the secret society he was a part of."

"The Society of Odd Fellows," Kat chimes in. "Winston Churchill was one, you know."

"Very good, Katerina!" I pat her knee as she wrinkles her nose at the use of her full name. "Yeah, so he started his own kind of junior offshoot. He'd found Old Josef . . . somewhere. And since the Odd Fellows used to conduct their meetings around a human skeleton, he decided he would too. Ours was supposedly an old saint and therefore covered in precious stones, so, eventually the members' nickname of Jewel and Bone stuck, rather than the pretty long-winded original: the Philanthropic Junior Chapter of the Society of Odd Fellows."

"Right." Cole sweeps the hair from his forehead and I spot a little frown line between his eyes. It's cute. "So we're actually part of this bigger society?"

"Yeah, which is why people go on to do so well. That original society has members everywhere. It's why we're practically guaranteed entry into any redbrick university we want, and as long as we put the work in, we will succeed." I tap the book. "Just like Bradley Harrison did."

"Before he lost it," Taylor mumbles.

"I am starting to wish I'd looked it up now, though." Cole laughs nervously. "Instead of just saying yes."

"You wouldn't have found anything, mate." Marcus presses a

closed fist to Cole's arm. "I'm glad you're my deputy. We weren't betting on all"—he spreads his hands wide—"this."

"None of us were," Kat says. "Plus, none of us really knew what we were getting ourselves into. We had notes pinned to our pillows last year, just like you did, then we had the official welcome ceremony followed by that stupid initiation, and—"

"Initiation?" Cole interrupts. "No one told me anything about an initiation."

"That's because they were banned," I explain, "after last summer."

"Last summer . . ." Realization washes over his face. "That girl, the one in the lake . . ."

"Morgan," Taylor whispers, glancing up at the wall from where the dead girls watch us.

"She died doing an initiation?"

We all nod, avoiding one another's eyes.

"It was her own fault," whispers Kat, her voice stripped of its usual confidence. "She made us take the boats out, wearing blindfolds. I mean, look at us—we're hardly bougie, none of us are sailors, are we? I doubt most of us even saw the sea when we were growing up, let alone learned how to maneuver a sailboat. Anyway, there was a collision on the lake. It was windy and we were all hyped up, invincible, you know? There were like, eighteen of us, all acolytes, all giddy as anything. It was carnage." Kat sighs, reliving the night. "But then the sailboats crashed and the boom on one of the boats went wild—it swung across and hit Liz and Morgan on the head, throwing them into the water and tipping the boat over."

"Morgan went in first." I take up the story, my voice quivering at the memory. "I remember the splash. Before I could pull my blindfold off, I was smashed in the head—I felt like one of those old cartoons, stars and tweeting birds flying all around my head." I raise my hand to the scar along my scalp. "Split my head open. I wasn't unconscious, though—I managed to cling to the upturned boat until someone came for me. But Morgan must have been unconscious. She was gone, floating facedown in the water, drifting farther and farther out to the middle of the lake." I choke out the last words and they taste of stagnant lake water. "That's all I remember."

"Wait, where was Patel during all this?" Cole says. "Did she know what you were doing?"

"She wasn't there, until . . . after. When we dragged Morgan from the lake to the chapel, that's when Patel appeared," Taylor explains.

"How do you know that for sure?" Cole says, his expression intent. "You were all blindfolded, weren't you?"

Taylor shrugs. "I guess we don't. God, this all makes the motto sound really sick, now."

"Motto?" Cole asks.

"Non fortuna nisi per sacrificium," she says, burying her head into Marcus's shoulder. *"Behind success lies sacrifice."* Those words ring so differently now.

I've read that somewhere—very recently. Then I realize where.

"That's exactly what Bradley Harrison's followers believed," I said, pulling the book around to my side of the table and skimming the article again. "Here." I start to read the reporter's words aloud. *" 'Harrison seemingly wanted his disciples to believe that their murderous acts would gain them a higher place in society—that their sacrifices would create success for them later. Reports on Harrison urging members*

to name him on their life insurance policies are currently unfounded.'
I bet he made them hand over everything and then planned for someone to kill them too."

"You know what we have to do now, don't you?" Kat says, her eyes twinkling. Oh, God, I already know whatever she's thinking is a bad idea.

"Find out if Patel was part of the cult," Marcus says softly.

"Find out if Patel was part of the cult," Kat confirms.

"How are we going to do that?" I ask, turning to face Kat. I'm still wrapped in her hoodie.

"We break into her office."

Everyone looks stunned, horrified, and then, slowly, we all nod.

"Fine," I agree. "But first you have to help me find out what Creepy Billy gave to Emily."

33

"I CANNOT BELIEVE YOU TALKED US INTO THIS," TAYLOR GRUM-bles from her spot behind the low wall.

"Shush, he'll hear us," I hiss. "You can moan at me later."

"Oh, I will," she says, but thankfully falls silent.

All four of us are crouched behind the little stone wall that surrounds the plot of land by the groundskeeper's house. It's dark and we are dressed all in black, per Kat's instructions. On the other side of the wall, Mr. Loomis potters about his plants—although why he's doing it in the dark is anyone's guess.

A strong hand grips my waist and I slap it playfully but let it stay. "You make a very hot cat burglar," Cole murmurs.

"Behave," I whisper, but I don't tell him to move. His arm pulls me a little closer.

"Spoilsport."

"Jesus, get a room," Kat says. Even though it was my idea, she has taken this *very* seriously, down to the black lines smeared across her cheeks. Camouflage, apparently. "We're already down a man. Where *is* Marcus, anyway?"

Taylor shrugs and pouts, looking down at her nails. "Calling home, I think. I don't know."

"Get down!" I snap. We lie in a jumble of arms and legs, our bodies pressed tight to the wall as a beam of light sweeps over us and we hear a voice.

"Mr. Loomis?"

"Who's that?" Kat hisses from somewhere near my left knee. "I can't hear properly."

"Because you've got your face in my chest," Taylor says, and Kat giggles.

"Sorry, wondered what that was."

I ease myself out of Cole's grip and poke my head over the wall, just a tiny bit. I'm grateful Kat made me wear a hat now—my blond hair would be glowing otherwise.

"Mr. Loomis," the voice repeats. "What are you doing out here so late?"

"It's Dr. Patel," I whisper, and Kat swears.

"We're dead if she catches us."

Maybe literally.

"Some plants don't like the daylight too much," he replies. From here I can see the flash of some lethal-looking shears, followed by the sound of water spilling from a metal can. "They like to be watered after dark. Funny things, plants."

"Quite," Dr. Patel replies.

"What can I do for you, doctor?" Mr. Loomis's voice seems to carry a touch of irritation now. I squint to get a good look at the plants, but honestly, I have no idea what I'm looking at. They could be marijuana or chrysanthemums, for all I know. From the corners of my eyes, I see the others untangle themselves and join me.

We all peer over the wall. If anyone looked our way, they would see four little pairs of eyes floating at the top of the wall. I suddenly remember playing Whac-A-Mole as a kid and stifle a giggle. How is it possible to be amused while my body is a twisting pit of anxiety? It must be nerves.

"Oh, nothing, I'm just out for a . . . stroll. It's a lovely evening."

"Right. Well." He points the shears toward the ground, moonlight glinting on the blades. "You should watch yourself out here in those shoes. Dangerous on the ground in the dark."

"Thank you, Mr. Loomis." Dr. Patel's voice is ice-cold. "You finished for the evening?"

There's a pause. "S'pose so," he tuts, clearly dismissed from his own turf. He gathers up his watering can. "I'll drop your herbal tea off in the morning, as usual. New blend. Couple of the kiddos have gotten some from me this week; they've had trouble sleeping as well—what with all the . . . you know."

"Yes, thank you, Mr. Loomis," Dr. Patel repeats, and we all watch him retreat to his cottage.

"Tea?" Taylor hisses. "Emily was getting *tea* from him?"

Minutes that feel like hours tick by. Sharp gravel cuts into my knees.

The headmistress doesn't move.

"What is Dr. Patel doing?" Cole whispers.

I shrug.

"Is she stealing plants or something? Poisonous ones?" Taylor asks, dropping back on the ground. Her back is pressed against the wall, and she's facing the main school building. I keep watching the plot of land, and beyond it, the gates that the delivery vans use.

That's when I see him. Walking through the gates, brazen as anything.

"Oh my GOD."

Dr. Patel's head whips in our direction, but we're already in another human puddle on the ground.

"Did you see him? Did you?" I sound delirious, even to myself.

"Who?" Taylor asks, untangling herself again.

"Look."

The four of us move as one, each head bobbing up within a millisecond of another. I almost expect Dr. Patel to be standing there holding a mallet. But she's talking in a low voice to the figure I saw.

"Oh, hell, no," Kat murmurs. "Is that . . . ?"

"Yes," I breathe. "It's her brother. Rikesh Patel is alive, well, and on the grounds of Morton Academy."

34

IN THEORY, THE PLAN SEEMS REASONABLY STRAIGHTFORWARD.
Except we've no choice but to execute it on one of the busiest days
on Morton's calendar. Plus, if we blow it, we've ruined our only
chance.

No pressure.

It's the day of Open Evening, so we've had the afternoon off
classes to prepare, to make sure Morton looks its sparkling best for
the prospective students. Most will arrive with their parents, wide-
eyed fifteen- and sixteen-year-olds clutching their ivory-colored in-
vitations, all hand-selected by Dr. Patel and the school board. They
will probably never have seen a place like this before, apart from on
television. Banners are up, uniforms have been pressed, and a sheaf
of letterheaded revision cards sit snugly in my top pocket, just in
case I forget the name of the artist who created the stained-glass
window, or what year the main staircase was added. I'm spending
the first part of the evening on meet-and-greet duties, and then I'll
be leading tours at six and seven for the prospective history candi-
dates.

I find the others in the common room, the only area that will be off-limits to visitors tonight—we'll show them the junior one, but this is where we can come between tours for a break. Even our bedrooms will be on show. Taylor finally agreed to relocate to the head girl's bedroom. It would seem odd if it didn't look lived-in, but she wasn't thrilled about the prospect of sleeping on her own.

"Are we ready for this?" I ask.

"I think so." Kat is scribbling down times and initials on a scrap of paper, her cake untouched. She *must* be taking this seriously. I scooch in next to Cole and feel a little tug of happiness when I see that he's made me a mug of Earl Grey.

"Thank you," I murmur, pecking his cheek before taking a sip, the powerful citrus aroma sliding down the back of my throat, coating it in perfume.

"You're welcome." He smiles, resting one hand on my leg without thinking. We both freeze for a second, it's still all so new, but when I melt into him, I feel his muscles relax too. I take another sip of tea and try to avoid the fact that we're planning to break into the headmistress's office. "One more time." I address the group. "What's the plan?"

"It's four thirty now," Kat starts. I glance at my watch and nod. "The first tours arrive at five. Liz, you and I are on meet-and-greet together—Cole, you're in the library, and Taylor and Marcus have to be in the head's office with Patel and Lucas for any questions about what it's like being head boy and girl, blah, blah, blah . . ."

"Wait a sec," I interrupt, "does that mean Emily will be in the office too? Cole, are you in there at any point?"

"Not that I know of." He looks worried, like he's dropped the ball. "Am I?"

"You should be for a bit, I think. Deputies normally stop in to say hello toward the end of the evening. She should be stationed somewhere, like you'll be at the library. Out of the way. Marcus can come and get you when I have to go for Emily," Taylor replies. She keeps glancing into a small, handheld mirror. The sore on her face looks red and angry now. She winces. "I can't believe I have to woo prospective students looking like this."

"You still look great, babe," Marcus tries, but it's hard to agree. Taylor's usually bright skin is dull and she's not smiling very big. You can tell she is in pain.

"OK," Kat continues, directing our attention back to the scrap of paper. "Great, Emily will hopefully be out of the way then. So, Liz, your first tour is at six, right?" I nod. "So is mine. They're meant to be half an hour, so we can meet in the foyer at six thirty. Cole, you're going to the office around half past six and declare some kind of emergency in the library that Patel will need to attend to. . . ."

"Er, some kind of emergency?" Cole's voice vibrates through my back. "What am I going to say?"

"I dunno." Kat waves a hand airily. "You'll think of something. So—you'll all run to the library or wherever. Marcus and Tay, when Patel realizes nothing has happened, you just need to make sure she stays out of the way for a few minutes—the parents should be in the foyer—use them to distract her if you need to. One of you will have to wedge something in the office door—"

"I'll do that on the way out," Marcus volunteers with a salute.

"And Liz and I will slide on in from the hallway and start digging around."

"How do we know when she'll be coming back?" I ask anxiously, running the plan over in my brain. All the millions of things that could go wrong are dancing before my eyes. "If we get caught, we'll be expelled," I whisper.

Quiet again. In spite of everything that has happened, none of us want to leave Morton.

"I'll keep watch and call you," Taylor says. "I'll step into the bathroom, call your burner, and just let it ring. You won't have to answer. When you feel yours vibrate, Liz, both of you get out of there. OK? I'll stash my phone in there now."

Kat shrugs. "Best idea I can think of. Thanks, Tay. What do you think, Lizzie?"

"Yeah, me too," I admit. I look up at Cole. "I hope this is worth it."

"It will be," Cole murmurs into my hair, and I let myself relax. He's right: it will be worth it. It will.

It has to be. I finish my tea and slide farther back into him.

"I'd like for this year to settle down already," he says quietly to me. "Think of all the time we could spend together if things were nice and boring."

"Hmm," I agree, enjoying the feel of his strong arms around me. "I miss boredom."

"All right, you two." Marcus threatens to spray us with his bottle of water. "That's enough, now. Liz, I didn't think I'd ever have to say that to you." He gives me a wicked grin.

"Sorry," Cole and I both say before grinning at each other.

"It's no good, Marcus." Taylor pulls herself away from the mirror, winking at me. "We've lost them."

"Come on, lovers, let's get ready." Kat stands up and straightens her uniform. Her usually wild hair is smoothed out and parted to one side. The ends curl around the lapels of her blazer and she is even wearing light makeup. "Ugh, I can't wait to put my leggings back on."

"You look great," I say to her before standing and turning to pull Cole out of his chair. "As do you." I readjust his collar, which really doesn't need readjusting, and let my hand linger on his broad chest for a second. It's a good thing we're not stationed together this evening. He would be *far* too distracting. The thought takes me by surprise.

"You guys ready?" I ask Taylor and Marcus. Tay has managed to arrange her hair in a clever braid across the front of her hairline, almost like a headband. She has fluffed and teased the ends of it. That, plus a deep part on the opposite side, covers the majority of her wound. "Hey, good job."

"Thanks," she mutters, touching her cheek self-consciously. "It'll have to do for now. I need to take care of this, though. I can't handle it anymore. Right," she says a little louder, "I'm going to stash my phone. We'll see you guys later, when all this is done."

Marcus grabs her outstretched hand and follows her out to the corridor. "Upstairs? Just after eight?" He calls over his shoulder.

"Yeah." I nod, taking a deep breath. "See you then."

Aside from my informal one with Cole, I've never given tours before, and my palms are damp as Kat and I walk to the main entrance. Dr. Patel is already there, dressed in a crimson pantsuit paired with glossy black heels and a slick of red lipstick. Her dark hair is shining, and she's rocking the most accurate eyeliner flicks I've ever seen, rivaling even Taylor's. Dangerous or not, the woman has got impeccable style.

She looks at us as we approach, all while giving out clipped orders and ushering people into position. I stand just inside the huge, open double doors and soak in the late-evening sun. Uncomfortable cramps clutch at my stomach again.

Kat heads outside to greet cars as I try to discreetly rub my stomach. She looks shiny and polished too, and I feel like an interloper for a moment. However cleaned-up I might look on the outside, I'll never feel that way on the inside. Another thing the shrink had me working on over the summer. *Self-worth.* Internally, I chant the little mantra she taught me, to the rhythm of my hand circling my stomach: *I deserve to belong. I deserve to belong. I. Deserve. To. Belong.*

Better.

I take a deep breath through my nose and out through my mouth, refocusing my attention just in time to see the first car approach against the backdrop of the quickly fading daylight. The nights are getting darker now, waiting for the clocks to turn back on themselves.

I plaster on a smile as the first family reaches the doors. "Welcome," I say, "to Morton Academy."

It turns out I'm actually quite good at this. I don't have to look at my notes once as I guide my first tour around—I have a head for dates and facts. I pause at the doors to each classroom and allow the prospective students to wander at their leisure, asking their questions to the prefects and staff stationed in each faculty so they can go away and settle on their two additional classes.

My cramps, though, are getting worse. I glance at the time and see we have fifteen minutes before Cole does—well, whatever he's going to do to create a distraction. I bite my lip as pain shoots through my abdomen. *Deep breaths, Liz. Ignore it.*

I spot a ladder over in the corner, near the top of the stairs. It was clearly used to hang the large welcome banner over the stained-glass window earlier today and no one has put it back. Patel will lose it if she sees it; everything was supposed to be picture-perfect and this is covered in white splashes of paint. I glance into the room and see that my charges are busy, so I make the decision to move the ladder. As I step toward it, I spot Emily coming up the stairs. *Damn.* I thought she'd be busy somewhere. She is the last thing we need.

I move the ladder carefully out of sight, away from the long draping lines that hold the banner up on brackets high above my head and race back to my station, hoping Emily doesn't decide that now is a good time to collar me.

"Excuse me, Erin, Mr. and Mrs. Walker?" The family I'm guiding around gravitate back toward me. "I'd like to show you the ground floor now," I say. "Once our tour is over, you can view the whole school at your leisure." I give them what I hope is a winning smile. "Please, follow me."

We head back to the main staircase and begin our descent when I realize Emily is still there, her eyes fixed on the banner high above us. She still doesn't look well, the circles under her eyes evident even beneath the foundation she has caked on. She's washed her hair, at least, but that eye is still twitching. She is not making a good impression.

"Er, excuse us, please, Emily," I say politely, guiding the Walker family around her. Erin, the prospective student, follows her gaze.

"Oh, look," Erin says softly, "the banner's coming down."

"So it is," I say, and laugh merrily, continuing down the steps. "Trust Emily to spot that! She is our deputy head girl. I suppose she has an eye for when things aren't perfect."

Emily looks at me coldly and calls over, "Fix it."

I blink. What? "I'm on a tour with the Walkers," I say through gritted teeth, gesturing to the family. There's no way I'm getting on that ladder. I don't do heights. "I'll mention it to Mr. Loomis once we're finished."

Emily rolls her eyes. "You are worse than useless," she mutters as the Walkers exchange glances and my smile cements itself in place. "Fine, I'll do *this* myself, too."

"Let's keep going, shall we?" I trill as the Walkers continue to watch Emily climb the stairs with the ladder.

"She's not really going to try to get up there herself, is she?" Mr. Walker, a watery man in glasses asks, rubbing the thinning patch on top of his head.

"No, of course not. She meant she was going to find the groundskeeper." At least I *think* that was what Emily meant.

We arrive at the bottom of the staircase and I try to distract them, pointing out the keystone that sits above the main doors. It's carved with the date 1838, the year the building was constructed.

"Please, after you." I gesture down the hallway and begin to escort the Walkers away from the bottom of the stairs. I don't want to go too far, as Cole will be here any second to distract Dr. Patel. I am showing them a small map of the grounds when a scream rips through the air.

It doesn't happen in slow motion, like I might have thought. No, when a body drops through the air from that height, it's fast, a sickening thunderclap, the visceral slap of flesh on stone.

I jerk my head up, even though it has already happened. The ladder hangs precariously over the uppermost part of the balcony, the banner still drooping idly at one corner, its ribbons hanging free from their mooring.

Silence rings in my ears as I turn to face the Walkers. Their faces are drained of color, their mouths open in horror as they stare at their daughter.

Erin stands frozen, dotted with red splashes from head to toe, a pool of Emily's blood spreading at her feet.

35

STUPID GIRL.

She was so predictable. Another Little Miss Perfect. I knew when I saw her leave her station that if I loosened that banner, her perfectionism would kick in. She would have to fix it herself, something she could be praised for.

Such a sycophant.

Shame I'd covered the ladder rungs in grease before she got to it. She wouldn't have had a chance—once she got up a few steps, either her hands would go or her feet would. If I was lucky, both.

It appears I am incredibly *lucky, which was a shame for Emily.*

I suppose.

36

NOW EVERYTHING KICKS INTO SLOW MOTION.

Hands guide me away from the bottom of the staircase and I follow blindly, barely registering as Dr. Patel hurries the families away from the scene. My ears feel as though they are stuffed full of cotton wool, so the cries of horror are muffled, but I do get a glimpse of Emily's blank, staring eyes. The huge pool of blood. One of the PE teachers, Mr. Coffey, kneeling on the cold stone floor, her limp wrist in his hand. His slow head shake.

"She's dead," I mutter, the hands still strong around my arms as I realize I'm being steered toward Dr. Patel's office. I turn my head, dazed. "Kat?"

"Shhh." She pushes me through the open door and shuts it gently behind us. "I know it's sick, but now's our chance. Jesus, Liz, I know we told Cole to create a distraction, but . . ."

"Cole didn't do this!" I gasp. "How could you even think that? I saw her, on the stairs, she tried to climb that ladder and . . . I think she was trying to fix the banner."

"Christ. Why would she do that?"

I shrug. "I don't know—she didn't look right."

"Christ," Kat repeats. "Right, well, we need to use it to our advantage. Get searching—look for anything that refers to the cult or to Patel's brother. There's got to be some kind of link in here."

"OK," I say, but my body is rooted to the spot. I search the room desperately, my eyes feeling like the ligaments that hold them in place are loosening, blurring everything at the edges. I raise a hand to my face to find my cheeks are wet and pull it away, expecting to see tears, but my fingers come away red, and bile rises from my aching stomach.

"Come on," Kat hisses, already flipping through a filing cabinet. "Argh, these are useless, just our files." She pulls out a brown folder. "Jeez, yours is big, Liz."

"All the medical stuff," I murmur, touching my head unconsciously. "You wouldn't believe the amount of appointments I had this summer."

"I bet." Kat smiles in sympathy and puts the folder back. I head to the far side of the room and pull open the double doors of a floor-to-ceiling closet that's built into the walls.

"Can you believe she keeps this stuff unlocked?"

"I guess she usually locks the office door. Anything?" Kat doesn't look over, just carries on digging through the filing cabinet. How can she be so calm, so focused?

"I don't think so. . . ." I scan lines of box files that blur together in uniformly neat, color-coded rows. I read the labels. WHISTLE-BLOWING POLICY, STAFF SOCIAL MEDIA REGULATIONS, CURRICULUM STANDARDS. A couple of spare jackets and a formal dress hang underneath and a large umbrella and a pair of flats sits at the bottom. "Nothing," I say as I part the jackets to peer into the back. A sudden, searing cramp has me doubled over and I gasp in pain.

"Are you OK? Don't think about what just happened, just . . . lock it away. Deal with it later. Liz?"

"Yeah." I clench my jaw against the pain as my muscles spasm. Emily's crumpled body lying on the ground flashes into my mind. My throat feels full of needles.

"Is it your stomach again?" Kat crosses the room to join me.

"Yeah." I take a deep breath, forcing the image of Emily from my mind. The pain recedes. "Ouch."

"You think it's something you've eaten? Or . . . drank?"

My mind flashes back to Cole handing me a mug of Earl Grey.

"No. Maybe. I just need to . . . ignore it," I pant. I drag out a large, worn box from the closet, more in an effort to distract myself than anything. "This looks promising."

It's pretty, made from smooth, polished wood and inlaid with patterns that look like mother-of-pearl. It's clean too, not dusty, as I expected. Like it's been opened recently. "How long have we been in here?" I ask as I ease the lid off.

"Not even five minutes, but we need to be quick."

"OK." We peer at the contents. Photos, mainly. Some folded letters on lined paper with ragged edges, as if they were torn from a workbook. They have clearly been read and refolded many times, some in the original envelopes, complete with yellowed glue and ancient stamps. "Is it a memory box?"

"I guess so." Kat pulls out a Polaroid photograph. The white border has MINAHIL'S WEDDING, GOA, 1996 written on it in faded marker pen and the picture shows a family of four dressed in the most beautiful Indian wedding outfits. Two proud parents stand behind a boy and a girl, all four of them beaming. One of the kids is obviously

Dr. Patel. The year would make her twelve or thirteen, I suppose, but she was already prettier than most girls her age. Smarter too, if she ended up being head girl here.

I study the picture carefully. Her brother looks slightly older, maybe fourteen or so, and he has a self-assured, almost cocky aura around him.

"It really was him last night," says Kat. "I didn't quite believe it."

"It's kind of sad, isn't it? They all looked so happy," I whisper, thinking back to the newspaper articles as Kat replaces the photograph. I thumb through the rest of the contents, finding more family photos and even some of Dr. Patel and other kids in Morton uniforms, all looking nineties-fabulous in their brown lip liner and skinny eyebrows. The boys have their hair parted in curtains. "Wait, what's this?"

At the very bottom of the box is another small, thick envelope addressed to Nikhita Patel. But the postmark is recent. Like, this year recent. I pull out the thickly wadded paper, pages and pages of scribbled handwriting, and my eyes widen. It's from her brother. "Oh my God. Kat. We were right." I thrust the letter toward her and she scans it.

"Harrison's out?"

"Looks like it." I glance through the other pages. One shows a picture of a small terra-cotta angel. It stares back at me, its face blank, barely sculpted. It's the Bernini I showed Cole. *My* Bernini.

"Is that the angel from the library?" Kat asks, plucking the page from my hand. "Weird."

"Is it?" My mind is whirring, trying to put the pieces together. "So, we have a letter from Patel's brother saying that Harrison is out of prison. And it sounds like her brother and Harrison stayed in touch all these years."

"Which is creepy, considering what they were both in jail for."

"Very," I agree. "But now *he's* out and her *brother* suddenly shows up. Even though he did time for *her* attempted murder? Dr. Patel clearly has no problem meeting with Rikesh. What if she's trying to help him? Help both of them?"

"You think Patel is actually part of the cult? And the deaths here are all sacrifices, like before?"

"It's a theory." I tap the picture of the Bernini. "But what does this have to do with it all?"

"I don't kn—" Kat is interrupted by the sound of the door handle. We stare at each other with wide eyes, then jam the lid back on the box and shove it in the cupboard, closing it just as the door swings open. I shove the picture of the Bernini into my waistband.

Kat drags me into a hug and strokes my hair. "Follow my lead?" she whispers. Then, more loudly, "Shush, Lizzie, it's OK, Dr. Patel will be here soon and everything will be fine."

A throat clears. "What are you doing in here, girls?"

"Oh, Dr. Patel!" Kat releases me as I make a show of wiping my now-dry face. "Dr. Patel, we were so scared!" The headmistress has kept her composure, but her pale face and shaking hands give her away. "We didn't know where to go after . . . after Emily . . ."

"You were there?" she asks softly. "When she fell?"

We nod and I look down at the floor, unable to meet her eyes. I see dull splatters on my polished shoes and bile rises in my throat when I realize what it is.

"Oh God," I whisper. "I need to shower." Patel's and Kat's eyes both travel down to my shoes and the reddish-brown splashes across the front of my white socks. My throat heaves and I clap a hand over my mouth.

"You should see the nurse," Patel says kindly. Well, kindly for her, anyway. I shake my head. "Fine, then. Off to bed, both of you. The school grounds are on lockdown until tomorrow at the very earliest—that means you do not leave your rooms except to use the facilities or come to assembly tomorrow morning. I have sent the head boy and girl to communicate this to the rest of the students. Do you understand?"

We nod mutely. Lockdown. I scramble to think what this means. How this feeds into Patel's plan, if she really is behind all this.

"Er, Dr. Patel?" Kat says. "There's something we think you should know." I stare at her, wondering what the hell she's playing at.

"Go on," says Dr. Patel.

"We saw a stranger on the grounds at Open Evening. But he wasn't with anyone. About this tall"—she holds up a hand—"and of Indian descent, I think."

"Thank you for letting me know, Ms. Paphitis." Is it just me or is Dr. Patel's pristine makeup now shadowed with gray? "We have had a lot of journalists snooping around recently. I will alert the faculty."

"Oh. Thank you." Kat leads the way to the door, and I follow in a daze as Dr. Patel walks around to sit at her desk. As I start to move, a wadded-up piece of paper flutters to the floor.

The Bernini.

I snatch it back up and shove it into my pocket, but not before I see Dr. Patel's face, her eyes burning a hole into my pocket.

"She's definitely rattled." Kat shuts the door behind her and leans on it briefly. We're both shaking. "Do you think she saw the picture, when you dropped it?"

"I don't know." We go to a storeroom to use the back staircase— I don't think we'll use the main one again for a while. "I hope not."

"Same," she mutters. She pulls the door open and gestures for me to lead the way. "Well, Lizzie," she jokes, "I didn't think I'd ever be in here with you."

"Hilarious," I say forlornly, thinking of Cole. "Do you think the others are still waiting for us?"

"I dunno." She glides past me, climbing the steps two at a time as I pant behind her. "Do you wanna check?"

"Yeah, I guess." I think of the mess on my shoes. "I really do need a shower, though."

"Ditto." She pushes the door open at the top and we emerge into the tiny cleaning closet. "Come on, let's go and find them first, then showers."

We walk the long way around the first floor in silence, past darkened classrooms, avoiding the main staircase again. There are no sirens, but red and blue lights wash over the walls of each teaching space we pass. The police are definitely here. There's a slight chatter of people, those guarding the scene and the final few outsiders being questioned. The Walkers are probably still here. Otherwise, the building is silent. Holding its breath. Dr. Patel wasn't joking when she said the place was locked down. She must have immediately kicked out every family that wasn't in the foyer. God knows how she's going to keep this one quiet, with members of the public here when it happened.

When we finally reach our corridor, all the doors are open and girls are wandering in and out of each other's rooms, some red-faced and bawling, others looking drained of color. One of the girls from Kat's English class passes us and Kat stops her.

"Hey, Beck, have you seen Taylor?"

"No, sorry." Her eyes widen as she looks at me, the specks of blood on my face and neck. "Oh my God, you were there, weren't you? Are you OK?"

"Thanks, Beck." Kat dismisses her and we carry on. Our door is closed and we peek in, hoping to see Taylor, but the room is empty.

"Upstairs?" I say.

"Yeah, she must be." We head to the spiral staircase and climb up, both unconsciously tiptoeing, as though we don't want to disturb anyone.

"Nobody here," Kat announces as she reaches the top. The lounge is completely empty. "Lockdown must be pretty serious. Let's try her room."

The door is shut. I knock but there's no answer, so I try the handle and it opens easily. The bedroom is empty and the bathroom door is shut. "Tay?" I call.

"Don't come in!" Taylor's voice sounds panicked through the wooden door. "I'm fine!"

Kat and I look at each other. "She doesn't sound fine," I say. Kat nods in agreement.

"Taylor, honey?" Kat inches toward the door and presses herself to it. "Is everything OK?"

"Yes!" Taylor's answer verges on a squeal and Kat looks at me wide-eyed, shocked by the hysterical edge to her voice. I shake my head. She is definitely not OK.

"Taylor, babe, I'm coming in. I just want to check that you're safe." Kat wraps one hand around the doorknob, ready to turn it.

"No, no, don't come in." Taylor's voice is too fast, breathless. "It's OK, I'm fine, honestly. I'm fine, I'm fine, I'm fine. . . ."

"You don't sound fine," I say loudly. No response.

"Tay, don't make me open the lock from out here. It's only one of those stupid turn locks, not like the dorm doors. I could open it with a coin."

"I don't want anyone to see me," Taylor wails from the bathroom. I take a deep breath.

"Taylor," I try, "did something happen to you? You can tell us, we can help."

There's a pause, then a click from the other side of the door as Taylor turns the lock. Progress. I nod at Kat and she grabs the handle with a shaking hand and pushes open the door.

Taylor is standing there in a white towel, facing away from us. Her red hair is wet, almost black, hanging down her back in thick ropes.

"Taylor?" I try again.

She starts to shuffle around slowly, her breath coming in ragged little gasps, and I hold my breath. Her head is bowed, as though she's praying, and strings of hair cover her face. She starts to raise her head slowly, making tortured little animal noises as she does. "I tried to fix it," she sobs. "I just tried to fix it." She lifts her head up and pushes the hair behind her ears.

Kat gasps. "Oh my God!" she says, and Taylor starts to wail.

"I just, it was so sore, the pressure was too much, so I started to squeeze, and all this green pus started to come out and then . . . then this . . ." She breaks into sobs again as I study the gaping wound on her face. It's blackened at the edges, like the flesh is rotting, eating her face from the inside out. "I don't know what to do!" she cries, taking deep breaths between each word. Kat races toward her to give her a hug when the smell hits me. The wound has been festering, all right, and the air is thick with the smell of sickness, infection. Then I see a flash of white inside the gash.

I can't help but think it's her bone.

37

LOOKS LIKE I'M GOING TO HAVE TO DO SOMETHING ABOUT *that nosy bitch. She keeps opening her big mouth, getting herself involved.*

If I'm not careful, she's going to uncover exactly what I'm planning to do.

I keep thinking about the memory box, the one with all those letters and photographs in it. The family photo is the most condemning thing, I think, along with the letter from Rikesh—I'll have to think about what to do with those. But they need to stay in the right hands. Mine, preferably.

I have time now, though. Lockdown will probably continue until the end of the weekend, at least. The police on duty are paid off and everyone else is confined to their quarters, staff included. That gives me three days to do what I need to do.

I know I can do it.

It's time to finally get what I deserve.

38

"I THINK YOU SHOULD STAY IN BED," I TELL TAYLOR BEFORE KAT
and I leave for morning assembly. We moved her back to our dorm
room last night so we could keep an eye on her. I stroke her hair as I
perch on the edge of her old bed, trying to soothe her back to sleep.
She let us clean and dress her cheek last night, and it looks slightly
better now, but the ends are still puckered beneath the Steri-Strips
that are holding her face together, the skin swollen and purple in the
morning light.

"No." She tries to push herself up but retches as soon as she's in
a sitting position. "I'm head girl, I have to be at assembly. Especially
after yesterday. Please?"

"No." I help her shaking body get back down onto the pillows, then study her face. "Are you sure you don't want to see the
nurse, Tay?"

"No, no, it's fine. She'll just want to put me on fluids, and I don't
even want to think about needles. I'll drink lots of water, I promise.
Do you have any more painkillers, though?"

"Here." Kat pulls a blister packet with two pills in it from her bedside drawer. "It's an anti-inflammatory—it should take the swelling

down." We watch as Taylor chokes them down with a glass of water before retching again.

"Fine," she says sleepily. "I'll stay in bed. But you tell me everything when you get back."

"Of course," I say as Kat continues to search her drawer. "What are you looking for?"

"My Tiger Balm, my neck is killing me. Have you seen it?"

"No, but here." I dig into my pockets for one I found in the bathroom the other day. "I found this one."

"Thank you." She grabs the little tub and twists the golden lid off, rubbing the greasy liquid into the nape of her neck.

"Hmmmm," Taylor says sleepily, her words barely strung together. "I love that smell, smells like Marcus. I could just eat it."

"Yeah, you don't wanna do that," Kat laughs. "It's totally toxic. I think like a spoonful can kill you."

"No way," Taylor says through a yawn, half engulfed in sleep. "Hmmm." Kat and I watch as Taylor's eyes finally flicker to a close and she settles down.

"Come on," I whisper to Kat as I shrug on my blazer. "Let's leave her to it. Should we lock the door?"

Kat thinks for a minute. "Yeah," she decides. "I'll slide my key under so she can relock it if she needs to leave for some reason. It's hard to trust anyone at the moment, isn't it?"

She turns the key with a click, her words ringing in the air.

The atmosphere in assembly is fraught with emotion. Assemblies usually take place on Mondays, Wednesdays, and Fridays, so this shouldn't be any different, being a Friday morning, but of course it is. The ghosts of Morgan, Jameela, Frank, and now Emily stalk the edges of the hall as students whisper to one another, conspiracy theories trickling down their neat lines. Silence quickly descends as Dr. Patel enters the hall, her spiked heels practically sparking off the stone floor, followed by the other senior staff. They climb the steps to the stage in a solemn procession and stand in a line behind the headmistress.

"Good morning." Dr. Patel speaks into the microphone, her voice calm, measured. "I will not keep you here for long—I'll get straight to the point of today's assembly. There was a most unfortunate accident last night at Open Evening. It is my sad duty to tell you that Emily Sinclair, our deputy head girl, passed away immediately following the incident." The hall instantly fills with muted chatter, especially from the juniors, who hadn't taken part in the event last night. Dr. Patel raises one hand and the whispers cease. "You will notice a police presence around the building. All the proper procedures have been put in place, which means that as of last night, Morton Academy is in emergency lockdown. No one leaves the grounds, and no one enters them, either."

"Liar," Kat hisses.

"I trust that you will follow the rules during this period. Classes have been suspended for today and the main staircase is off-limits. You may use the back staircases or the elevator normally reserved for students with disabilities. Once you return upstairs, you will be expected to stay on the second and third floors, in your dorms or the appropriate lounges. Do you understand?"

A chorus of shocked agreement ripples around the hall.

"Excuse me, Dr. Patel?" My skin shrinks as Kat raises her hand—and voice—above the crowd.

The crowd falls silent.

"Yes?" Dr. Patel raises her perfectly groomed eyebrows while her lips tighten.

"Why exactly are we in lockdown? If Emily's death was an accident."

Dr. Patel sighs into the microphone. "Because, Ms. Paphitis, we do not believe it *was* an accident. We believe Emily was pushed."

The hall empties out in shocked silence and I scan the crowd for Marcus and Cole. "There," I say, grabbing Kat's hand and bumping through the crowd to intercept them at the door.

"Hey," I call as quietly as I can. Cole's head whips around to the sound of my voice and I feel an ill-timed flush of pleasure. He grabs Marcus's arm and points out to the hallway. We follow them, detaching from the rest of the crowd, which is heading to the back staircase. Cole drags me into a hug immediately and we allow the crowd to disperse around us.

"Thank God you're not hurt," he breathes into my hair. I squeeze him as tight as I can.

"Hey." Marcus narrows his eyes as we release each other. "Where's Taylor?"

"She's in bed." I wince, thinking about her face last night. "In our room. She didn't text you this morning?"

"No. She didn't reply last night, either. I just thought she was in shock or something. Is she OK?"

Kat and I glance at each other, clearly thinking the same thing—

why didn't he just go and see her? We might be in separate dorms, but that hadn't bothered him the other night, when he flouted the rules by coming up to the girls' lounge.

"No," Kat says slowly. "I'm not sure if she is." She explains the scene we walked in on in Taylor's bathroom last night. "We left her in bed to rest, but honestly? I think she needs to see the nurse."

"I'm going up to see her." Marcus's jaw is tight. "It could be sepsis. God, why didn't I notice? Was she sick?"

"No," I say, "but she did feel sick earlier. She was retching this morning, even after water."

"And does the wound smell?"

"Yes," I admit, nervous now. "It did last night. But, Marcus, she's a clever girl, she knows about this stuff, doesn't she? If she was worried—"

"You don't understand." He cuts me off. "Taylor is exhausted. She doesn't want anyone to know, but she's on the verge of failing her classes. She's been studying at all hours and, when I followed her out of the library the other day, she just broke down. There's no way she'd take time off to go to the nurse. She's anxious and her immune system will be useless because of it. And I haven't helped. . . ."

He shakes his head, leaving the sentence hanging, and starts toward the storeroom.

We follow him up, through the first-floor corridors and up to the senior girls' dorm rooms, silent and breathless. What if Taylor really is that sick? We arrive in our hallway and I am suddenly out of breath. I stop a minute and lean against the wall. Cole pauses with me.

"You OK?" He holds a hand out and I grab it gratefully and he takes my weight as I straighten up.

"Yeah, I think so."

"Is it true—were you there? When Emily . . ." He focuses his sad brown eyes on me and I remember what a horrible start he's had here.

I nod and look toward our room. I don't know if I'm OK or not.

Kat and Marcus approach our door farther down the corridor. We hover behind them.

"Liz, do you have your key?" asks Kat.

"What? No, I thought you did!"

"No, I slid mine back under, remember? Oh, God, we've locked her in!" Kat wrenches the handle, but the door is firmly locked. Her voice begins to rise as panic grips her. "Taylor?" she shouts, pressing her face up to the door. "Taylor!" she tries again, banging. She turns to me with desperate eyes. "Liz, are you sure you don't have your key?"

"I'm sure," I whisper so quietly, I'm not sure she hears me. I watch as she hammers on the door, unable to do anything. It's like I'm frozen to the spot.

"Move," Marcus growls. Kat takes one look at his face and does as he says. "These doors are useless; one of the seniors last year managed to kick one in." He eyes the wood, searching for weak points.

"It's a fire door," I croak, finding my voice. "Some of them are hollow. You might be able to break through it."

We move back in unison, giving Marcus space as he bounces up and down on the balls of his feet. "Right." He drops his center of gravity and launches himself at the door, using his shoulder, aiming for the center. He pulls away and we see a faint depression in the middle.

"Yes, it's hollow. Keep going," Kat urges. "You can do this."

Marcus steps back and runs a hand over his hair before launching himself again. This time there's an audible crack and it seems to spur him on. He throws himself at it over and over again, the wood veneer splintering beneath his shoulders. When there's a fist-sized hole in the middle, he fires instructions at Kat and the two of them start kicking out bits of wood until there's a space large enough for Marcus to squeeze through. I hang back, shoving my hands into my blazer pockets, unsure of what to do. My hand closes around something cool and the blood drains from my face. *My key.*

Kat ducks to look through the door and I gently withdraw my hand.

"Oh, God, oh Taylor, no!" Kat throws herself through the opening and fumbles around on the floor, retrieving the key and unlocking what's left of the door for us. I trail slowly behind Cole.

"Taylor?" I whisper. She's lying in the bed where we left her, her eyes shut and her mouth crusted with vomit. The room smells putrid, like something has . . .

"No, no . . ." Marcus's keening cry needles into my ears. "Taylor, Tay, baby, come on. Please, I'm sorry, I'm sorry." He goes to pull her up into his arms, but Cole stops him.

"Marcus, stop. Marcus!" He turns his wild eyes on Cole. "Come on, remember what we've got to do. Recovery position, all that stuff."

"I can't." His voice catches. "I don't remember. . . ."

"Well, I do." He holds a hand over Taylor's mouth and nose. "Shit, she's not breathing. Kat, go and call for the nurse—you can do that on the phone in the hallway, right?"

"Yes, right." Kat leaves the room seemingly on autopilot and I shrink back into the wall, letting Cole take control of the situation.

"Marcus, trust me. Give me some space. Liz, can you get some water?" I nod as I grab a half-drank bottle from the side table, not taking my eyes off him as he gently lowers Taylor from the bed to the floor. Her arms flop uselessly and her skin is gray against her shock of red hair. While Marcus paces behind him, he goes through the first aid motions, bending her knee and rolling her onto her side. He tilts her head back to open her windpipe and waits a second for her to start breathing again.

Nothing. Cole looks at me with huge eyes, his assurance fading. Marcus continues to pace behind him, his face in his hands.

"Clear her throat," I say, remembering, though I can barely hear myself. "Clear her throat," I repeat.

"Yes." Cole nods and opens Taylor's mouth, checking for any foreign objects. I squeeze my eyes shut as he forces his fingers into her throat.

Still, nothing.

"The nurse is on her way." I peel open my eyes at Kat's voice just as Cole is about to roll Taylor onto her back, psyching himself up for CPR. "Oh, God. Oh, Taylor," Kat groans, sinking to the floor, clutching the doorframe so hard, her knuckles are white. We can do nothing but watch in mute horror as Cole pinches her nose between his thumb and forefinger and expels two deep breaths into her, her chest rising and falling. He leans back on his heels and starts chest compressions that I count silently along with him.

The only sound in the room now is the faint cracking of Taylor's ribs and Marcus's sobs.

"Come on, Taylor," Cole growls before leaning down and pumping two more breaths into her. He starts compressions again. One-two-three-four—

Taylor's eyes pop open.

"Cole!" I scream and he stops, his eyes wide with shock. Taylor starts to gasp for breath, her windpipe rattling as he quickly turns her back onto her side so she can cough up the vomit that was clogging her lungs.

"Taylor?" Marcus drops to his knees behind Cole, tears streaming openly down his face. "Oh, Taylor, thank you, thank you. . . ."

Cole moves out of the way to let Marcus sit by her but stays close, rubbing her back as she coughs up the last of it. I hand him the water and he pours some into her mouth, but it filters straight out again as Taylor's eyes roll back in her head.

"No!" Marcus screams as Cole grabs her wrist.

"It's OK, it's OK. Her pulse is strong—she's just unconscious."

"Jesus, we have to get her help *right now.*" Marcus scoops her up from the floor as though she's nothing but a rag doll. She looks dead, the way she is hanging there, limp in his arms. One of her pajama legs is pushed up to her knee and I have a crazy need to push it down so she's not embarrassed when people see her.

"The nurse is on her way," Kat tries again, louder this time, but Marcus steps over her and starts to carry his girlfriend down the hallway, her head bobbing with each huge stride, while the rest of us stand uselessly in the shattered doorway.

39

I POUR A SPLASH OF MILK INTO THE DARK CUP OF TEA ON THE counter, watching it swirl as I add a heaping spoon of sugar and stir. I balance it on a saucer, my hands still shaking, and head back to where I left Cole, on the sofa closest to Taylor's room in the senior lounge. As usual, it's deserted—everyone else must still be in the corridor. We left practically all the senior girls gawking at the hole in our bedroom door after Marcus left with Taylor, Kat sprinting behind them.

"Here." I place the cup down in front of Cole. His color is starting to come back, but his hands are still shaking and his eyes are unfocused. "Here," I say, pointing to the cup. "You're in shock. You need some sugar in your system. A police officer once taught me that."

He nods, puppetlike.

I sit down, careful not to crowd him, but I reach over to take his hand. "What you did back there was amazing—you know that, right?"

"I thought . . . I thought she was . . ."

"I know," I soothe, moving closer and pushing a lock of hair behind his ear. "I know. We all did. But she's not, because of you." He grips my hand for a second and releases it, reaching for the cup instead. He takes a gulp, even though it must be scalding, and his eyes clear a little.

"This is good, thanks." We sit in silence as he drains the tiny cup.

"Do you want another? I'd have brought it in your mug, but it's hidden downstairs."

"Behind the fireplace in the common room. I know." He smiles. "No, I'm fine. I could sleep for a week, though."

"Do it, then. Here." I edge to the corner of the sofa and balance a threadbare cushion on my lap. "Lie down."

"You sure? Do you think they're OK?" he says weakly.

"Yes. Kat texted me and said she'd come back as soon as she had news. It's been less than half an hour. You need to relax. That was a massive thing you just did." He nods and leans back, gently placing his head in my lap, his long legs stretched out along the sofa. We're both still in our uniforms, which seems absurd, and he tugs his tie loose, undoes his top button. He closes his eyes as I fight the impulse to stroke his perfect face or trail my fingers along the dip of his throat.

"Thanks for looking after me," he whispers, raising my hand to his lips and kissing the back of it.

"Of course," I whisper back, watching as his breath starts to settle, his chest rising and falling. I envy his ability to fall asleep like that; I haven't been able to do it since my accident. I give in to my urges and trace one finger across the arches of his upper lip. It's a perfect cupid's bow, mesmerizing. His nose twitches and I pull my hand away, but he grabs it back sleepily and places it on his cheek.

"Keep going," he mutters.

I gently run my fingers across his cheek before moving my hands up to his hair, combing my fingers through, using my nails to trace little circles as his body relaxes even more deeply into mine. I don't know how long I watch him sleep, but the next thing I know, a hand is gently shaking my shoulder.

"Hey." Kat edges around the sofa and perches on an armchair. "How is he?"

I rub my blurry eyes and glance down at Cole, who is still breathing deeply. "He's tired. I must have nodded off too. So, how is she?"

"Should we wake him up?"

I really don't want to, he looks so peaceful, but she obviously wants to tell us something together. "Yeah, I guess so. Cole?" I brush the hair from his forehead and give his shoulder a little shake. "Hey, Cole, Kat's here. Wake up." He starts to blink and lets out a huge yawn. Kat stifles one too as she watches him.

"Kat?" he repeats, his voice thick with sleep. "Kat!" He sits bolt upright so fast, it makes me jump. "Sorry, sorry, Liz." He pats my leg. "Kat—how is Taylor?" He grabs hold of my hand and we both stare at Kat expectantly.

"She's OK." Cole lets out a sigh of relief that's half sob and half laugh and I squeeze his hand. "Well, she's not, really, but she's alive. Thanks to you."

"Oh, thank God." He pulls away from me and presses his face into his hands. He stays that way for a second.

"Did they say what was wrong with her?" I ask.

"They think it is sepsis, like Marcus said." Kat shakes her head. "I can't believe I didn't realize, I mean, she was so sick."

"It's not your fault," I try, but my voice is quiet. "None of us did anything to help her, did we? We've all been too busy with . . . everything." The deaths of our classmates hang like specters in the air between us. "Poor Taylor."

"How serious is it?" Cole asks.

"Pretty bad. She hadn't regained consciousness by the time the ambulance arrived, so—"

"Ambulance?" I butt in.

"Yeah. Nurse Templeton and Marcus went with her. I think someone called her parents, but they live so far away. . . . I didn't realize how bad sepsis could be—they had to get her to a hospital before her organs started to shut down."

"Jesus," I whisper. "When will we know more?"

"I dunno. I asked Marcus to text me. Get this, though—Patel tried to stop them."

"What do you mean?"

"She tried to stop Marcus and the nurse from calling an ambulance. Said we could deal with it here, that we were on lockdown, no one in, no one out, blah blah blah."

"Seriously?" I ask. "She said that? What the hell is she doing?"

"I don't know, but whatever it is, she doesn't want anyone coming onto the grounds right now."

"To the point where another student could die?" Cole asks, his face incredulous.

Kat leans forward. "What if this lockdown, Emily's death—what if it's all a cover for something else, something bigger?"

"Like what, though?" I ask.

"I dunno," Kat admits. "Cult stuff? What if they bring in Bradley Harrison and just *kill* us all?"

"Jesus, Kat, are you serious?" Cole stretches and shoots me a look.

"Yes," she answers, then shrugs. "No. Oh, I don't know. I don't have a clue what the hell is going on."

Cole gets to his feet. "In that case, I'm making more tea. You guys want some?" We both nod as he glances sleepily around the room. "Where am I going?"

"Over there." I point to the patio doors. "There's a little kitchen around that corner."

"Thanks." We watch as he ambles off and almost immediately, Kat's smile fades and she grabs my wrist.

"I need to talk to you, now," she hisses, low, so Cole can't hear. My eyes drop to her iron grip.

"Kat, you're hurting me."

She loosens her hand. "Sorry. I'm just—I'm scared. I think I've figured something out and I don't want to say it, but . . ."

"Tell me." I glance toward the kitchen to make sure Cole is still there and hear the reassuring clank of cups being pulled from cupboards and the kettle starting its low hum.

"I've been thinking about all the people who have been . . . hurt. I think that's where the connection is. I overheard Templeton talking about Emily with one of the cops while we were waiting for the ambulance. Emily's hands and the soles of her shoes were coated in something that smelled of menthol. Like Vicks. Or it could have been Tiger Balm, I guess—they smell the same."

"What?"

"I know. If it was on her hands and feet, that must mean it was on the rungs of the ladder. Someone put it there on purpose, so the next person to use it would fall. You know, like they greased it. Premeditated."

"But how would they know it would be Emily using it next? Or that *anyone* else would touch it?"

"I dunno," she admits. "But I'm not finished. When I heard that,

I went back to our room and checked the ingredients on the pot of Tiger Balm I have. Do you know what the main one is?"

"No, but it's poisonous, right?"

"Right. Camphor. But nowadays most camphor is synthetic. Like the one used in Tiger Balm. Do you know what the scientific name for synthetic camphor is?"

"No. Kat—where are you going with this?"

"It's trimethylbicyclo heptan." She stares at my blank face. "Remember? The chemical we found in Jameela's inhaler when we did the gas chromatography! The chemical that shouldn't have been there."

"What? How do you know what synthetic camphor is called?"

"The pharmaceutical name is on the label. It was right under our noses the whole time, literally. Someone must have filled the mouthpiece of the inhaler with it and when Jameela started having an asthma attack, she must have sucked it right in. She practically ate the stuff. Her lungs were already under pressure—she didn't really have a chance."

"So it *was* murder," I whisper. "But what about Taylor? The scratch on her face was because of a loose nail in her blusher brush. Do you think someone put it there?"

"Maybe, I dunno." Kat shrugs as I glance over to see what's taking Cole so long. I see him leaning on the kitchen counter, staring out the window, the kettle sending up puffs of steam behind him. "I haven't had time to think about that yet. But look at the others." She starts ticking off dead girls on her fingers. "Morgan, drowned. Officially an accident. But she was an excellent swimmer, she nailed the records last year—she even set a new one for the hundred meters.

We didn't think Patel was there, but honestly, most of us don't remember, do we? Next there was Jameela. Another tragic accident. Only, not. And what did Jameela and Morgan have in common?"

"They were best friends," I say, "and so was Emily. They were all so tight, like they'd known each other forever."

Kat shakes her head. "No—I mean, yeah, you're right, but think about what *else* they were. Head girl, Lizzie. They were all head girl, or were next in line to be."

I know this, but I try to follow. "And you're saying Frank fits this pattern because he was deputy head boy?"

Kat frowns. "I don't think that's why Frank was killed. In fact, I'm not convinced his murder was planned, not like the others, anyway."

"So . . ." She's on a roll and doesn't let me finish.

"They all had a huge future ahead of them, thanks to Jewel and Bone. A future that Patel didn't get to have, because of her brother. He ruined things by snitching on Harrison. But now Harrison is out of prison. Finally, they can enact the sacrifice. Patel can achieve the success she always dreamed of—if she sacrifices everyone in line to be head girl this year. . . ."

"Right," I agree, incredulous. "And Emily was deputy, so she'd have been next. . . ."

"After Tay, who was the new head girl . . ."

"Now there's hardly anyone left in the running, is there? Not really—I mean, there's Ayesha, and Beck and Caroline, but they came after us in the hunt, so . . . ," I say, reality dawning on me.

Kat nods. "No one else but us, and we're the ones sticking our noses in." She stares directly into my eyes. "What did that message on the mirror say? When you were in the shower room."

" *'Dead girls can't win.'* " I say it slowly, the words dripping from my mouth like poison. I start to shake. "What do we do now?" I ask.

"We need to stick together," says Kat firmly. "We're the new head and deputy, or will be, which means we're next on the list. We don't leave each other alone for a second. And we get all the evidence we can to prove Patel was involved. Deal?"

"Deal," I reply, realizing we have no other choice.

40

IT'S FINALLY TIME.

All of Morton is on lockdown and no one is coming in or out for the foreseeable future. I made sure of that.

There are just a few things to do first. A few idiots who think it's a good idea to get in my way. And then I'll have it. Everything I want, everything I deserve. Everything I have dreamed about for so long.

Tonight, this ends.

41

"THIS WASN'T WHAT I HAD IN MIND WHEN YOU SAID WE should stick together."

It's Saturday morning, we're still in lockdown mode, the weather is glorious, and the gym is empty. Plus, it smells: a combination of old sweat and lemon cleaning spray.

"Listen, it'll be good for you, I promise. If nothing, it'll take your mind off Tay until we hear something." Kat pulls on a pair of gray weight-lifting gloves, and despite the situation, I still look at her co-ordinated outfit with a touch of envy. Everything matches, from her cropped mesh hoodie to her brilliantly clean sneakers. "Come on, you can spot me first. I'll show you what to do. I'll take it easy on you, promise."

"Yeah, right." I follow her over to the weights, a section of the gym I wouldn't dream of going to on my own. I normally come in for a half-hearted jog on the treadmill while Taylor does sprints, or maybe go on the bike so I can sit down. The weights section intimidates me.

Taylor. I wonder if she'll be OK.

"Let's try a simple bench press first." Kat talks me through how to push the weights onto the bar and secure them with clips at each end, before sliding herself beneath the barbell, one leg hugging either side of the bench, feet on the floor. "Right, so you just stand over me and if I need it, you help me lift the barbell back onto the rack."

"I guess so." I stand behind her head, looking at her upside-down face beneath me. "Er, how much weight is on here?"

"Sixty-five pounds." She smiles. "Starting light."

"Light? That's almost half of me!"

"I can do a solid one forty-five, but I have to warm up to it. Ready?" I nod, even though I know there's no way that I can lift sixty-five pounds if she's in trouble.

Kat clasps her hands wide apart on the bar, wriggling her gloved fingers around to find her grip. She takes a deep breath and pushes her arms up, lifting the bar into the air. I step back and watch as she brings the barbell down to her chest and pushes back up, locking her elbows at the top.

"Kat, that's insane!"

She grins at me through gritted teeth. "Count," she puffs.

"Oh, right. Er, one." She keeps going like a machine until we reach ten and her arms wobble. I grab the bar and help guide it back onto the rack, but I feel utterly useless.

"Right." Kat stands up and takes a long gulp of water. "Your turn."

"There's no way I can do even one of those," I protest.

"Oh, don't worry—here." She starts to undo the clips and slides the plates off one side, so I copy her, removing the other. "We'll do it with no plates on. The bar weighs forty-five pounds on its own, so let's try that." She smiles at me expectantly, and I realize it's my turn to lie on the bench.

"I don't think I can," I say, my voice small.

"You won't know unless you try," she says encouragingly as she removes the plates from the bar. "If you can't, I'll grab a lighter bar. Just give it a go. For me?" She turns her big, brown puppy-dog eyes on me.

"Fine, but you need to save me if anything goes wrong, deal?"

Kat laughs. "Deal."

I slip beneath the bar like I saw Kat do a few minutes ago and stare up at her.

"Ready?"

"No."

"You are. Here." She pats the bar. "Hands here, evenly spaced out but not too wide. You want to take a deep breath when you lower the bar and force all your air out when you lift it back up. Ready now?"

"I guess so." The metal is cool against my sweaty palms, the cross-hatch pattern on the bar already etching into my skin. I wonder if that's why Kat wears gloves to do this. I hold on tight and push it up, Kat's hands guiding me. I feel a tightness around my ribs and back, every ligament and tendon extended. God, it's heavy.

"I'm going to let go now, but I've got you," Kat says. I don't even try to respond. The tops of my arms start to burn and a band of muscle I was not even aware I had strains across my chest as I lower the bar. "Good, halfway there. Now—big breath out and push up, press your back into the bench if you need to, that's it! Push your feet into the floor. . . ."

I follow her instructions as best I can, but it's like there's an invisible giant sitting on me. I squeeze my eyes shut and push with all my strength. It's so heavy, I'm worried I'll pop something, but it's as if a barrier breaks and suddenly my arms straighten up, elbows locking painfully.

Then relief as the bar is taken from my hands.

"Lizzie, well done!" Kat squeals, replacing the bar as I pant up at her. "You did it!"

"Barely," I choke, pushing myself into a sitting position. "Jeez, how do you do that all the time?"

"Practice," she says, handing me my water bottle. I take a deep swig and go to stand up, but blackness starts to crawl across my eyes, creeping in from the corners. I sit down again.

"Whoa," I say thickly. My ears are full of a high-pitched whine. "Woozy."

"Aww, no." Kat sits next to me and eases my head down between my knees, where I take several deep breaths, my vision clearing, the darkness receding. "I'm sorry, I didn't think it'd mess with your head."

"It's OK." I wave a hand at her and take another swig of water before sitting up carefully. "I've been a bit off recently, anyway, with that bug or whatever it was that I had."

"Bug? You mean, those stomach cramps?"

"Yeah," I say. Kat looks uncomfortable. "What is it?"

"Lizzie, will you do me a favor? Don't take this the wrong way, but . . . just don't take any more mugs of tea from Cole. For now, anyway."

"What are you talking about?"

"You got ill after both of them. . . . It's probably nothing." She brushes it off and busies herself with loading the bar up with weights again, but I dwell on her words. Cole—she suspects Cole?

"I think that's it for me," I tell her. "I'll wait for you, though."

"Oh, don't be silly. Go for a shower and I'll just have a quick session; we can go back to the dorm when you're ready."

I look around the deserted gym uneasily. "I thought we were supposed to stick together."

"Lizzie, you'll be a wall away. And anyway, look at all those dumbbells." She points to a shiny rack beneath a mirrored wall by the door to the wet room. "I'm pretty sure I'll be able to defend myself if I need to."

A hot shower does sound good. "If you're sure?"

"I'm sure. We really need to get you back in shape, though. It'll help your recovery so much. That can be our goal this year."

"If you say so, boss." Kat gives me a squeeze with one arm and pulls me up to standing.

"I do. Now go and relax. The gym showers are a hundred times better than ours."

"Thanks, honey." I grab my bag and head into the shower room, the thought of washing my troubles away spurring me on.

42

I DO WISH I'D HAD A CHANCE TO PLAN THIS ONE MORE CARE-
fully, but there's not much time left. Not every police officer can be
bribed, after all. They're bound to come in the end, asking questions and
gathering evidence.

Or worse, the press will arrive. Vermin.

The gym is quiet, which is normal for a Saturday morning, as most
students sleep in. Lazy. You don't get to the top by sleeping in.

It's so quiet; in fact, she's the only person here.

I watch from the doorway as she does some absurd exercise, lying
on the floor and lifting a heavily weighted barbell with her hips. She's
in the most perfect position: legs pinned to the ground and her upper
body raised up on a bench, facing away from me. I can hear the music
thumping in her headphones from here, almost as loud as the shower
running in the other room.

There's no way she will hear me.

I trace my fingers along the rack of dumbbells, two pounds all the
way up to fifty-five. I settle for something in the middle, selecting a thick-
handled weight. It's evenly balanced, two heavy black hexagons attached
by a silver bar. I wrap both hands around one end and swing it through
the air experimentally.

That should do it.

I approach her. I'm so close, I can see the sweat beaded on the back of her neck, small swirls of brown hair curled around the nape. She's lifting the bar with her lower body, evidently struggling now but still going. I haven't come across a person this determined in quite some time, and I feel a pang of something like regret. She could have been quite brilliant.

I wait for her to lift the bar again and raise the dumbbell over my head. As she pushes up with her hips, I lower it as fast as I can, the dull thud only slightly less sickening than I thought it would be. Her hands go limp in shock and the barbell crashes to the ground across her hips, pinning her in place. Her head drops back onto the bench and she locks her fuzzy eyes on mine.

"It's you," she croaks.

"Yes," I respond, lifting the dumbbell into the air again, before bringing the weight down onto her pretty face. "It's me."

43

"LIZ? LIZ!"

I emerge from the shower with my ears full of water and quickly use my towel to clear them.

"Cole?" I start toward the bathroom door with my towel around me and he pushes the door open, blocking my path. He looks sick.

"Oh, Liz, oh, thank God." He wraps me in a bear hug.

"What's wrong? Has something happened? Is it . . . Taylor?" My mouth goes dry at the thought and he lets go, running one hand over my soaking hair as I try to desperately keep the towel in place.

"No, I mean, I don't know. I haven't heard from Marcus yet. But . . ."

"But what? Cole, you're scaring me."

"Get dressed," he orders, looking over his shoulder and into the gym as I hesitate. "Now! We have to get out of here."

"Why?" I whisper, fear pooling in the pit of my stomach.

Cole closes his eyes.

"Kat's dead."

* * *

I can't remember when or how I got dressed, but the next thing I know, Cole is guiding me out of the gym, one hand covering the side of my face to try to stop me from seeing her.

But I do.

There's a gap between his fingers and through it I see my friend, her body thrust back in an unnatural position. Her face is thick with blood and a heavy dumbbell has been discarded next to her. My throat fills with tears and a scream starts to build in the pit of my stomach.

"Come on." Cole practically pushes me out the door and onto the path between the gym and the lake. "We need to go and find somebody."

"Dr. Patel?"

"No." He grabs my arm and starts to drag me along the path. He's twitchy, agitated.

A Cole I've never seen before.

"Wait," I say, yanking my arm free. "How did you know where we were? School's on lockdown, and no one's supposed to leave their rooms."

"Which is precisely what you two did." He glares at me before letting out a huge sigh, his shoulders sagging. Behind him the lake twinkles in the morning sun, surreal after what we've just witnessed.

"I'm sorry," I whisper. "You're right, we shouldn't have left. But you know Kat, once there's an idea in her head, she's like a dog with a bone. She doesn't let it go."

"Didn't," Cole corrects me.

Silence drags between us.

"I had to tell you something," he says. "That's why I was looking for you."

"What?" I ask. What else could possibly go wrong?

"It's Patel. I was out on the boys' terrace and saw her walk into the woods, you know, where we found . . . where we found Frank. When she came back, she was with that man." My ears prick up.

"Her brother?"

Cole nods. "I think so. I couldn't see too well, but he looked like the guy she was with the other night."

The cogs in my brain kick into overdrive. All these deaths and an original cult member is back on the grounds—one who has possibly been living *on* the grounds all this time. "Do you really think they're behind all this? I mean, Kat did, and look . . ." The sentence sticks in my mouth. Look what happened to Kat.

"I don't know." Cole throws his hands in the air. "Liz, this is insanity. There has been nothing but death since I got here, and now the one person we're supposed to trust is sneaking a former cult member into school! What are we going to do?"

My mind calms. Kat was the decisive one. The one who put things together. But now I have to do that for her. For all of us.

"We face her," I say, "and we stop them."

"Are you sure this is a good idea?"

"No," I reply.

Cole and I are camped out in the storeroom later that night, sitting with the door cracked open so we can see down the corridor to Patel's office. The door to the back stairs is propped open with a huge box of tomatoes, in case we need to make a quick escape.

"Then what are we doing?" Cole asks, handing me a squashed sandwich. I take a bite, but it's like sawdust in my mouth.

"We're waiting."

It's now ten thirty, which means that upstairs lights should be out. It seems everyone but us has actually kept to the lockdown rules, only leaving their rooms to collect the trays of food that were delivered for dinner.

"I think we should just call the police, Liz," Cole sighs, brushing sandwich crumbs off his jeans. "It's too dangerous. Look what's happened so far. . . ."

"We will. Here." I take my phone out of a pocket in my bag, which is still full of wet gym things, and press it into his hand. He puts it in his pocket. "Just not yet. I have a feeling Patel's up to something tonight, and if we can catch her in the act, surely that will be better than calling the police with just suspicions. Don't forget, I'm pretty sure she paid off the local police. Plus, I bet she can talk her way out of anything."

Cole sighs again. "I guess you're right. I wish you weren't, though."

"Thank you." I lean forward and press my forehead against his. "You've kept me sane through all this, you know."

"Same." He smiles faintly. "How are you dealing? Seriously? I want you to know you can talk to me."

"Honestly, I feel . . . numb, I guess?" Is that the right word? "Like none of this is real. I mean, Taylor, and now Kat." Her name catches in my throat as I see her battered, bloodied face again. "They were my best friends, Cole."

"I know." He strokes my hands with his thumbs, a soft, soothing motion. "At least we have each other, right?"

"Right." I let him pull me into a hug, his chest strong against my back. I lean into him and close my eyes.

I'm so tired.

"Hey." A whisper in my ear saves me from the brink of dozing off. "What was that?"

I hold a finger to my lips and push onto my knees, crawling back toward the door. I can't see much from here, but I can see enough.

"Patel is leaving her office," I hiss.

"Alone?"

"Yeah, looks like it."

"Should we follow her?"

I sit back on my heels and look at Cole. He's so beautiful, even when the world is falling apart around him. I want to keep him safe forever.

"Not we. Me." He opens his mouth to argue, and I hold up a hand. "Stop, I'm not negotiating. I'm going to follow her, and you're going to wait here."

"No chance."

"Cole, listen. If her brother is still in her office, you need to follow him so you can warn me." I point to his jeans pocket, where the phone sits. "If something happens to me, I need you to call the police immediately, do you understand?" He opens his mouth to argue again, but I lean forward and silence him with a kiss. "Please? We don't have time to argue."

"Fine. I'm going to check her office and I'm giving you ten minutes, then I'm coming to get you, no arguments."

"That works," I say. I stand up and stagger slightly, still a little faint from earlier. Cole jumps to his feet to steady me.

"Be careful," he says, burying his face in my hair. "I need you back in one piece"—his lips move to my ear, his breath tickling me—"because I think I'm falling in love with you."

I lift my head in shock.

"What?"

"I wasn't going to say anything, but . . ."

I plant my lips firmly on his. "Shut up," I demand, pulling away. "I think I'm falling in love with you too."

We take a second to stare at one another before I remember I have something to do.

"Right." I give him one final kiss before I pull the door all the way open and step out into the hallway. "Let's finish this."

44

"I WONDERED WHEN YOU WOULD SHOW UP."

Dr. Patel is exactly where I thought she would be. The library is dark, only some dim security lights lining the exterior walls. Shadows fill the room and I hesitate at the threshold.

"What made you think I would?" I ask, my voice smaller than I would like. I take a step onto the polished monochrome floor.

She sighs. "Because you're the only one left." I walk slowly forward as she unlocks a glass cabinet with clipped precision, her dark nails glossy even in the gloom. "And you, Elizabeth, like every other Jewel and Bone wannabe, cannot help yourself. The thirst to succeed outweighs all else, am I correct? *Non fortuna nisi per sacrificium.*"

I don't say anything, just walk slowly forward, glancing over my shoulder at the empty room. Cole said ten minutes. Would that be enough time?

"I know what you're doing." I stop a few feet from her, my eyes adjusting to the dark. "I saw your memory box. You and your brother and Harrison—you've been behind everything, haven't you?"

"My brother?" She laughs but it's cold, humorless. "My brother.

What a disappointment. You can't choose your family, though, can you?" She narrows her eyes slyly at me. "You would know all about that, Ms. Williams."

Ouch.

"Oh yes, I am very familiar with your file. As I am with all your little friends. Taylor—her father is in prison, did you know that? Armed robbery when she was twelve. Real daddy issues. And Marcus, he's not as sweet as he seems, oh no. His son is two now, though I bet he's never mentioned him."

"You're lying," I spit, moving around to get a better look at what she's doing. The cabinet containing the Bernini angel is open. "Stop trying to distract me."

Patel shrugs. "Maybe I am, maybe I'm not. I'll leave you to find out, if they ever return. But you." She taps her chin with one finger, the nail filed to a stiletto point. "You really did have an awful life, didn't you? A useless father figure, a mother who would rather do anything but spend time with you. Never actually neglected you enough for social services to visit, though, did they? Just emotionally scarred you. Made you feel like you'd never be good enough. Well." She pulls open the cabinet door and removes the statue reverently. "We know what that feels like, don't we, Elizabeth?"

"Is that what your family did?" I say. I need to keep her talking, get her to admit to everything while I can. "Is that why you joined the cult? To show them you were worth something?"

"Joined the cult?" She laughs again and it's a chilling sound. "I never joined that pathetic bunch. They were insane—imagine thinking that killing people would get you anywhere in life. No, I was head girl, the brightest, shining star. I was destined for big things."

She places the angel carefully on a nearby table and locks the cabinet again, before producing a long-handled screwdriver. She waves it around as she speaks. "My darling brother put a stop to that, though. My parents were so ashamed. And my name was sullied—no one wanted to help the sister of such a high-profile cult member. Bad for their image, you know? No more sponsors for Nikhita."

"But we saw your brother here the other night." I keep my eyes on the screwdriver and take a step back. It looks sharp. "What did he want?"

"He wanted what he always wants from me. Money. Somewhere to stay. The only way I can get rid of him for months at a time is to give him what he wants." She pauses, her face a furious mask. "He's very . . . persuasive. He always promises it will be the last time, but as long as he can find me, it never will."

"So he ruined your life?"

"Bingo!" Patel squeals, her voice edging on hysterical. "My dreams of a shining future were over. I had to scrape a living, training as a teacher, of all things. But I was in it for the long game— I knew if I bided my time, a job would come up here and I'd be able to charm my way in as a hardworking alumna. And look at me now." She gestures to her sharp black pantsuit with the tip of the screwdriver. Even when she's losing her mind, she's still the most glamourous adult I've ever met. "I'm the goddamn *principal.*"

"You must be proud of that, right?" I wonder how many of Cole's ten minutes are left.

"Hardly," she sneers, taking her attention off me. She focuses on the small silver lock on the cabinet and pushes the tip of the screwdriver behind it before pulling down on the handle. The lock snaps immediately and the glass around it cracks and splinters. Patel pulls it out and smashes the weakened area with the handle, once, twice, three times, until it shatters.

"Perfect!" she trills, gently taking a statue from its perch on the top. "This way the statue doesn't become damaged, you see?" She stalks over to another case, smashing it, repeating the motion over and over until we're surrounded by glittering, deadly shards of glass. She crunches back toward the table where she had left the angel and smiles triumphantly as she picks it up. Her lipstick has smudged slightly, and she has a manic gleam in her eye. "Now that idiot Officer Whipsnade can bring the police in and declare a robbery, like the corrupt little man he is. Once they realize nothing else is missing, that the whole scene was staged, I'll be long gone."

"You're stealing it?" I ask. "The Bernini?"

This wasn't what I expected.

"I think of it more as . . . taking what I'm owed, after I was denied the life I deserved." She strokes a terra-cotta wing gently. "It was always my favorite. Do you know how much something like this will go for? There are so many private collectors on the black market. My brother was good for that piece of information, at least. He didn't have the balls to do it himself, so I will make millions." I shake my head, mesmerized. "Millions," she repeats, her eyes sparkling. "I have a buyer lined up and they have a helicopter waiting for me. Can you believe it? I can spend the rest of my days living the way I deserve to. However . . ." She turns on one spiked heel to face me. "I can't have you ruining all my hard work, can I? No, I'll have to . . . deal with you."

She's serious.

"You'll never get away with all this," I say, not taking my eyes off her. She's no longer holding the screwdriver, and I try to remember when she put it down. Where.

"Oh, really? No one suspected anything until you found that picture in my office, you little brat. So now it looks like there will be one more death at Morton before the headmistress mysteriously disappears. Boo-hoo, another head girl—how tragic."

My head snaps up. "Head girl?"

"Yes, you're next on the list, aren't you? A cursed position, in my opinion. Ms. Fox is on life support—I've spoken to the hospital, even if she pulls through, she won't be back this year. It was a shame about Ms. Paphitis; she was a smart girl, or so I thought. Now, Elizabeth, that leaves you. The next contender in line." She places the angel down again, looking at it fondly. "We don't want to damage you, my lovely," she croons to it. "We wouldn't want to get any . . . fluids on you." She smiles, turning back to me. "Terra-cotta can be so porous."

Then Patel's smile fades.

Because *I* am holding the screwdriver.

45

"WHAT ARE YOU DOING?" HER VOICE FALTERS AS I APPROACH her. Images flash through my mind. Morgan, her face blue and gasping. Jameela, dropping to the ground in her silky pajamas. Frank, Emily, Taylor. Kat.

I've had enough.

"You said you read my file?" I say, stepping closer. Patel starts to back away and I circle her, the two of us trapped in a macabre dance. "Well, did you? Did it tell you what I did last summer?"

"Yes," she croaks. "You spent the summer in and out of the hospital. A head injury you sustained here last July."

"That's right." I turn the screwdriver in my hand. It's much lighter than the dumbbell. "Temporal lobe epilepsy, it's called. It's triggered when someone has a massive head injury, like I did. Causes blackouts, funny turns, that sort of thing. It also causes other . . . problems."

"Like psychotic episodes?"

"Not quite." I laugh coldly. "I'm not a cliché, Dr. Patel. No, when the temporal lobes are damaged, it can cause personality and behavior changes. If that happens to someone who is already displaying . . .

problematic . . . behavior, it can be very, *very* bad. You said you read my file? Liar. You'd have seen that my old school was quite worried about my conduct. They couldn't wait to get rid of me."

"I don't understand." Patel is trying to stall me, her eyes wild, looking for a clear path out of the library.

"Well, *doctor*," I mock, "if those symptoms go unchecked for a while, like mine did, thanks to my pathetic parents, it can become a real problem." I play with the screwdriver, watching the dim light glint off the sharpened tip. "I've always had a little trouble deciding what is right and what is wrong—well, by societal standards, anyway." I rap my knuckles on the scar in my hair. "Seems like this just exacerbated everything." I lean in conspiratorially. "I mean, it's not like epilepsy turns you into a murderer, does it? No, I have more . . . issues than that. Never actually had a fit, though, so the pills must be doing something." I look up and see that the truth is dawning on Patel. Clever girl. "Who else did you think was killing the students? Your brother? You said it yourself—he's pathetic."

"I . . . I thought he . . . maybe Harrison . . ."

"What, you thought he was providing the perfect distraction for you to carry out"—I gesture at the cabinets—"whatever *this* is? So, after all this time, you still thought you were covering for him? Pathetic," I spit. "It was *me*. I read about the cult online. There wasn't much else to do over the summer. And hasn't it all fallen perfectly into place?"

"You're lying, you little witch."

"I'm no-ot," I say in a childhood singsong. "You see, I never really belonged anywhere," I explain, "until I got here, to Morton. I made sure I blended into the background. I was the *nice* girl, the *reliable* girl. I would have been head girl much sooner if I wasn't playing so nice, if I hadn't helped Taylor and Kat in the hunt. I gave them the answers. I was so desperate to look *normal.* Then, that night, we took the boat out and Morgan fell in. I really was trying to help her, at first. But I hit my head and when I came to, it was like everything was suddenly clearer. If I could get rid of her, I'd be one step closer. And you know what that feels like, right? The promise of a successful life ahead? I know *you* understand." I lift the screwdriver and point it at her face. "Answer me," I whisper.

Her face goes slack. "You're insane."

I smile. "No. I just stopped pretending to be *that* girl. The girl who lets everyone walk all over her."

"Liz!" Cole's voice echoes through the library and I'm momentarily distracted. Patel takes the chance to charge at me.

"Cole!" I squeal as we both go down, Patel on top of me. "Help me! She's got a screwdriver, she's crazy!"

But she doesn't have the screwdriver, does she?

I ram the weapon up into her chest as hard as I can, aiming for something vital and twisting the end for good measure.

I look her straight in the eye as she lies on top of me. I know she's dying, I can tell. A warm pool of blood pours from the wound the sharp tip has made, and when the light fades from her eyes, I push her limp body off me and yank the screwdriver out. Even in the dark, I can see the bright red arterial blood spray across the room before I drop the weapon to the floor and watch the life drain from her.

"Liz! Liz! Are you hurt? Liz . . ." Cole drops down and starts running his hands over me, checking for injuries. Creepy Billy is behind him, barking orders into a cordless phone. "Oh my God, all this blood. Are you hurt?" he repeats.

"It's not mine. I . . . I think I'm OK." I make my voice small as Creepy Billy checks Dr. Patel's pulse and shakes his head. "She jumped at me with the screwdriver, and as we fell, I grabbed it from her . . . ," I say, my voice shaking. "And she landed on it." Cole pulls me to my feet and I look him in the eye. "She was going to kill me, Cole."

I mean, I'm not lying.

"Oh, Liz, I should have come sooner, I—"

"It's OK," I say quietly. "You got here in time." He gently pulls me up and leads me away from Patel's body. "It was her. She . . . she killed them all, Cole." I start to sob.

"Hey, I've got you." He holds me close despite the blood and I imagine what we must look like, silhouetted by the long library windows as red and blue lights start to strobe up the driveway, sirens blaring. "I've got you," he repeats.

"It's over?" I ask.

Cole kisses me on the forehead.

"It's over."

46

I PIN THE SHINING BLACK BADGE TO THE LAPEL OF MY BLAZER *and admire it in the mirror. Head girl suits me.*

I still want to grow my hair longer, but I've styled it this morning and I'm fairly happy with it. I knew there would be perks to having your own bathroom.

I sit on the bed in my room and study the contents of Dr. Patel's wooden box, trailing my fingers over the mother-of-pearl inlay. I select each of the items one by one, turning them slowly in my hands.

It now contains my trophies.

Morgan's photo from that first day, the one I passed to Jameela, her friend's eyes scratched out. I dropped it in the doorway on my way in—I knew someone would pick it up. I was quite pleased to find it in Frank's pocket after I killed him.

Jameela's inhaler and the little tub of Tiger Balm I stole from Kat, most of the contents used.

Taylor's blusher brush: the one I planted the rusty nail in and the little jar of ointment I gave her. It smells awful now—the raw meat I mixed in it has turned rancid. I definitely need to keep the lid on that.

Then there's the almost-empty packet of caffeine pills, the ones I'd been "lending" to Emily. I might have . . . misjudged the dose, though.

The eye drops I put in my tea, to cause stomach cramps. I couldn't be the only one not affected, could I? That would have been suspicious.

Kat's gym gloves. I've tried to scrub the blood spatter off, but that stuff is hard to remove.

I add the picture from the newspaper now—the one of Cole and me walking out of Morton, police wrapping us in foil blankets. We were hailed as heroes, the couple who stopped the Morton Massacre in its tracks.

I'm interrupted by a knock on my door.

I replace the lid on the box gently and slide it under the bed, smoothing out my skirt and checking my badge one last time. I open the door to see its twin pinned to another blazer.

"Hi, gorgeous." Cole smiles down at me.

"Back at you." I grin, standing on my tiptoes to kiss him. My Cole. Mine, mine, mine.

"You ready to face a new week?" he says, leveling me with a serious gaze.

"I think so," I say, glancing at the silver label engraved with ELIZABETH WILLIAMS, HEAD GIRL *on my door. "But there's just one thing."*

"What is it?"

"I want to leave all that . . . stuff behind, have a fresh start."

"Right." He looks worried.

"Not you, silly," I reassure him. "No—I've always hated the name Liz. It's what my parents called me." And they are utter trash.

"You want to change your name?" he says, his brow furrowed, though I see a shadow of relief on his face. "Are you sure?"

"Not change it, exactly," I explain. I hold my palm over half of the sign. "Just use a different part of it."

"Beth," he reads. "Beth," he repeats, smiling at me. "I like it."

"Me too." I smile, already visualizing my life as Beth. Liz can stay where she belongs, in the past. The girl with the pitiful family who melted into the background.

"In that case, my lovely Beth, let's go." Cole sweeps an arm out and I follow him into the lounge. He's taken to being head boy just like I knew he would. Marcus didn't come back after Taylor died. Some people are weak. I look up at the new portraits of Emily, Taylor, and Kat that decorate the wall, alongside Jameela and Morgan. All those dead girls.

I smile as I follow Cole down the spiral staircase, already daydreaming about our future at Yale together. The school board has agreed it will be all-expenses-paid after our terrible ordeal, and even though Jewel and Bone disbanded after the scandal, I'm sure we'll find our way into another society when we get to Yale. It's going to be amazing.

And what Cole doesn't know won't hurt him.

Right?

ACKNOWLEDGMENTS

On to the thank-yous. Where do I begin? There are *so many*.

This book *tested* me but ultimately turned into one of my greatest achievements. I knew where I wanted to go with it, but it's just not that easy to get thoughts from brain to paper—coherently, anyway. It really does take a village, and thankfully, I had one.

Thank you to my editors, Ruth Bennett, Genevieve Herr, Yasmin Morrissey, and Sophie Cashell. Ruth and Gen, you helped me polish this book within an inch of its life. Thank you. To the rest of the team at Scholastic—Lauren Fortune for believing in my hideous ideas, Jamie Gregory for yet another *stunning* cover, Ella Probert for the most delicious graphics, and Peter Matthews for making sure everything was perfect—thank you. Harriet Dunlea—I aspire to your levels of brilliance and organization; you're the best—thank you!

Thank you also to the team at Delacorte Press, particularly Alison Romig. You will never know how much it means that you took a chance on a girl from the Northwest of England. Things like this don't happen every day, and it's a dream come true to know my book will be in the hands of US readers. Let's do this!

My agents, Stephanie Thwaites and Isobel Gahan. Izzy, thank you for all you have done this year. We got there, and I couldn't be happier.

Thank you to all the booksellers, bloggers, and of course *readers* for embracing my books. Thank you, thank you, thank you. You're amazing and I hope to horrify and delight you for years to come. To the GoodShip2021 and all the other beautiful souls I have met in publishing—thank you for your advice, knowledge, and support. It's such a pleasure to watch your successes—may they long continue.

Georgia Bowers. You are literally the only person who asks me whether it's too much for a child monster to eat vocal cords. I love our brainstorming sessions (and our moany ones). You are the best and are destined to do wonderful things with your writing. Please don't give up. You've got this.

My friends and family. How I wish I had seen more of you over the last eighteen months—hopefully we can celebrate this book together. Emma Bolton, for your scientific expertise—any gas-chromatography mistakes are definitely mine! Donna, your pride in my first book makes me cry every time I think about it. Thank you. Mum and Dad, thank you for pushing my book into the hands of everyone you have ever met—you are the best parents and cheerleaders ever. I love you all so very much.

Loli—I know you can't read (well, I don't think so), but you are the best assistant ever. I'm looking forward to writing my next book in my new office while you bark at people out the window. All the chewy sticks for Loli!

Luke. My brightest shining star. You and Loli have made me

smile every single day during my pandemic writing sessions, and I know I wouldn't have got through it (sanely) without you both. You didn't bat an eyelid when I swapped teaching for full-time writing, and my heart is ten sizes bigger because of it. You work so hard to provide us with the best life and I am always so, so proud of you. Five years ago, we weren't sure what was going to happen. Now I feel like I'm living my dream. Thank you. I love you, I love you, I love you.

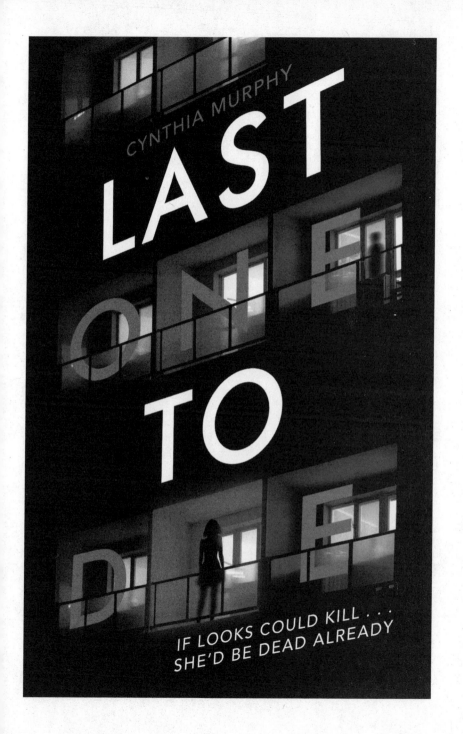

CYNTHIA MURPHY

LAST
ONE
TO
DIE

IF LOOKS COULD KILL . . .
SHE'D BE DEAD ALREADY